Portrona

Norman Malcolm Macdonald

Birlinn

First published in 2000 by
Birlinn Limited
8 Canongate Venture
5 New Street
Edinburgh
EH8 8BH

www.birlinn.co.uk

ISBN 1 84158 073 2

British Library Cataloguing-in-Publication Data
A catalogue record for this book is available
from the British Library

The publisher acknowledges subsidy from The Scottish
Arts Council towards the publication of this book

Typeset by Palimpsest Book Production Limited,
Polmont, Stirlingshire
Printed and bound by Creative Print and Design,
Ebbw Vale, Wales

For James Shaw Grant

An ataireachd bhuan,
Cluinn fuaim na h-àitearachd àird

Hear the euphony
Of the eternal surge
Of the high sea

(*An Ataireachd Ard*: Donald MacIver)

Funeral Fund

A LEWIS HERRING GIRL died in Fraserburgh 150 years ago. Consumption, hurried along by pitiless night-and-day working on gluts of herring, gutting and packing barrels and ships to feed the hungry of Eastern Europe.

The fit girls could take it for the time, a hard but well-paid season.

Not Catherine MacKenzie. This was her year to fail. We may be sure she knew, but like a well-born Hebridean lass, she went through with it until she could no longer raise her head and the nurse tried to contact a doctor, sending a note at the same time to an undertaker of her acquaintance. Payment for the funeral was not an issue. She knew her girls; they would take care of it from the weekend filling-up money.

What the Church nurse did not know was that the crews of women from Lewis had ordained that she would rest in the machair at home with her relatives, looking out over the Western Ocean, hearing the eternal surge of the sea. Not in some stony, overcrowded cemetery outside a grey Eastern anonymous town. So they set up a funeral fund to take her home by boat and train.

It is yet in existence, the Funeral Fund, collected annually by lady volunteers, a pound a time, and anyone who dies away will be transported home for burial if their name is down.

Sand is the preferred abiding resting place of seafaring folk of course.

How can we know the past today? We desperately want to, whether we admit it or no, in the context of the experience of our ancestors, many of whom audaciously traversed the known universe, others who stayed in the same house all their lives.

The past is not something to be escaped, avoided or controlled. The past is something with which we should come to terms, which involves an acknowledgment of limitation as well as power. We islanders have more access than most to details of our past.

There are important parallels between the processes of history writing and fiction writing. Only through the struggle with fictions based upon 'facts' can we come to alight upon parts of our human story that make sense for us and help us to live for today – and tomorrow.

So not only are we here setting the scene and background, selecting the themes for our stravaig from *Bounty* to *Iolaire* through the 'true' history of Lewis, town and country. We are also going to give to the process known to academics as 'historiographic metafiction'. A mode of writing which sets out to cause problems for the making of both fiction and history. These two are inextricably linked, your own memory weaving the threads that try to stitch some sense into it.

Post-modernism does not merely reproduce the past as nostalgia (as we are used to doing), but reveals it as always constructed by others to suit their own views. The big question is not about *the* 'truth' but *whose* 'truth'. We want that truth to be ours.

Stay with me and I'll tell you a bit of the way in which many writers of today attempt to find out what actually happened. You may say: 'What a hope!' but as the Bard said, 'Yet still we sing.' Now and then we can tell that the truth has been touched, often through music.

You see a lonely granite stone standing by the far fence in a Lewis cemetery. 'Catherine MacKenzie' died away in Fraserburgh, July 18, aged nineteen. The clues are all there for those who know.

The reconstruction begins from our vast oral knowledge of the great herring industry that gave us our being from the time of feeding the slaves to the coming of the purse-net and, with it, an unlimited bankers' loan, enabling fishing boats like battleships to destroy it all.

But is this how writers have always worked? Who can tell the twists of intuition and where they may take us?

Someone has said we all live immersed in narrative. Those who object to this immersion in our past say it has been at the expense of history. But it all just depends on your definition of history. Too often, we get both the story and the story-telling of the losers and right or wrong, we Gaels have seen and are still seeing ourselves as losers. It is more than time for a change in this perspective.

But why begin with the Funeral Fund? Not because of the familiar Lewis fascination with death, oh no. But because the Funeral Fund is at the centre of the Lewis experience; there are only two places in the world important to a Lewis person and they are Home and Away.

From the late 17th century to mid-20th century this experience revolved around the herring fishing each summer.

God's Providence is Our Inheritance with a picture of a fat full herring: Stornoway's coat of arms.

A full fat herring: a sked as these miraculous fish were known to the populace of Stornoway and Lewis in the vernacular (Gaelic sgadan).

So the Funeral Fund started by the Lewis herring gutters, with the assistance of a sympathetic Stornoway curer, so that their friends could rest at home tells us a lot about the ways of mind of the thousands who left the island each season and returned with their little monies and wooden kists of goodies each autumn. A few would follow the English fishing to Yarmouth but most would return for the harvest.

Men went too. Some as hired hands on East Coast boats, some proudly skippering their own. But their experience does not excite us the way that of the girls can – aged from fourteen to *Chan innis mi dhut* ('I'm not telling, I can still twist the gut from a sked every second and I never miss the right selection basket').

And in this, the Year of Our Lord 2000, the millennium, the Funeral Fund still operates. You may join it if you wish. You don't have to be a herring girl!

That is the kind of folk you are talking about here.

Even the scientists have recently taken to talking about subtle genetic differences between us and others. Dangerous loose talk, but the idea that we may be like the Icelanders does have its appeal; many of them got their wives here on their way through. The point to make is that the past is not something to be escaped, avoided or controlled – the past is something with which we must come to terms, which involves an acknowledgment of limitation as well as of power. People have access to the past today only through its traces – its documents, the testimony of witnesses and other archives. Unless you are from Lewis, in which case you are steeped in the knowledge handed down to you of *Na daoine bhon tàinig thu* ('the people you came from').

And always you must be aware of the important parallels between the processes of history writing and fiction writing. So much so that you delve into the 'fictional' artefacts of your ancestors (still available in this tight little community, as seldom elsewhere in the world) giving your fictional findings a sheen of historical truth.

We have plenty of old photographs; but how 'true' are they? Did my great-aunt really hold the cutag at that unusual angle always, or did the photographer place her hand for a better shot?

Similarly documents are not, by any means, innocent reports. Who wrote them? Think of any committee meeting lately attended! The best part is, however, that story-telling is a bond between the teller and the told, within a context that is historical, social and political. We live immersed in narrative, creating our own life and memory.

Two small revolutions took place in the Highlands and Islands during the 1840s.

First, almost unnoticed, the old clan chiefs gave over their lands, sold out their people to the new rich entrepreneurs, 'Rich as Croesus', in the case of he who purchased Lewis, 'one MacDrug' who made limitless cash exploiting the newly discovered 'riches' of the Far East. They are there to this day, the company, although the Chinese are slowly and patiently (it is their way) regaining the ascendancy.

The chief sold out, the rich man came in, built a new castle, planted thousands of exotic trees outside Stornoway, got married (he was in his forties) and started a new-type Highland Dynasty.

Busy in London with his mark to make in politics, a suitable seat to be won, within a number of years he succeeded, erected a huge white marble effigy to his young wife overlooking the herring town and had been persuaded by a member of a powerful English family to place a bright young woman *in loco parentis* to run the Lewis end of the estate. MacRoe, a very powerful factor, was put in charge, but Lady Emily Percy gave a certain cachet to the place as the administrator (in name only).

The other revolution, beneath the notice of rich landlords, was the upheaval in the Church in the Highlands and Islands, but also on the mainland, that led to the creation in 1843 of the Free Church of Scotland, one of the most honest and heart-lifting changes ever to take place in Highland religious life.

If the movement lacked anything (and it was not courage)

it was women; women who were prepared to act out of their own feminine convictions. For how can you have a whole way of life, a culture, religious or any other, with only the male side showing forth?

Be this as it may, for a hundred years the Free Church steadied and led the people of Lewis through many traumas. Those days are long gone and the power and the glory of the Free Church is dissipated on petty squabbles.

The Church led the people in the direction of owning (or having a say over) their own land. Riots resulted but with no bloodshed (a tribute to the discipline of the Church over its people): Royal Marines shoved bayonets up to crofters' throats and they responded with laughter. 'Away and kill a hen!' (My ancestor and by God I'm proud of him!)

Crofters got some jurisdiction over the land and their lives but then the hell that broke over Europe in 1914 engulfed them just as they might have thought they were gaining some kind of human equality.

Between the nineteenth century and 1914, the landlord saw a growing 'surplus' population as a problem. These people had no legal rights, nowhere to plant potatoes or oats to feed their families. A great problem – squatters.

The answer: emigration. Various attempts were made to transport some of the 'surplus' from Lewis to overseas colonies, during this time. These attempts were hopelessly inadequate in the face of a population explosion. My grandmother had nine children of her own and raised another three.

Many did, however, emigrate between the riot times of the 1880s and the War of 1914 that was to change everything for ever. Young men ceased to haunt shipping line offices and succumbed instead to the blandishments of recruiting sergeants for Highland regiments. The older men were already, thousands of them, numbered among the volunteers of the Royal Naval Reserve.

When the lights went out over Europe in 1914, Lewis

responded. The number of volunteers per head of population was unsurpassed anywhere in the lands then known as the British Empire.

This is the modern background to the story of Portrona and its Herring Fever, which is dealt with in the following pages.

Portrona

THE HERRING FEVER IS once more on Portrona. It strikes each year in May, anytime between 1789 and 1919, years associated with two distinct vessels – HMS *Bounty* and HM Yacht *Iolaire*. Why should our chosen year be any different?

The fever is something immutable. It was happened always and will go on for as long as the seas teem with herring.

So it was and would ever be to the thousands of women and men for whom Portrona was at the centre of the world in the month of May.

The web of the world, whose filaments reached to far places, visited by only a few, and yet nearer places visited by the many; Shetland, Wick and Yarmouth.

The herring fishing, says our Portrona man of a hundred years or more ago, makes our bay, our shores and our streets bright and busy in May and June. Boats from as far away as Fife and the Isle of Man begin to appear. From our windows we see them enter the bay. We count the brown sails with joy, for their coming means an influx of fresh foreign life to our isolated town.

Thirty miles of sea divide us, he goes on, from what they call in Gaelic 'the great land', the Scottish mainland.

The founder of Portrona must have been some searover with a good eye for a refuge. We can imagine the time, now long ago, when a few poor dwellings dotted the shore or sheltered behind the rude castle of the chief of the Lewis MacLeods at the elbow of the bay. That primal simplicity has given way to the town of today.

At this minute we are thinking of one person coming to life in the town: Henny, whose new husband went to sail on a Portrona-built schooner and never returned. He had stepped ashore in some alien port and, apart from a glimpse of him in the company of a brown girl in a dockside bar, nobody from Portrona had set eyes on him since. Henny is therefore neither a widow nor properly married; she has ceased to meet the local ships returning from long trips; the brown, burned men have nothing to tell her. Sometimes she acts moonstruck but that is understood and her boy-man son is treated like the Holy Fool of the town. Norman Daft, not Daft Norman, Norman Daft, the Gaelic inversion. Follower of funerals.

Speak of Henny's man who went off on a Portrona schooner and never came home, his envisioned life with the brown girl under the coconut tree raises the shade of Jim Morrison, who sailed to Leith and then London many years before him; who came back later one time for a three-month story-telling about his paradise island in the vast Pacific Ocean where he was a King, some said, but you ken how the rauts grow. We can know nothing of Henny's man nor of thousands like him who went off and never came back, since the coming of civilisation, but Jim Morrison is another matter. Not only did he write his own story, he worked himself a berth on the best kent ship ever to sail out of England. If there is one way to guarantee your name liveth forever more it is to get yourself noticed (preferably adversely) by the English establishment.

What better than to be appointed bosun's mate (though already a midshipman but without friends in high places) on *HMS Bounty* in 1789? Very well, she sailed in 1788 but the mutiny took place in 1789. This could well be the same year when a cousin of Jim's drowned in the Minch. The loss became the catalyst for the greatest tragic ballad in the Gaelic language. Alan Morrison lost his slim black ship of oak and his own life within the sight of Anna Campbell of Scalpay, on the way to their wedding. Tahiti and Scalpay, think of the difference. But I never heard that the songs are better when the living is easy.

We even have a physical description of Jim Morrison, our mutineer (or should we call him that?). They never did hang him although he came pretty close. Here he is, in the words of Captain Bligh himself, after his astonishing voyage in an open boat, adrift on an ocean: James Morrison, boatswain's mate, aged twenty-eight years, five feet eight inches high, sallow complexion, long black hair, slender make, has lost the use of the upper joint of the forefinger of the right hand, tattooed with a star under his left breast, and a garter round his left leg, with the motto *Honi soît qui mal y pense*. Has been wounded in one of his arms by a musket ball.

Tells you a lot about him, a boy from Portrona who had an adventurous and dangerous life a good bit more than 200 years ago. But the Navy was aye that, for instance, the musket ball in one of his arms, the partial loss of the use of a forefinger, these are the hazards normal to a ship's master gunner in action. Best of all, the tattoo of the garter around the left leg. Our man awarded himself the Order of the Garter and why not? Who was the star under the left breast for? A brown princess?

When Henny is in one of her wild moods, as they say, the cooper will take advantage of her behind the wall of barrels. The refilling time, topping up with best skeds, holding tight to the round wood barrel lid, waiting for the cooper to come around and fit it delicately on top of the tender bellies. She was the best gutter on the quay and Madame Wolkova sent her a telegram every April from Petersburg. Madame knew her worth as she knew the quality of Portrona best matjes, top season fish. The time of the herring was the time of excitement for many more than Henny NicKenny. Purple ink in Petersburg, for instance.

The two-month season coincided with the only true summer weather of the island year in the north and west. The sun burned on a metallic sea, some days, white winter skin turned scarlet, full herrings lost their freshness by noontime, powerful odours blossomed on the quays. And people everywhere, more women than men, eager about their work, a touch of fever about them.

Now Henny's workmate, the too young bride of last season, Anna, now in black, widow of the white water on the sea wracks, despite her new place in the castle there across the bay. Anna enters the leather and rosin ambience of Hector the shoemaker with a black bible open on his high wooden counter. Anna stands patiently in front of the blackened wooden counter and watches Hector at work. He mumbles at her through a mouthful of what she knows to be nails. The nails now reveal themselves one by one, propelled by his tongue between pink pursed lips, to be delicately picked between finger and thumb, placed and struck into the sole of the boot he is working on; rapid taps like soft drumbeats, that leave bruises on the resilient leather, dimples that appear to move. Anna wonders what would happen to Hector were he to swallow a nail. The she recalls hearing how it would do him no harm; the powerful acids in Hector's stomach would melt them, the flux acting as a tonic enriching his blood, clearing his brain for argument. He blows out his lips and a shower of nails descends into a box beside him. She asks for her seaboots.

'Pay me after the season, lass.'

She smiles and sweeps the refurbished boots from the counter, then walks along the length of Point Street to reach Number One Pier. There she stands looking down at the gently heaving wooden ramparts of the gathering boats, their masts lying, soon to be raised and socketed ready for the brown sails, lettered and numbered from KY to BCK, from BF to INS to

PA itself. Looking down; hugging her boots, they smell of her and last year's toil, shaped and sculptured by her body. She turns to stare across at the castle, at the window of the room where she sleeps, next to Miss Percy, not a maid's room, a guest's chamber. She thinks of young Iain, him only three months and miles away with Mairi, her own never seeing life, giving him suck instead of her, turning into a lady at the castle, Henny said. She squeezes the supple boots against her swollen breasts.

To give our namer another few words before we leave him behind us, he says others have birthplaces enshrined in history, whose memories the whole world knows. Yet the clamour and glory of history (he means world history, whatever that is) strike lightly enough on the common heart. Even in a great town the citizen has his own history, trivial and unimpressive for others, great and poignant for himself. That is the only history he has read at the sources: the rest, resounding and fateful as it may have been, is but a pale reflection in comparison. With the greatest and best of cities, Portrona has its interests and sacredness for the children it cradles. It can stir thoughts that range wide and dive deep.

May you be proved right in this writing, my friend! But is it not a human attribute to fictionalise everything? It's not just you and me – everybody else does it too, all the time. It's how we remember how we live. Example: the north-west corner of solid Europe in a golden age, always recalled, where a people dwell on the brink of the ocean, living solely off the food in it. Pure without question. And to this very day. Portrona has had its Men Who Make Things Happen, always to their own advantage. The time of our herring boom gave great chances to such entrepreneurs and the one we've chosen is as clever as they come. Does he not charm the lady at the castle and the milkmaids at the shielings in the same breath? He asks money from the banker, has friends in Liverpool and New York and a bright scheme that fits the history of the day, with the East Europeans who used to eat most of the salted herring from Portrona now heading across to Ellis Island and the country beyond. New York! New York! Emigration is the other great industry of the century and even emigrants have to eat, preferably something that reminds them of home. Like the best Portrona matje herring, only full-gutted now, to suit the higher aspirations of men and women who seek the new world and its better life. Do they need special herrings in America? Our MacAllan is the man to convince those that matter that they do.

Now Hector is not just a shoemaker, a clichéd character there for the mummer's chore of giving Anna her symbolic gutting boots that remind her of the boots worn by Jim Flett the last time he went off to fish, a day trip, round home coasts, for haddock, the gale unexpected and fierce for the time of year. No, our leading shoemaker of Portrona is but one of a long line of philosopher-theologian-historians that reaches to the day you read this and hopefully beyond. Opposite Hector's counter is a long wooden bench, made specially for Hector's ancestor, upon which the thinking men of the town settle for their daily deliberations in the course of the Portrona Perambulation, undertaken by all men of sufficient freedom and importance to be able to leave off their daily toil for an hour or two without any loss of their income. The *Highland News* and the Holy Bible are the material they chew on at Hector the Shoemaker's and they spit out each their own particular nail.

Ever since theology entered into the soul of the place soon after Jim Morrison came home from his sojourn in Tahiti after leaving the *Bounty* to Christian, men have savoured religious debate in Portrona. Not that Jim Morrison had anything to do with it, him going off again within weeks and never coming back, although plenty were inclined to follow him after the rauts he told in the change house. No, the theology came from much closer to home and revolutionised the whole place, made men think twice before they took even a black bottle of porter, never mind a fierce clear dram of the local whisky. Before? They just took it and thought nothing about it and amazingly, the hangovers were quite unremarkable. The stuff paid the rent, warmed your breast, was so innocent that shame would keep you sober.

I thought I could maybe take the poet's place but I'd better have him there. Too bad it could not be a blone, 'cept there are a fair number of them already in the story. What with an English lady at the castle, our tragic heroine, Anna, Henny, her hardy friend who knows her local town, woman of experience, Madame the Ruskie, sophisticate from Petersburg, a goodly representation of the distaff side, bound to make for plenty of intriguing action, not to mention the brilliant girls of the shielings, the antipodes of our seamen.

Here he comes then, our poet Rob, stravaiging the eager quays now they are to rage for a couple of months. Sniffing the air for herring roes, he spies on the millionaire's exotic forest behind the castle. Soon he'll be found about the gutting boards, making himself useful to the foreigners. A bit of translation of language or mores, a go-between for all, never lost for a word or phrase, connoisseur of slang, masticator of discourse, Robin Ard, as his name sounds to Madame W, only he cares not for money. That's not what empowers him. He's reciting, for its sound, a bit of new Gaelic verse:

– *Chan eil àite air talamh tròcair/Air làithean ùr an t-samhraidh /Cho bòidheach ris a' Ghàidhealtachd /Na h-àirighean cho àlainn /A' chlann-nighean annt' cho brèagha* – He lights on Anna, crouched on a barrel with her boots in her lap. She gives him the kind of smile he clichés to himself as wan. She makes an effort for the positive poet.

– Shielings comfortable? Bard's licence, Rob –

He gets words to his tongue in an instant, without thought.

– They lie on beds of heather bells that ring with summer's pride!

14

Her little laugh emboldens him to take an unfortunate tack.

– *'S e obair a' bhainne/Sin obair nam mnathan* – The work of the milk is the task of the women –

O Rob! Heedless he plunges deep, his muse rising for him in front of the black long hair and white skin above the strange boots.

– The milk you suck makes you what you are. Milk maketh man, and woman too.

Fostering Anna, and here comes comfort for her, is he conscious of what he is saying or is it just his fine intuition working.

– Fostering is our Gaelic pride, Anna ye ken what we say of it. Milk is ten times thicker nor blood when it comes to relations. We have always loaned our children and they are aye the better for it –

So cease from playing the bereft Madonna and look kindly on the young lady in the castle. That last sentence stays in his head as Henny comes round the ranks of white skinned empty barrels, lined in tall tiers on the parade ground of Number One, blotting out the sight of the castle across the water of the inner harbour. Lower the tone, Henny, and she does!

– Yuus, Anna Rai, yon room at the castle you're in has a window as big as the side o' my house, the maid says. Last year skolting skeds, this year a lady, who ever heard the like, Rob? –

– Fate, Henny, an unpredictable lady, chust like her across the water –

Rob heads away, nose up, a scent of fresh herring already, the Close Season broken again?

The bard gone, the ladies get to the real talk: about earnest-money from Henny.

– Ah'll tell the Russian dame ye'll be taking the arlish again this year, Anna Rai, yir boots are ready there –

About her new life from Anna, ignoring the reference to her

boots. Can one not walk beneath wet trees behind the castle, do boots mean only fish in this wee town with one track thought. Say it out though I'm not ready to decide.

– Henny, dear, may I tell you Lady Emily has asked me to accompany her to England –

– England, wiv been there, on frozen Yarmouth quay, salt and ice how they burn on cut fingers! –

– It's Cambridge, the college town, Henny, it's not easy for me over the castle –

– Twas yourself decided to go there, nobody here ever made out what the honey was for you there, nor what the castle posh blone sees in you above the other disaster widows –

– Because I am alone with a child, is what she says, Henny –

– Anna now, plenty other women here alone with babies, the invite they get is the poor house not the castle! –

Henny ruminates on twenty years of raising a simple son with no help from anyone, poor Norman wanting his morning roll and she cannot think now if she gave him the meek to buy it with. God in Heaven, he's older than Anna here!

They watch the man who passes now, flickering eye and lip but not speaking yet, weighing up the quays and the conditions, ready to finalise his new scheme for Roddy Banker, pull all the ends together, the local man, with the community knowledge and unusual confidence when meeting the incomers with their superior savvy of the ways of money. MacAllan, who hopes he has the biggest credit in Portrona for the coming season. Did he not cure plenty good stuff for Germany last year when it hit top price, luck or skill? Little does anyone know it but our entrepreneur is planning a brilliant ploy that deserves to succeed, selling salt herring in New York of all places. He had holes in his trousers when he was an apprentice cooper, Henny remembers, look at him now spinning his stick and fluffing his cravat. That cove makes me proud, one of us, clever or crooked, he even got an invite to the castle, another of Lady Lapag's charities. Anna see a piece of glass flash on his waistcoat, fob or monocle, he tips his hat at her now and did he wink? I can see why Emily likes him.

This Emily now, this Lady Bountiful, bluestocking from Cambridge, what can Portronians and country folk know of her, what can I do to show us what Lady Emily Percy is really like? But then she is but a woman, crammed with knowledge out of books rather than out of field and bed and sea. What can even Anna make of Emily?

– Do please call me Emily –

Anna knows nothing of Shakespeare or Hardy or anybody in between. A *tabula rasa* so far as books but the Bible, but my God, for life itself, that's why Emily is so taken with our Anna. She can see living and dying glowing out of her green eyes, drawn on her handsome face, in the very stretch of Anna's pouted lips.

Emily might say to herself when faced with the tall child-widow as now designated in her *Diary of My Sojourn in the Western Islands*: when I was eighteen, I was still taking dolls to bed. Aye, she probably says something like that to herself as she sits in the hothouse staring through the misty glass across at the swaying boats in the inner harbour, gathering for the Great Herring Hunt of May and June that year; pen and embossed paper to hand alongside her opera glasses to watch the town with.

But where, you ask, is your villain amongst all these couthy coves and blones of Portrona in the second half of the last century, a fair long way from the millennium which bates our breath now? Do not fret my friends, read on to find that he lives, MacRoe, lives to this very day. His memory and his deeds are known to all who touch upon our history. The thesaurus alone can describe him fully, get his flavour. Only the fact that his shadow lived can give us dramatic licence to include such a base, blackguardly, cruel, diabolical, evil, fiendish, hateful, inhuman, malevolent, opprobrious, ruffianly, sinful, terrible, vile, wicked character in our performance, which can not be a proper production without him. Black Donald MacRoe, gauleiter of crofters and persecutor of squatters, a people that would have had to be invisible if they were to escape his spite and malice, I was only carrying out my orders, who was blind and who was loose? And don't forget he is the public face for the same powers as is our kind Lady Emily, with private rowing boat to skim his bulk across the inner harbour whenever he needs another signature, not to waste time by going the long way round by spring cart. No horse to nourish either, a boatman feeds himself.

One of the questions regarding the infamous MacRoe is how much did the aura of the Fantom of the Moor, the one whom folklore credits with twenty murders (the last one, the hangman on his very scaffold) come to be his? The Fantom, known to all as *Mac an t-Srònaich*, who became the projected black Other for the people of the island, as they at the same time tried to come to terms with their terrible sinfulness (a peasant population of ladies and gentlemen, naturals, one of the great innocent societies of all time) had now to confront the darkness spoken of in their souls, projected onto the dangerous and dark figure who haunted the wet caves of their hills, minds and glens, who regularly was reported to have killed, although there are no bodies to be found in the criminal records. Did he eat them? The one common statement about the Strònach was that he was always hungry, a state and condition that the people were very familiar with. Now there are children's videos about him, attempting to show him as an empty coat, but this exorcism is futile. We need him, or someone like him. What has been changed by the writhing images?

Magumerad's body is buried to his hips in the grave he is gouging from the niggardly stony soil of Portrona cemetery. He is working near the shore and expects soon to see the salt water seep through into the hollow at his feet, sinking with him as he picks and scrapes his way to a decent depth. I hope to God I can get a lair in one of the sandy graveyards on the machair for myself, this is no place to spend eternity, much as we Magumerads come from a long line of wandering Frenchmen, I have Viking blood too, like everyone else on this wet island and no decent Norseman would consider for a second burying his friends, or his enemies, in this smelly gravel bed. Much as they loved the sea they preferred to sleep in sand. Only shopkeepers without souls would come here to make a burial-ground. I hope Norman remembers to fetch my piece. He'll know there's been a death.

On cue comes our innocent, silver spade on shoulder, singing his triumphant burial song, handed down to us,

– The spade one day/Thee low will lay/The sod twill break/ The grave twill make/The spade/The spade/Hoh, hoh, the spade! –

Magumerad clambers out of the grave, Norman Daft leaps into it, after letting Magumerad take a brown paper bag from the pocket of his shabby black overcoat.

– Easy there, Norman, leave some work for me –

Amazing how that wee silver spade from the castle grounds has lasted out. Norman's delving, him strong as one of MacAllan's Clydesdales. Crowdie again, can a man dig graves without meat?

Magumerad pick pick stones for Norman spade lift out of sleep-outside place for people gone away when wake them who sleep in ground Magumerad Magumerad gone to sea danger sea for wash hands before meat a cruel trade it has the spade.

Norman worries everyone in Portrona, naturally. To think that someone so daft is so versed in the ways of the end of all, they don't want to think about it but he makes 'em, grins our gravedigger, his tombstone teeth now flecked with cottage cheese. His mother, Henny, he troubles most of all, as last week on the quay when he went into a fit after overdoing his song following an extended session of Timmarree with the boys picking him, as he likes them to, as the Drum, pounding his broad hollow back to their weird tune with clenched fists.

– Timmarre, Timmaroh, Timarradie Oh! Lay on him Braggimore! –

His head buried in the stomach of the leader, the rest lining up for their turn, each assigned such names as Braggimore (*Breug Mhòr*, Big Liar), Sinidore and Heavens, Pots and Pans. Norman's chest resonates. Then rehearsing his Song of the Spade with an unusual excitement for the lounging men and women on Number One (still awaiting a landing of early summer herring) did Norman not collapse with a twitching and a foaming never seen outside before. Henny rushes to his aid, slackens his mouth with a twist of her shawl, whispers in his ear, helps him to his feet, he stands shivering with the life dawning anew in his vague grey eyes. MacAllan tips his hat at her and speaks first.

– He will fall over the quay one day, Henny, and drown! –
– God in heaven forbid, MacAllan. He'll do his turn and me quiet in my grave –
– You should listen to them who would help you send Norman away where he would be safe, Henny –

No reply to that from a loving mother.

Roddy Banker now, Portronian civic leader to his fancy boots, made and measured in chamois and best sole by Hector, he belongs to the town in the special way that the sons of successful incomers do, a foot in both camps, with relatives in thatched cottages in the country round to balance against doctors in Bearsden and lawyers in Morningside.

This was how Rob the Bard thought of him, though not Henny, who was regularly summoned to one of his offices to discuss the possible fate of Norman among other things. The offices were three: the banker's sanctum in Sandstone Buildings which Henny never saw, the provost's office in the Town House which she visited at times when the need was urgent and the business office in The Octagon set square in the space between Cross Street and the quays, final goal of the herring entrepreneur with its sales floor for the curers surrounded by many small offices of odd shape. This office was familiar to Henny, especially during the herring season. Summer and winter, for Roddy dabbled to a cautious extent in the herring curing industry, by shipping out full barrels and importing salt. Others who maintained a presence in The Octagon included Madame Wolkova of Petersburg and MacRoe, who had a space for some of his dealings, none knew quite what, legalities to do with land perhaps, for did he not act for the castle as well as the Crown?

– I can keep my eye on things –

Roddy Banker had been putting it about for years each season as it came, that he intended setting up as a curer. But he never did. Perhaps it was an excuse to discuss herring gutting and packing crews with Henny, the recognised top gutting foreman in the town. To try to persuade her to send Norman away to the mainland for secure care, which he may or may not be in need off.

It is to the Town House office that Anna has been summoned by the provost, asked (or ordered?) by Lady Emily, who fails to see why Anna should refuse help from the Disaster Fund, even although she is receiving emolument for her work at the castle. It baffles many why Anna refuses to accept money collected on her behalf, and on behalf of the other widows bereaved by the sudden summer storm last year. It may be that Anna herself would be inarticulate on the matter were we to stop her now on Dempster Street and insist that she say what she has against taking help.

If the provost thought to overcome the girl from Eye with his mammoth mahogany and leather desk, his fat chair, the lurid painting of him in his chain on the wall, he was too late. Her days at the castle have granted Anna confidence to live among rich people's things, whilst her contact with Lady

Emily gives her natural dignity a polish that appeals to the bluff man before her, one who can slide easily from the talk of the men's room on the quay, to the florid maunderings of municipal meetings. There are those raised among simple things who find no difficulty coming to terms with the artefacts provided by money and Anna was one of them, not that rare a person on the island, just a mite more confident than most, arrogant even, enemies would say.

It took only minutes for the provost, despite using all his banker's wiles, to have to admit defeat. This girl widow before him was not going to go back on her rejection of what she called 'southern charity' whatever he may say to her. He felt his admiration and physical attraction (she's young enough to be my daughter) giving way to exasperation and anger, not knowing how to react to one who so plainly did not have any respect for money. She rose and he tried one last gambit.

– To accept money from the fund would be to include your son in the obligation to Lady Emmeline? –

Got you, lady, as Anna stills like a deer who hears a strange sound.

– My son is being looked after down in Eye –

– Lady Percy wants to be a mother at second hand, is that it –

She turns after withering him and flees down the clattering concrete stair.

Anna strode along the street that took her to the quays, no thought of turning to the bridge leading to the castle grounds. By the square stone box of the customs house, she paused, hearing voices over water, the knocking of oars. Raising her head to breathe in the crisp morning sea air, she sees the castle across the anchorage, its false turrets looming above the exotic trees. The glass panels in the greenhouses gaze blindly back. I wonder if Emily is there now, with her opera glasses aimed at me?

The rows of raw whitewood barrels with their hoops of cane

had grown and there was a fresh mound of white salt at the end of Number One, sparkling like a snowdrift, too soon for it to melt down and add to the slush under foot which would start to spread when the first herring arrived.

Now Anna becomes aware of the unique scent of a fishing boat, overwintered and not yet fished this year; tar from Russia, cutch bark from the tropics, and behind these odours just a sickening whiff of rotten bilge water, the stench that turned the coiler lad's stomach, crouched in his wet cubbyhole, fighting to subdue the streaming line of black rope, the feared apprenticeship of all fishermen, the badge of manhood, a season past coiling, a belly of iron at last. Will herring guts be carted this year to Laxdale, where potatoes and herring will blend in the land, the symbolic joining Rob says the women with knives make possible?

From the edge of the quay she sees someone she is vaguely aware of already, Donald MacDonald, brother-in-law of Mairi, baby Iain's wet nurse. She watches him work on the newly barked lugsail hanging half over the side, fingers rapidly undoing knots, totally concentrated. She raises a hand, he does not see her, she turns away to the path to the bridge at the end of the inner harbour, that takes her to the drive that leads to the front door of the castle.

– You must enter by the main door, Anna, always –

Donald MacDonald has straightened his long wide back and is staring after her.

Donald MacDonald, son of a squatter on land leased to his father, with no chance for a piece of his own, a fisherman though by choice. Devilish good excuse to put your back to acid soil next to peat cuttings, look out ever the unfathomable sea surrounding the spreading race, the growing numbers never coped with by constant emigration, encouraged or voluntary, now entitled to wear a skipper's cap, paid for by his scrawled name on a crackling paper he can barely read, *took my chance with Aeneas*. The herring's a gamble, if you don't take a throw you never pick up. Weird the way Anna's been since Jim Flett was drowned, lucky for her my brother Murdo's wife lost her baby the same time Anna had hers or she could not be a swell at the castle the now, her son a god child at Mairi's breast. Oh, just see the pride of her walking there into the very porch of Portrona's castle!

He thought of the cronies who appear now from winter quarters to eke a living from odd jobs around the quays. These old men, retired fishermen and sailors, were useful during the season, with much wily experience to draw upon, willing to work slowly for a few hours on some seaman's task for the price of a twist of black tobacco and a glass of equally black rum. The cronies are another small part of the summer scene, tolerated reasonably well, although they are prone to gossip and tale-telling. Whilst they await the Great Bosun's Pipe to join their shipmates in the cemetery, they are able to ease the work of many a hard-pressed skipper who cannot afford to pay a man full-time. Donald bethought himself as to why he had a mental picture of cronies whilst contemplating Portrona Castle, gave up, remembered he would need advice on stepping the new mast. And the Old Man in the Castle has gone to his eternal rest of course, not in stony ground nearby, but in a posh London mausoleum.

Prior to persuading an amenable crony to his boat, he is greeted by our peripatetic bard, smart to make a living without getting his hands earthy, his feet wet, or making orthodox use of his education, today giving out on the kippering of herring, talking to that newspaper man who's taken to hanging about town and telegraph office now Portrona's on the map of the world herring industry.

– Hey Donald. Saw you speak to young Anna there, some blone, eh? Been telling yon scribbler about smoking kippers, this town going to go on the map for Portrona kippers, mark my words, the girls split the herring down the back, all the guts are out of them, chust like MacAllan's fish for New York, if they ever get there, only he splits them down the front, the fires of oak shavings and sawdust, the smoke would choke you, it smells nice tho', always the danger of fire. Donald, think, this morning's finished kippers on sale in Billingsgate the day after tomorrow –

– Slow down Rob, help me lift this, stop talk of kippers till we fishermen land some decent skeds first –

– Chune herring in its own chuice! –

Wonder if I can teach Norman Gòrach how to nail up kipper boxes, make himself a few wing in the season, millions of kippers in small caskets of white soft wood, a dozen pairs per box, the smokey scented greasiness oozing. Pity the best June kippers never catch the new potatoes, August's pink marbles with the skins peeling, you can taste the summer, short as it is.

There is a bellman in the town, forerunner of all hucksters. His jacket is Victorian but his breeches go back almost to the time when Jim Morrison went off to join Bligh and MacKenzie, went to Hudson's Bay, already studying the blank rugged map of Canada he was to cross. Be sure our bellman had heard of them in some garbled style, the town's very own fictioned version of pieces of its past. Now the bellman calls for pilots for the arrival of the first salt boats, ready to discharge a mountain of brackish hailstones on the main quay, from other exotic isles, Sicily and the Balearics. Every grain of it will eventually pass through the fingers of a woman, imagine, to cling to the fish.

The bellman is an extremely useful fellow worth more than his salt.

Barrels by the million, each stacked eventually with succulent herrings, rolling from western Europe to Russian steppe, made by that aristocrat of the curing industry, the cooper, stave and hoop and craft and later the cure itself, the cunning blending of fresh fish, fresh wood and fresh salt in his wise hands. Only he can do nothing without the girls who connect the aspects of his glorious trade by gutting with enormous speed and every care each fish on which the cooper's mystery relies.

And top of the trade, in June, the world famous brand, Portrona Maiden Herring, so celebrated the cure that, paradoxically, the barrels need not be stamped by the brand inspector at all, the very name of Portrona enough, the German buyer knocking out the bottom of the barrel to suck a mouthful from the back of one of the selected fish that have been specially put in the bottom tier to fool him. Maybe he knows, the dour man from Germany, just plays along, listening as the packer ladies call to the cooper for him to pass it:

– Bottom tier! –

He knows the quality runs from top to bottom tier, maybe some lesser fish, tornbellies, here and there, in the middle rows in the whitewood barrels, he knows they know he will not ship two bad consignments in a row to Stettin, nor will Madame Wolkova to Petersburg.

Emmeline, which she prefers to Emily among close friends, speaks to Anna in the small drawing room of influences on western civilisation, from Homer, Aristotle, Plato to later men whose teachings built that empire which reddens the globe at the time. Major writers always emphasised what was put into the heads of our children with no care for what was put into their hearts.

– Very few books have been written, Anna, for the purpose of educating people about their feelings –

– Emmeline, we have to suffer before we know what is true, that is what the men say and I believe it now –

– Oh Anna, you have gone through so much, so young –

– I saw the boat, I saw my man's boat, flooded –

– Anna darling, open your heart! –

– You have no notion at all of the power of the ocean. Other men were with Jim in the boat. I was not seeing

them, only him, the beautiful lad who put movement inside
me –

– You are so courageous –

– She was fast on the Sgeir and you could see her, shaking
like an animal, the water breaking over her. Jim took off his
boots, to swim, you understand, Emmeline. If you do not take
off your seaboots, they trap the air when you go into the sea,
your boots full of air, they push your head down, push you
under the water and you, and you, and you –

– Oh darling –

– Drown, Emmeline, drown, you are drowned by your own
boots! –

– Open your heart –

– Yes. I found Jim's boots before I found him. In the tangle.
The big boots of the man of the sea. A cross of nails on the
sole. That's the mark he had on them. A cross of nails on
the sole –

– Do go on, dearest Anna –

– I knew these boots well, many's a time I drew his boots
off him. Yes. Between my knees, dragging them from his feet.
Then, peering down, the stockings, with the pattern I made
up myself. It is on the stocking pattern the women know their
men, who are spoiled, Emmeline, by rock and by crab, their
faces, Emmeline, so that you do not recognise them –

– Oh my poor brave darling –

– *Gu leòr*, Emmeline. Enough –

Every culture needs prophecy or how could we go on, just
because the true seers foretell disaster and death more often
than triumphant life is no reason not to listen to them. As for
Portrona it was a crone who had the gift, yes a cliche of a crone
could tell your coming life just as soon as you put a coin in
her palm. She studies you and makes her prognostications, just
like a doctor: you will not drown, you will be safe, you will
return, even going off to war, one might tell you (rarely later
during 1914 to 1918) you will be safe, you will come home,

I see you crossing the tidal ford without your rifle. Our time is before this, but the cailleach (she had a name, once, but is now cailleach (old woman) only, her feminine power that of telling us what's going to happen to us. Power enough, (God wot) a fisherman, not allied to any church yet, a boldish young fellow, he comes to her in the sight of all on Portrona quay today as the boats make ready to leave to start the season, the Buckiemen having broken the close time, the curers out to steal a march, though how with skin and bone skeds that a starving seagull would cock a beak at. Our man with rope and coin stops the roving cailleach and asks her curse or blessing and she tells him true what he wants to hear: first, you will be safe, but she does not tell him if they'll cross the path of shoals. Being alive is enough and if you're going to be alive and working the season, surely the fish will come too?

It was winds they sold, a piece of your sheet rope they put three knots in. We shall reveal the details of the Rope Spell in good time. It was himself, the first really long story writer, told us about Portrona's wind seller, to wit, Walter Scott, a man who knew more things than any single person has a right to know. As for wind sellers, well our cailleach is almost the last of her race, engines have started to come in and man assuming yet more power over nature, what need did he have of bothering himself about the vagaries of the wind?

Our fearless young man (or frightened superstitious cove, take your pick and more) is the very boy Donald MacDonald has chosen as mate of his new boat. Now he produces a piece of rope from around his waist and asks her to knot it thrice. Does Donald approve, will he know, there being the danger of excess tied in with the Rope Spell? Storms.

Doubtless both he and Donald are of the type described at the time when it was fashionable to speak of types as strong manly fishermen, tall like all men of their race, their heads proudly set and carried on kingly necks, some fair, some dark, with waving locks, gleaming eyes that can persuade or threaten, since we are on the subject, Norse and Gael mingled.

Their sisters and lovers no less impressive to the friendly stranger, the sunny good humour of the fishergirls and the gladness of their faces. Nothing though about the beauty of their bodies, the colour of their heads or even their carriage, which would bedeck a catwalk. Today those ladies with long backs and legs set to packing the herrings in the barrels in particular, only they would not consider modelling as work. Even today so little has really altered, their attitude towards the world one of constant endeavour to make things pleasant for the stranger and to acquit themselves of their best in difficult circumstances.

And the curers? We have met a couple, from Portrona and Petersburg, add canny Fifers and bluff Norfolk men, those who know the ways of money and who savour the risk of it. There's no gamble greater than playing with nature, casting your chips into the sea itself, sitting safe in harbour and letting your money take men and boats out night after night, waiting to see their dawn return, trailing a cloud of herring gulls and lying so low the fallen fish slide over the side on the tack or high and slow and empty, no tail of birds, either way impossible to predict the price the fish will fetch. Supply and demand drives a man mad, the superstitious crime of dumping fine herring into the harbour.

Let a fisherman of the time tell us what drew him. Donald speaks of the sound of the sea, the sough of the wind, that all at home listen out for. Sometimes you are scared but strangely sometimes you are not, always you scan the water (remember how close we are to it) with its depths of green and indigo, looking out for the smoking signs of the herring. It is better when the water is dark, you can imagine the shoals swimming below. When the water is clear as you sail over sandy bottom, there is nothing to imagine, green smooth sand on the ground, nothing between you. A crab slips along sideways, a speckled plaice stirs up the sand like a puff of smoke that goes at once like blood in water. My brother was lost one year, after a good fishing. The Zulu boat heeling, the water hissing past her, she leans so far over, the loose herring on her deck slip from her back into the sea, young Iain watches, the dipping yard swings over fast, he's over the side his head bobbing far astern in a second, she cannot go back for him. We like the dark purple sea, hides the fish from us, we say they are down there, millions, a year's money in one night. After planting the nets and singing the psalm and breaking our fast we haul off the throbbing capstan, shake out the gasping fish glittering in the dawn, gold not silver, the hold fills, the boy coils coils in his cramped cubbyhole, his heaving world wet black rope. We turn for home, Portrona beckons behind the pearl sky, the wind with us, she takes it, straining boards and sheets and canvas. Hear her chuckle past Tiumpan, Bayble Island, the Chicken, Holm, the Beasts, Arnish, Goat Island, to Number One. We are not the first but we are not the last, either.

Anna looks out of her window high up in the castle, has a mental conversation with Mairi and her son who are miles away, she speaks softly. If I stand on my bed and look out of the top window I can see the dark rocks at the mouth of the harbour, the Beasts of Holm, the sea licking their spines, monsters floating in the water, rising and falling, up and down. Of course it is the sea that moves, the rocks do not, yet they are never the same, not for one second, it makes me tremble, Mairi, tremble, to see the Beasts in the water, rising and falling, rising and falling, the Beasts of Holm, floating.

Does Mairi not appear that same day with the child on her back, tight-shawled like a traveller woman's wean, at the outer door of the back kitchen of the castle and ask one of the undercooks, Chrissie, a local girl, to tell Anna she was there and with permission from the head cook she did so (discipline having slackened just a little since the death of the old lady and the advent of Lady Emily Percy) and Anna runs now in front of Chrissie, down the wide wrought metal and mahogany stairs, along silent carpets, on to clacking tiles, then over the sea sounding slabs of Caithness slate that floor the long passage to the kitchens.

– Mairi! Is my darling well? –

– Very well, Anna, sorry I came here, but I have no meal left and Murdo went off to Buckie last night –

They speak in Gaelic naturally, but it is well to supply some kind of translation in an English narrative. Chrissie comes in to the back kitchen.

– Lady Emily says you are all to go to the small drawing room –

She speaks in Gaelic also. What's more she smiles and tickles young Iain under his chin, Anna holding him eye to eye.

Murdo went to Buckie last night does not need translation for anyone in Portrona at the time. It means that Mairi's husband is one of the many island fishermen who travel to the east coast of Scotland every summer to help make up the crews of the fishing boats working the North Sea (a Buckie skipper is wont to say when asked the number of his crew for the season: six and a Hielanman).

To the surprise of Anna and the discomfiture of Mairi, Emily (or is it Emmeline today, I fancy?) stands there waiting and now goes to the child, trying to be like any woman, thinks Anna, then feels ashamed at the thought.

– Oh, isn't he precious! Fast asleep –

It is Mairi who replies, proprietorially, emboldened by Anna's presence and her closeness to her, being part of her.

– He is good at the sleeping, my Lady –

– Oh Anna, darling, a madonna you look standing there –

She goes now, sensing a private mother's need to talk and a mite embarrassed too, to pore over the red bound ledgers of crofters' rental accounts, scrawled in MacRoe's spidery hand too often with angry notes about non-payment. She finds it difficult to visualise the state and condition of those who exist in what she thinks of as crude, unfinished cottages of undressed stone and straw.

Meantime, the mother and the wet nurse discuss pressing matters in careful Gaelic, after Anna has handed Mairi a gold coin to buy a boll of oatmeal, the bedrock supply that ensures daily nourishment and represents riches to those with no money, fish or potatoes.

– The carpenter made me a cradle, Mairi –

This cradle made by the castle carpenter-in-chief, from exotic timber imported, the plantation trees being yet too young to work with, though he has his eye on some slow-growing exotics, yet to be planed even now a century and more since he underwent the neutral offices of Magumerad: the carpenter chose carefully and sawed and planed and cut and grooved and made a cradle for the child of a girl young enough to be his daughter. His eyes dimmed with tears when it was polished for he had no-one, being a Gall, a tradesman incomer who put his craft in front of felicities such as marriage and children, who never managed to learn a word of Gaelic to chat in (unconscious rejection?) but now he has made a true work of art in his own terms, you just cannot see the joints! It tilts to the touch on half-moon rockers. Most of all, he is proud of the canopy of scented cedar from the East, bent to a one piece semicircle with advice on steaming wood from the head cooper across the water, a strong and elegant arch to protect any child fortunate enough to spend its infancy in this cradle the castle carpenter has made for young Iain.

– It will outlast me, Anna! –

– I have him in bed with me –

– Better you use the cradle, I'll send someone across with it –

Mairi is reminded, as so very often, that Iain is not hers, that her own was taken away in a small box wrapped in white linen, a few months ago.

– Oh the cradle, Anna, the cradle –

– You'll have another child, dear –

– Not while I'm looking after yours, Anna –

– Are you making enough milk? –

– Oh yes, Anna, yes, if we have food in –

– You will have that now, Mairi. Are you staying with Murdo's parents while he's away? –

– No, Anna, Murdo wants to build –

– Build, how can he build with no land, no lot of his own? –

– His father has given him part of his own lot –

Anna looks towards the big desk at the window, the heap of account books, hears the susurration of stiff pages turning, sees the frown on Emily's face, remembers hearing about the present preoccupation of the estate officials, the population 'explosion' on the island, the crowding in of too many people on too little arable land resulting in the growth of a new class that begins to strike fear in the landlord class, the squatters.

– Murdo built a bothy till he can start the house at the end of the season –

– A bothy is against the law, Mairi. Murdo's father has no right . . . –

Mairi feels an understandable surge of anger and envy.

– You in a castle, Anna, your son in a bothy –

– Do your duty to me, Mairi, and to my son –

Mairi is overcome with remorse and grief and fear too, perhaps. She promises with vehemence to do all for baby Iain, for his mother, for as long as Anna wants.

– You lost your own, Mairi, I am giving you mine –

– Yes, Anna, yes, yes, yes –

– We shall leave it like that, Mairi. Go now, I'll send his cradle over –

As though she understands Gaelic by some osmosis, Emily slams shut a rent ledger and turns to the mothers abruptly.

– Someone will see you out, Mrs MacDonald. Anna, the

water was not hot enough this morning, speak to the house-keeper. Also, you will inform the maids, and the kitchen staff, they must set standards equivalent to those in the South –

– I think coal would be better than peat for heating this huge luchairt of a place, Lady Emily –

– Peat costs nothing, Anna –

That's what you would think, my leddy, but under her breath of course.

The assumption that peat for use as fuel is easily and freely available is one held by many who come to the islands of the west; watching a pair of self-righteous incomers struggle and sweat to cut a straight trench in the moorland and produce workable slabs of fuel at the same time is to view the start of the fading of a dream; when you visit the site after rain and find one of your sheep drowned in the bog thereby created, then does your rage rise and it is unreasoning rage and can lead to the kind of incident that both settlers and islanders deplore.

The bold MacAllan has requested that Lady Emmeline accompany him to the moorland shielings later this summer and it may be she will discover something about the hard and skilled work of peatwinning then, although she has no inkling or interest now, being drawn purely by pictures in her mind of lovely shepherdesses in gay gear, singing songs to many-coloured cattle, by wine lochs (lakes?) with sedgy green edges, seat of the lone shieling and the pure spring with healing waters. She has learned from her reading that the shieling time is the real time for the maidens and especially for the young men, for whom it means the chance to approach a caravay without having to pass the dog and to avoid the noisy ambush set by the girl's mother of tinny utensils to trip over in the sneaking dark. Emmeline had memorised the words: the milkmaids on the moor love to play the Romany with scarlet kerchiefs on their hair. And more, a little play between the moorland nymph with fine dark eyes whose power over the ignorant town boy is almost absolute.

– On the shielings you can find crofters' daughters with all the dignity of carriage so famous in the women of Castile –

Lady Emily is far from such thoughts of Emmeline's at the moment as she waves Anna away, asking her to send in the Sheriff Clerk who has been squatting bulkily in a wicker chair out in the inner hall for several minutes, in his coat of many seal skins with its right hand pocket full of snuff, hugging a cracked Gladstone bag, bouncing it on his knee now and then as though it were a strange hairless animal or even a child.

Sheriff Clerk is another of the titles held by the ubiquitous Donald MacRoe. His task as he sees it is to shape the world around him in accordance with the dictates of certain laws that provide him with a mental configuration which authorises his despotic actions towards the people of the town and the island. He has yet to find out what kind of a principal is Lady Emily Percy, who has lately been handed the reins of the titular head of the estate. He anticipates no difficulty and the bobbing of the bag of legal papers on his lap reveals not anxiety, rather his impatience to get on with his many tasks, each authorised by a legal instrument made out by himself, under one title, granting him permission under another hat, to carry out without fear or favour, this or that business of the law as Donald MacRoe understands it. The crack-skinned creature on his knee is the focus of his being, that and the roll-top desk in his main office in the court house, although one cannot be sure how aware he is of this particular fact.

MacRoe made a dire impression on thousands during his reign of many years and he may have inspired a three-decker novel eventually, where someone very like him appears as one Factor Donald Black (Black Donald/Satan, Gaelic inversion), who delights in abusing, in Gaelic (what additional power this gave him, his ability to speak their language, oppressors seldom speak the language of the oppressed) all who come before him, whether they have the rent money or not, eviction and emigration an ever-present threat.

The puritan mind thrives on chewing at the sinews of legality; laws, rules, regulations, local or national, meat and drink to it (is this why the USA is besotted with lawyers?) and MacRoe is a fine example. Even now, his pen scrawls in his head on thick cream embossed paper making the words for the latest document of eviction; a lovely case, clear indisputable breach of the estate regulations against building without consent, the Sheriff's signature already in place, merely confirmation from the estate needed now, a simple initial from Lady Emily to show the Sheriff when the accused failed to comply with the eviction and MacRoe could ask for the Order to Demolish; and fail to comply he surely would. Can a man cast his wife and family out on the sitig (dunghill) and him off to the East Coast for the summer fishing?

– Timing is vital when enforcing the law –

He has cast his skins in the outer hall and confronts Lady Emily with gaping bag, retrieving with thick fingers, papers from its maw to place them, next the rent ledgers, spreading them out in front of her with a hint of a flourish, starting to read:

– Petition to Interdict against Murdo MacDonald, Fisherman, by Lady Emily Percy, for the Pursuer; the abovenamed Pursuer submits to the Court the Condescendence and Note of Plea in Law hereto annexed and prays the Court.

– I find Scotch Law to be confusing –

– Leave it to me, dear Lady –

Just so we know what the law intended and why, let us explain that Murdo MacDonald built a temporary cottage near his father's house last autumn in order that his wife and expected child be accommodated whilst he is away this summer earning his only annual income as a hired hand on an East Coast fishing boat. This proceeding, though unlawful in the eyes of the estate, is commonplace, the only alternative being either that young couples crowd in upon their parents, or give up the notion of marriage altogether. We may presume that the unfortunate couple presently pursued by MacRoe is by way of example to the other squatters, and we will consider them doubly unfortunate in that their first child was born dead soon after they moved to the bothy that they hope is the beginning of their permanent home.

Here is part of what confused Lady Emily, who wrongly imagines that the use of English law would make her work easier:

TO INTERDICT THE DEFENDERS (Murdo's father is included as having given permission for his son to start building) *and all others acting for them or him from proceeding further with the erection of the dwelling house (hereinafter called the new dwelling house) now in course of erection on the lot of land occupied by Malcolm MacDonald as tenant thereof under the Pursuer and which new dwelling house adjoins the dwelling house presently occupied by the said Malcolm MacDonald, FURTHER TO ORDAIN that the Defender demolish such part of the said new dwelling house as may have been already erected.*

Plus six other pages of legal clauses meant to ensure that neither Murdo nor his father had any chance of evading the orders of the estate, ensuring that vigorous young couples are not permitted to settle and will thereby be encouraged, or forced, to emigrate. This fear of the growth of population in an area with hundreds of thousands of empty acres can only be understood as the unconscious terror of the few against the felt need of the many to obtain justice. God can testify their wants were few; simple food and basic warmth and comfort, yet they were being denied even this, a people renowned for their eagerness to work.

When the Sheriff has granted the above, which is a formality under the present law, MacRoe can then proceed to obtain the Order to Demolish. If the unfortunate Murdo (at present in a fishing boat bucking the North Sea swell) does not demolish the part-house already built, where shelters the little family he left behind him, the Sheriff Clerk's men will do it for him (at Murdo's expense!). Straight and crooked is the law, say the old folk here.

Suddenly tired of MacRoe's presence and wanting free of this sure and surly official, now oddly Lady Emily initials where indicated, politely dismisses the factor, wonders whether Madame is really as outrageous as she thought last year.

Can you believe in our Madame Wolkova? A lady with thick eyebrows and wide mouth, boot swaggering, cigar smoking, fur-collared, great-coated, who comes each summer all the way from Petersburg to Portrona to buy and cure herring for the Russian hinterland. Of course we believe in Madame W (or is it Madame V?) and we know why we can believe in her; there *was* such a one in Portrona, in its long gone golden time of fishy prosperity, so Madame Wolkova is for us another in that great company of characters who make the past times so much more absorbing and inspiring than the prosaic present.

Madame appeared each year at the same time as the first strange sails; she booked her usual room for six weeks at the top of the Quay Hotel, then sailed past the counter into Roddy Banker's inner temple, where a flirtatious exchange of vodka for whisky took place and Madame's monogrammed accounts ledger was taken out of the safe and placed on the corner of the banker's desk.

– Anozzer season comes, Roddy –

Glasses clink (Madame does not smash hers) and then the clerk appears with crunching canvas poke to empty into Madame's money belt. Now for Henny NicKenny and the signing on of the gutting girls, put a gold coin in one hand and touch the other with the pen for a cast iron con-tract.

– Knife ladies for Madame Wolkova's company! –

Ah, but can you also believe the other, the non-business Madame Wolkova, who winters in Paris, buys new paintings for a gallery in Petersburg, who works herself in water-colour? Women and boats as a rule. You can?

The presence of such a one in Portrona, if only for the summer season, is not lost on Lady Emmeline and an invitation to the castle for Madame is a not unexpected eventuality. When she can spare the time, but then, there are great intervals of empty time at the curing, interspersed with periods of furious mind and body bursting action. Madame, unlike her rivals in Portrona, savours the alternating periods of sloth and frenzy, but then she has the soul of an artist.

Madame's neat boots (from Hector, made to measure) beat like a soldier's on the hanging wooden bridge erected by the carpenter we have heard about, the maker of the exquisite cradle, the span designed to give a short cut across the ravine below the castle, his own idea, although MacRoe and Lady Emily imagine it to be theirs. She inhales the scent of the newly awakened trees, fails to identify any predominant fragrance, only delights in the strange bouquet, trees from the East and from South America, flourishing in the soft climate of the West, awaiting the rushed two months of warmth that gives them life for the year to come. Chust like the peoples here, eh, Madame (she referred to herself thus in her own mind, when speaking the local lingo, so how should we know her forename? She would lose both authority and foreignness). When thinking in Russian or French, she gave herself her baptismal name, which may be later revealed. Now she is on her way to see Emily, having promised last year to call again and bring Emmeline a gift of a painting, on a certain famous theme, for Madame is shrewd in her judgment of people and understanding also. She pauses now at the end of the timber pontoon, looks down at the burn below, drops her cigar butt into the biggest pool, startling, we may be sure, the plump speckled trout lazing there (a favoured spot for feeding them, the goldfish having failed to thrive).

Emmeline sees the approach of Madame through the windows of the small drawing room and this contributes to her hurried dismissal of MacRoe, her failure to think through the implications of appending her initials to crackling papers proffered by the Sheriff Clerk who is at one and the same time the factor of the estate, giving him the position to abuse both offices.

When Madame is shown in and they have held hands and kissed each other with murmured words in three languages, Emily the Administrator turns into Emmeline the Romantic and relaxes with relief into a role without responsibility, coquettish, keen to hear of the vast world beyond. But first a question:

– I saw you approach across the ravine? –

– One of my skippers rowed me across, Emmeline –

She goes on to explain how she contracted certain skippers to supply her with their catches, paying them large bonuses, in competition with other curers, for this was before the setting up of the daily free sale of all fish on the fish mart, and how she could not find a gig to bring her around the bay and up the castle drive to the front door.

These two foreign women, alien to the place, and to each other, how do they react to one another, standing in a fairy tale castle on a lone island in the Western Ocean at a given time between the Mutiny of the *Bounty* and the Disaster of the *Iolaire*? Both women of privilege, yet not cushioned sufficiently to be able to lead a life of leisure, although one is led to suspect that either would have chafed at a position where they had little or nothing to do. Lady Emily, following education, demanded work of her peers and was sent to administer the estate of a distant relative. Madame Wolkova, in her European travels, had hit upon the perfect industry to subsidise and excuse her itinerant pursuit of art. They converse:

– Madame! How very glad I am to see you! –

– Anozzer herring season, how the years go round, Emily, how well you look! –

– I return the compliment, Madame. But then you are free, oh will you not tell me where you have been since you left us last year with a ship full of herring barrels? –

– Heh, in many places, Russia, Germany, 'Olland – still they love West Coast herring in Dutchland – to make you jealous, Emily, I spent the Vinter in Paree –

– Oh jealous, jealous, Paree! This place is so distant from the culture of Europe! –

– Ah, but you bring a breath of the great world outside to Portrona, no? –

– Yes Madame, oh yes! The Ladies' School . . . –

– But you will remember, no? They have their own culture?–

– It is dreadful here during the winter –

– But the Summer Festival now, yes? The Herring Carnival! All ze people chase the fish, chase the money, yes? Madame Kupper chase the women! –

– Chase the women! –

– Sharp knives, strong hands and long backs. That one reason I come to the Islands –

– The gels; of course. To what other reason do we owe your most welcome annual visitation, Madame! –

– Ze sweet soft herring you have here! Big Minch matjes, so tender! –

– Oh you may smoke if you wish –

– A cigar, Emily, non? My best girl is now with you –

– Anna Flett –

– The very lady. Best girl I effer had. The others follow her –

– Madame. We wish Anna to progress in her education. Can you not see that Anna can no longer be part of the ugly, dirty world of the herring gutting? –

– So, Emily! Dirty, ugly vorld of the herring curing, eh? Millions live off the shining fish. Best eating on earth –

– Oh Madame, forgive me! –

– Zat okay. But remember, Emily, remember is dirt everywhere! –

– I am so sorry, I did not wish to . . . –

– Think nozzing of it. Ze Russian woman care Damn All about blood on her boots! –

– Anna brought her boots from the shoemaker . . . –

– Oh the girls with their sea boots! The same boots as their men. I am wearing a pair myself. Good shoemakers in the town of Portrona –

– Will you, will you put nails in the sole? –

– Every boot has its own nail, Emily. I have many girls already. A woman from the town, Henny, she find them for me. You know her, Emily? – She have son – big fellow, walk about with a drum on his neck, no funeral happen without he know and follow, beating his drum, beating, beating not everyone like the bang! –

– Anna speaks of him. Norman Daft – why not Daft Norman? – Norman Daft they call him. People are frightened of him and I'm not surprised –

– Why do they fear a Man with God? That is what the Russians say of a man like that. A Man with God. Is that not sweet, Emily? A Man with God. Norman Daft, a Man with God –

– A Man with God . . . I like that. I shall tell it to Anna. Anna is a very understanding girl, Madame –

– Henny tell me she want Anna to work with her. To sort the girls into crews, you know? It sure, Anna will be very much of use to us in this season –

– I am sorry, Madame, but I shall have to say to Anna to take no notice of you or your foreman! Much better things await Anna than to be guddling amongst your herring, Madame, be they matjes or midgies! –

– Good you go, Emily! You stand up straight for you, *comme une true* English lady! Ve vill see vot Anna says! Good day to you now –

She goes in a cloud of smoke, only to return at once carrying a large wrapped framed picture.

– There the painting you vont so much, Emily, one of your dear Madonnas, yes? –

– Oh thank you, thank you, thank you! Oh how can I repay you for this, Madame? –

– Zee beeg fat Maidens from the Minch will pay! –

She goes, laughing. Emily stares after her, then eagerly starts to tear the wrappings from the picture.

Lone Shielings

NOW WE COME TO the other face of the island, the mysterious moorland plain of russet heather, laced with dark lochs and ale-coloured streams with green banks, the antipode to Portrona, summer home to milk burdened cattle and their attendant nymphs. On this island the natural order is reversed: the sea masculine, the land feminine; this purely because the sea is the domain of the male whilst the moor is the feminine hinterland, here in summer, the secret goal of the growing boy, during the same two months of burgeoning herring.

At least one grown man in Portrona has an inkling and it is one reason why MacAllan has prevailed upon Emmeline (definitely it is her today on the moor), she having read of shielings and proud-stepping milkmaids like the women of Castile, being compared to our maidens on the moss, a few miles inland from Portrona; why should they be astonished to find sure treading dark haired damsels with bright kerchiefs here, when they are to be seen everywhere else?

Now Emmeline is to proud-step, it is easier than it might be, May having brought its dryness, yet Emmeline has mud on her silk stockings, peat rather, that will dry and harden and can be brushed away before laundering, though Emmeline does not know that of course. She is aware of little, beyond the humming silence, softly yielding to tussocky ground, tiny bright flowers, bunches of heather in places like twigs, a shimmer in the air, the sea on the horizon, another world. The man toiling beside her (for he is a townie) has indicated that they have some distance to travel before coming to the shielings and is engaged with his own inner rumination. We can accuse him of being mundane, considering the price of salt herring bound for New York, perchance.

Or it may be that MacAllan is dredging up from the bottom of his memory what he had heard from his grandmother in the fetid close in Portrona where he had been raised; stories of a wide fragrant space with unlimited sweet water, and milk and cream and curds and butter to fill up a hungry boy's empty belly until he was afraid to bend over!

> Thug mi 'n oidhch' a-raoir san àirigh
> 'S bidh mi nochd gu càirdeil, coibhneil,
> Ma' ri maighdeanan na h-àirigh.

Emmeline stopped like a startled stag hearing it and in response to a demand for a translation, he ventured: I was last night in the shieling / And shall be tonight merry and affectionate / With the maidens of the shieling.

– It is the most common shieling song, Lady Emily –

– Is that all you know of it, Mister MacAllan? –

– I hardly listened to my Granny. Wish I had, now –

– Do the maids sing to the cattle when milking? –

This is getting close to personal revelation but they are out on the moor, surrounded by empty miles of personal and private space and there is no chance that one of the rough and ready men of the quays and the change houses will hear of Alistair MacAllan's dabbling in soft stuff of this nature.

– They do –

– Will they sing for me? –

He refrains from informing her that the girls sing to the cows to encourage them to give down their milk and at the same time he feels a surge of lust towards the tall woman striding awkwardly but with determination beside him. What is it about her?

This expedition of Emmeline's to the moorland shieling is not quite such an aberration as MacAllan and others may have it. It had been customary in olden times for gentlemen farmers and the proprietors of estates even, to go to the moor on occasion at morning milking time in order to gladden their hearts by seeing their calves thrive, get a draught of rich warm milk and enjoy the sight of bonny women doing the work thought most congenial to them.

We are indebted to the excellent Mary MacKellar for most of our information about the vital work at the summer shielings, that and oral history, there being little notice taken of it by those who came early to write about Gaelic ways; probably because it was confined to the summer and happened on the distant and difficult moor, out of sight of habitation and roads. This may be why Emmeline is determined to discover it, that and her interest in Anna, who should perhaps have come along today as her companion. But Emmeline is keen to find out for herself (and MacAllan wants her to himself, urging her that no companion is necessary in this situation and he is surely right, such not being mentioned in any known book on etiquette). Although MacAllan's Gaelic is townie and rusty it is adequate for interpretation, so we can leave Anna in the castle.

The rearing of cows and caring for their welfare was a matter of great importance to the Highlanders of the past. Milk, in its different forms, was the food on which they chiefly depended, and their store of butter and cheese largely represented their winter provision. It was therefore of great consequence to them to have their cattle so fed that their yields of milk would not only be increased but enriched. They spent most of their summer shieling time among their herds, they had fresh breezes and pure rills of stream and fountain, beauty and grandeur around them and if they had no couches of down they had heather beds. The affection in the hearts of these good women for the animals they reared and watched over was very intense.

It was a matter of great concern to them, when they moved from the village to the shielings at the summer's beginning, not to meet with an unlucky foot. They hated a lean, hungry-looking person to meet them or a covetous man, or anyone known to be even distantly related to a witch, who could not only make cows cast their calves but even kill them. They could take their milk from them, or take the virtue out of it, so that no butter could be made, and people with the evil eye could injure them in the same way. They did not like anyone to look at and praise a cow without their wetting their eyes with their own saliva, taken up on the point of a finger. Nor did they like anyone counting their cattle without invoking a blessing on them. The snipe was the most blessed creature they could meet on the moor, because it was the bird that met the Virgin Mary on her way to her Son's grave on the morning He rose from the dead.

MacAllan, some sediment of childhood memory stirring when Emmeline suddenly shied into him, alarmed by a snipe exploding into flight at her feet, told her:

– The snipe told Mary her Son was risen from the dead –

She was too agitated to answer, but his words made a deep impression.

The girls on the shieling enjoy their residence there, free from all restraint; they can sing and dance to the music of their own innocent hearts without fear of minister or elder. There are generally four girls in each shieling and they occupy a large bed made on the floor, from rushes, bent and hay. Between this bed and the fire of heather stalks, there is built up a couch of turf for sitting on. Wednesday night (is this because that night at the home village finds parents and elders confined in church?) is the night the girls' sweethearts come to visit, bringing Jew's harp and chanter for dancing, and the girls sing the Gaelic songs that are too often forbidden at home.

They hospitably entertain the young men, the usual feast being curds and cream; and when the lads go to the East Coast fishing, they bring presents back to the girls who were so kind – shoulder shawls of tartan, ribbons, combs, penknives, brooches – which are lovingly treasured.

Emmeline has recently been gathering notes for her diary from local members of staff at the castle (those few not too shy to speak to her of their way of life) and recalls now what she has written and re-written about the trek to the shielings by the calf-maiden, the sturdy girl who lures the calves to the shieling ground. A little company of calves does its best to keep up with a robust maid, who has a curious drum-like utensil covered in cowhide strapped round her breast and resting upon the pad formed by the bunched gathers of her drugget skirt in the small of her back. As the girl moves over the uneven mossy ground, streamlets of milk are jolted out of a hole in the lid of the drum, and trickle down the skin; it is these white droplets that attract the following calves, eager to lick them up. Indeed, this is the object of the cunning churn or imideal to lure the little creatures out to their summer grazings, and when the maiden arrives with her attendant small herd, why, the movement and warmth of her body will have made butter in the churn!

There is a completeness, a most satisfying closure, to the (true) story of this luring of the calves simultaneously with the making of butter in a portable cowhide churn, that Emmeline finds deeply mysterious, exciting, and revealing in the power of Art to inspire and arouse, though not to explain.

These discoveries of a life alive here now and dead in England (so Emily believes) are what made her decision to come to the island worthwhile. If only the winters were not so long and so wet and so windy, the summers so short; two months, but what months!

And in some mysterious way, young Anna, the child widow, seems to Emmeline to conceal a key of some kind, an explanation, a clarification, however partial, of that mystery that appears to slumber behind the low hills around.

They breast a heather hill and abruptly confront a multitude of multi-coloured cattle, intently tugging with eager tongues at the lush greensward covering the lawnlike banks of the narrow river MacAllan names the Donnburn. It winds its serpentine route through the depths of the peaty plain to the faraway sea, spilling rich minerals as it goes.

– This grass has grown up in a couple of weeks, Emily –
– So many colours, brown and white and black –
– Scotch and German breeds mixed, grand milkers –

Emmeline (or is it Emily?) stops, stares down at the grass that already has stained her walking shoes; she bends to work some in her fingers, vaguely alive to the uncanny transformation of it into milk.

Then all of a sudden they come upon the shielings, ancient stone-walled cots, refurbished with fresh thatch, low box-chimneys venting aromatic grey smoke, the clatter of tin and knock on wood utensils being scrubbed with fine gravel in an eddy of the burn. The light swift flurries of the movement of the milkmaids are unfamiliar to Emmeline, who stands now stock still at the edge of the river-side clearing where most of the àirighs are situated, a stranger from unknown drawing rooms, transposed to this tiny enclave of young women in a secret part of the hidden interior of the island. She turns to MacAllan with such a look that he tosses away his hat, shouts for milk and is given back joy and laughter and two cogs of milk, one warm (this morning's milking) for him and one cold, from the river, for Emmeline (last night's milking). The Portrona man's down to earthness dispels the shyness of all, for is it not said in town of MacAllan, that you can take him anywhere? But what do we make of the fact that the boldest of the moor maidens already knows he prefers warm morning's milk to cold night's? Possibly nothing, beyond recognising his sociability in town and country.

Alistair MacAllan, a pasha of the East, moves to the centre of attention, hands over his cog to the Scarlet Kerchief and in his expansive confidence, here on the moorland enclave given over to the work of the female, finds words to mock the leading woman of town and island as Lady Emily is perceived since taking over the running of the castle (and proving herself capable).

– Heilan' morning milk to warm an English lady, Emily –

– You go too far, MacAllan –

Unabashed, with a swarm of his own women moving around him, just two bold enough to talk, the others (he reckons a dozen not counting those further off) chivvying the cattle away from the bogs and switching their backs when they show aggression to each other, he acts up to his reputation for risk taking:

– Nah, nah, Emily, do not the old yins tell us, one teat of a milking cow is better nor a boll of meal! –

This sounds insulting in English and Lady Emily bridles visibly as the cliché has it and, naturally, says nothing. He is risking losing her respect though he does not think of it as clear as that. If she wants to learn about the Gaelic ways, she shall hear them from me as they are. But now he loses his nerve:

– Bheil am feur math am bliadhna? I am asking them, Emily, is the grass good this year –

Emmeline has gone and Lady Emily is in her place, cool but not sulking of course.

– And is it? –

– The usual, my lady –

The Scarlet Kerchief has spoken directly to her and it is Emmeline who responds:

– What do you do with all the milk you must get from so many cows and how is it that the calves do not take the milk away from you? –

– We do not let them near, we have a special place to keep the calves and we give them milk morning and evening –

– They make butter and cheese for the winter, Emily –

– I know that already, Mr MacAllan –

MacAllan asks Scarlet Coif her name, Ciorstaidh. Lady Emily understands it as Kirsty, is told these young ladies have little English, yet Emmeline feels bonds of sympathy beyond the bounds of language; she notes the need for changing the ladies' seminary curriculum to include more English at the expense, perhaps, of fine embroidery. Meanwhile she is alive to more than MacAllan suspects, now expounding in Portrona twangy Gaelic to the amusement of the girls, especially those two who have been mutely deputed to look after the anomalous guests; Ciorstaidh's friend is Murdag, a title she hates (because she has been named after a man, Murdo, as so many girls here are), insisting on being known as Dina or Deena, depending on your accent.

A generation or two ahead, the milkmaids will need to be kept off compulsory schools (all English and no Gaelic), in order to look after the cattle, the parents in a constant bind as to whether to have their children educated away or to (selfishly?) try to keep them at home (and ignorant?). Meanwhile there is only the church school in a cottage by the shore, where boys get some Gaelic during the day and adult men learn a little at night, maybe navigation, something useful, or psalm singing, now an art.

The Portrona entrepreneur, raised in a close, now turns his charm upon Emmeline (he hopes) and points out the various facets of a traditional shieling. Then Deena grasps the attention of all, describing in an excited mix of the two languages how her father courted her mother upon that very stone bed in front of you! Maybe she was even conceived there, on the very slab you have your hand on ... Who is amused, who is shocked, who knows, but breeding will out!

Lady Emily coolly queries:

– Alistair, how does this bothy compare with those erected illegally by the squatters? –

– Ye'll need to ask MacRoe, that's his department! Ah'm a fish curer, no a landlord's factor!

– I just thought you might have an opinion, as a local person –

– Aye, sure, Emily. The shieling is made for summer living. Keepin the milk. A squatter's bothy, on the other hand, needs to keep out the gales and rain o winter. And it's much bigger, with ambition to be a house one day –

He pauses, adds carefully:

– It is all down to the rules of the estate –

– The rules lay down, Alistair, that if the roof of an illegal bothy is stripped by the storm, the young couple are not allowed to go and live in the home of their parents –

– Does that no bother you, Emily, as the legal representative of the estate? –

– Although it is my duty to apply the regulations of the estate, it does not necessarily follow that I fully agree with all of them –

– Spoken like a true lawyer! Some will be gey glad to hear it, Emily –

Although he intuitively sympathises with the landless poor of his home island, MacAllan's true interest lies in what can be won from the sea. He knows well the sour soil can never provide more than a hazardous hedge against hunger (even for those who have access to it), whilst the hidden riches of the ocean are without limit. Those have already set a corner boy from a crowded close on his way to a mansion on Goathill, thanks to an instinctive understanding of the ways of borrowed gold in relation to the silver largesse of the Minch. Charm and confidence are assets he is vaguely aware of, and he has the eternal optimism of the man who wagers against the waters returning him their bounty, throw after throw after throw.

– Ahm wanting smart girls who can gut the big skeds full and clean, Kirsty –

– Murdag and me, we been away at the sgadan, Mister MacAllan, and plenty more from here –

– Come to town to MacAllan and I'll see youse all get top money –

– Who will learn us this full gutting? It will be slow, poor money in it –

– Special rates, ahm getting Henny NicKenny and young Anna Flett, they done special full gutting in Yarmouth –

– You must speak to me about Anna, Alistair –

The double ploy of Alistair MacAllan (to get Emily alone on the moor and intrigue her with the summer magic of it, plus recruiting fresh gutting crews) is thus startlingly and unknowingly interfused in his mind by Lady Emily, causing him to blink and shake his head, giving the women to think the midges had come despite the zephyr.

– I'll put the word about your wanting crews, Mr MacAllan –

– Tell them I'll top whatever the Russian dame is offering –

– Who is wanting them big full gutted skeds? –

– The Yanks: I'm shipping them direct to New York –

Lady Emily now decides it is time to inject some reality into the sanguine ploys of Alistair MacAllan:

– How do you propose sending a cargo of herring barrels across the Atlantic, when there are no sailings from Portrona to America? –

MacAllan has long been looking for a way to broach the delicate subject of the shipping out of emigrants with Lady Emily. Now the chance is gifted him, confirming his belief in his special luck. Cast!

– Has MacRoe not said yet, Emily? I suggest he'll soon be wanting to charter a ship to take away a load of emigrants, with all the back rent that's owing to the estate –

– The free emigration scheme is in abeyance, Mr MacAllan –

– Aye, but the fund is still there, Roddy Banker's sitting on it, the money to send them away as don't pay their rent for two years running and there's more than enough of them to fill a ship. MacRoe is desperate to get rid of them.

– I'm sorry but I cannot discuss estate business with you here – Change the subject:

– When, pray, did the Americans develop a taste for Portrona herrings? –

– New-come Americans, Emily, Polaks, Slavs, Bohunks, harping for a taste of the oul' country –

– What about Highlanders in America? Do they not want a taste of the old country?

– The teuchters in New York would not be seen dead eating a sked –

The girls have been absorbing, with patience, interest and some understanding, talk seldom heard at the shielings; now Murdag speaks:

– Can I come on your herring ship to New York, Mr MacAllan? My sister's there already –

– You and a couple of hundred more. Go up the town, give your name to Rob the clerk in the factor's office, pass the word to them as don't want to pay the rent this year again –

– Have a care, for Heaven's sake, you go too far, MacAllan –

– It's a free country, Lady Emily, though you lot haven't twigged it yet –

The look Lady Emily bends upon MacAllan now has taken a thousand years to develop, but he is nevertheless gallus enough under it to succeed in changing the subject in his turn (and into an area that he senses will be one day to his advantage); he nods at Kirsty:

– Aye, well. Show the lady the white stone well, blone. It's what we came to see, at the end of the day –

Kirsty leads the way to a very lush area of the river bank.

Fuaran na Cloiche Bàine. The White Stone Well, my Lady, there the white stone, there the spring water bubbling, bubbling –

MacAllan stoops, gathers clear water in cupped hands, tastes and Murdag cries out to him:

– Take care, Mr MacAllan! You know what the White Stone water will do to you! –

– Full of sulphur and plenty more besides, must be good for cove or blone –

He cups water in his hands, offers them to Emily, she ignores him, stoops to the hollowed slab that fills and empties endlessly, kneels suddenly, sucks up three mouthfuls, rises with a deep breath, droplets on her chin, the other three watching her benignly, now await her judgment:

– It tastes like many a holy well. Strange, is it not, they should all be so alike? –

The girls are smiling at her, waiting to tell her, patient, though. They look at Emmeline with a sort of love, they say nothing, MacAllan breaks the moment:

– Give us the raut, Murdag, about the special gift of the White Stone Spring –

– The girls will not drink from it, my Lady, unless –

– Unless? –

– Unless they want a baby –

Emily turns the look on MacAllan but is it softer? He thinks so anyway.

Kirsty speaks now:

– There is one more thing, my Lady –

– One more thing. Tell me –

– It will not work unless –

– Unless what, for pity's sake –

– Unless you are a virgin, my Lady –

Emily (or is it Emmeline?) rests her head on the nearest shoulder which happens, naturally, to be MacAllan's.

The thatched cottage where Henny NicKenny was brought up and still lives in with Norman Daft is at the far end of Iomair Sligeach (Shell Strand), beyond the bulky white houses of the master mariners, in one of which, in times past, Jim Morrison was raised and to which he returned, for a few months only, following his fortunate escape from the gallows.

Henny had heard (and so had her roaming husband of short duration, more to the point) of the tight roll of papers found in the shottle with the jammed lid (but now lost again) – Morrison's own writings of his time in Tahiti; his part in the Mutiny, perhaps even his vocabulary of the Tahitian language.

The papers must have been a first draft only, for the journal and account of the mutiny and the Island of Tahiti would turn up in the Library of Brisbane in the early 20th century, much too late to make our Jim famous. Yet his bold writing preserved his neck and that of young Midshipman Heywood, whose family borrowed Jim's journal (the fair copy?) to help with the young man's defence and never returned it, it following the family to Australia eventually, praise them for preserving it, anyway.

Whenever she thinks of the papers in the shottle (which is seldom, now) Henny gets a strange feeling that her husband (also named Jim) had seen these mysterious writings; but what if he had, he could not read, so far as she knew. Nevertheless, there were those in Portrona who could read and were not slow to tell others of what they had learnt. English, of course; it never occurred to Henny or to anybody else that Jim Morrison would have written his story in any other language, although he was a fluent Gaelic speaker and could get by in Tahitian. His bilingualism made him a natural interpreter.

Reading to Henny and to many others like her, then, was a mystery, but its lack made their minds keener to keep what they had heard and so we may be sure that many scenes from Jim Morrison's adventures have come down to Henny and are pictured in her brain, awaiting the right trigger to bring them to light, after so many wakeful nights listening to the restless Jim MacKenny, whom she vaguely senses now went off to find something of what Jim Morrison may have thought he had found, at first. In the South Seas, total freedom, whatever that may mean to someone raised among Puritans.

Twenty years before our time, then, here is. Henny, maybe carrying Norman, maybe not, yet stretched by Jim MacKenny in the straw-packed box bed with the canvas screen hearing the whine of the south wind around the straw roof above her in the house at the far end of Shell Strand alongside Jim's sensuous whisper:

– 'Never heard a word,' Jim Morrison said to the ship master when he asked him was he with the mutineers, 'Never heard a word about it'. I don't believe it and him telling the boys long ago when he was home after it, about the soft living on the Island of Tahiti and him being a big friend of the Queen and all –

Hiding in his warm words is a small part of the vague history of the Portrona quays, touching on the pliant brown women of the far southern seas, already an element of Henny's fancy.

('Never heard a word about it' comes to us today direct from the official court martial transcripts, a literal translation from the idiomatic Gaelic: Cha chuala mi facal air, James Morrison's language turning pure Gaelic in the dangerous moment, accused of mutiny, although his English learning, as we shall see, is marvellous, and he has no intention of being taken for a teuchter in London or any place else, not after the way the Highlanders are still mocked, a mere generation after the march to Derby.)

Back in our time Henny stands erect on Portrona Number Three Wharf in front of the tiers of empty white casks. She holds a new barrel above her head at the reach of her arms, a hand gripping each end; she flexes her elbows, rocks from toe to heel, testing her body's fitness for the desperate toil ahead, half wishing for a poor season, the very first empty barrel she chose this year held high in supplication to the Herring God?

With a sudden flick and jerk, a memory gesture, she drops the barrel at her feet so that it strikes the planks of the quay with a hollow boom peculiar to empty butts falling from a certain height at a sure angle, propelled by cunning hands. It rolls away rapidly, a true piece of the cooper's art, not deviating an inch in its flowing run from the course Henny set it on. Her eye still good.

A sprightly booted foot meets the rolling barrel, it slows it and turns it neatly into one of the fragrant pine-smelling alleyways between the tiers; a voice familiar yet strange calls Henny's name. Rapid footsteps tattoo on the boards and then Petersburg and Portrona are face to face:

– Why have you take my best girls away to MacAllan and you too, Henny, why? –

Shame makes Henny's blood mantle her face. The fierce shame of the islet, where no secret is possible, in a place where the standards of behaviour are yet ruled by the severe rigidities of fundamentalism, too soon after taking it over for the culture's basic tolerance to have tempered it. Yet the isolation of her state comes to her aid now. MacAllan is a local man, courageously taking on strange monied men at their own game, you have to admire him and support him. If he sails too close, even if he cheats, you say nothing. There is a need for bias here, how else are we going to draw ourselves up to meet the outside world, with its new and dangerous challenges? Naturally, Henny thinks none of these things, as she ducks her head in front of the imperious Russian lady, but she would have, given the chance.

– I'm sorry to leave you, Madame –

– Has Madame not treat her girls the best of all for years, yes? –

– We broke the record for you, Madame, barrels to Petersburg! –

But Madame Wolkova cares nothing for such reminiscences or such records. Bankers' promissory notes and prepaid orders for thousands of barrels of the sweet Minch summer fish yet uncaught (are they even there, this year?) preoccupy her now. The cultivated lady who risks the assessment of a new painting is not to be discovered in a Portrona summer, unless for a brief hour at the castle. Her strength lies in her ability to focus on the need of the moment and the Portrona herring season is making the money to enable the dilettantism of the rest of the year. She has a lot in common with MacAllan and she realises it more than he does, he never having had the opportunity to savour a rounded education. There lies Madame Wolkova's power over all the locals, simply in her superior schooling, the same as with Lady Emily Percy. Above all, in the confidence (arrogance?) such a background brings with it. There is no fairness to be found, you are marked by your place and situation from birth. So play to your strength and ignore snobbery, like the Portrona skemp, MacAllan, now appearing on cue.

He arrives swiftly out of the cathedral of empty barrels, dapper for the coming season, white silk muffler partially hiding his face. When the herring come, it is said, MacAllan forgoes his white silk, removes his soft overcoat, allows his watchchain and fob to dangle, even leaves off his hat. Some say his costume quirks affect the coming through the Minch of the fish, but then we are dealing with a bunch of gamblers here, large and small. He'd rather not hear Madame's sharp summons. Truth is, he is just a little afraid of her, a woman of authority, her and Lady Emily, but there is the fascination with fine ladies of confidence that maybe has something to do with the grandmother who was supportive to a skinny boy in a crowded close; she had the one room in Havelock that was not full of bodies and noise and bad smells; the haven of peace and the unique scent of Shenvar's attic.

MacAllan speaks direct:

– No time for one of your conversaziones now, Madame. All our barrels ashore yet, Henny? –

Madame knows his type, what is the difference between the

kulak on his way up in Petersburg and in Portrona? Language is all, a peasant is a peasant, unsophisticated notions of right and wrong in business, above all the low cunning of the ambitious underdog.

– Lissen, MacAllan, you take a big chance and you Henny also, skets to New York full gutted, pah! –

– We ken fine in Portrona we dinna measure much on the big map of Yourup where you go stravaiging all winter, Madame, but we ken fine also a market when we sniff one –

He is emboldened by the presence of Henny, albeit she is loth to add to Madame Wolkova's disapproval of her particular piece of low kulak cunning. MacAllan is not content to equal all the fishcurers from away, he must surpass them, in order to feel equal to them; and he depends upon the goodwill and tacit support of the local Gaelic people, especially those from the bottom of the heap, from the teeming closes in the town and the rough cottages thrown up on the outskirts by landless men and wandering sailors. He had known all along it would not be hard to persuade Henny to desert Madame and come to him, the enormous pressure on her to support the local man gave her no choice. It may be that Madame has some inkling of this behaviour, which is why she is not as angry as she could be and would be about a betrayal without pressure, for purely selfish reasons.

Madame however decides something must be said; she does not wish to alienate Henny, needing her local knowledge still, aware that Henny knows of scores, hundreds of girls in the villages near and far, ladies of all ages, experienced or not, from which to recruit afresh this season's crews, and quickly. Madame, after a number of years coming to Portrona, has a huge respect for the women of the island, their strength and honesty and eagerness to work, they too subject to the power of the community's opinion of them. But there is plenty pride as well.

– Have I not treat you well, have Madame not treat you girls the very best, better nor the men? –

– You have been good to us, the cailleach Ruiseanach is famous all over the island. You can get plenty more girls, no bother, but Mister MacAllan's paying us every Saturday, guaranteed money, Madame –

– Madame's money is good and sure certain at the end of the season, it lies now with Roddy Banker, waiting. Have you ready money waiting MacAllan, bet you, no! –

Henny is stung into a loyalty that surprises her, an anger she does not expect:

– Mister MacAllan's the richest man in Portrona! –

Madame decides on a small lesson in the intricacies of business finance, whether in Portrona or Petersburg, yet knowing it will not register with Henny:

– Henny NicKenny, hear you what I say to you and all the girls who work at this crazy fullgut for him. MacAllan has big credit, from bank, but is risk money, not same as ready money, no big fish to fullgut, no money to pay his crews –

Henny is ready for her, in full flow on the side of him who gives her home and world a sense of the worth of a cove from a close, a blone from the pungent Ocrach end of Shell Strand, who has nothing given but does not give up.

– MacAllan will pay us, fish or no fish, every Saturday night! –

– Henny, listen to me, how can he pay if no herring and he want special big fat fish, unnerstan Henny, fullgut no good on small sweet fish, must be big fat specials, no fish, no money, no money, no pay, Roddy Banker foreclose on him –

Henny now reveals another facet of the local women that Madame temporarily forgot, their dignity:

– Mister MacAllan was good to my Norman, and I stand by my local man! –

MacAllan has said nothing while the women debate his worth. He realises that Madame Wolkova has seen the hazard at the heart of his scheme (no big fat specials, no money) and that his promise to pay his girls every week (unheard of in the curing trade) is both a gamble and a means of controlling his expenditure. Better than leaving all debt to the end of a season that may prove calamitous. And does she feel threatened by his boldness? As for being good to Henny's crazy Norman, he cannot mind it, an impulsive man of sudden kindnesses, instantly forgotten, but never repudiated. Always thought Roddy Banker wearing his provost's chain was the one who was nice to Norman Daft and Henny too and she to him? The uneasy tableau is broken by the appearance of one of these lone fish gutters who moves from port to port, working on their own, people wary of them, yet ready to take a chance in order to get short term gluts of fish through the system. This is Betsack from The Broch, at least in Portrona she is Betsack, she is bold and knowing and she walks right up to Madame Wolkova:

– You wantin' a good foreman, Madame? –

Madame looks sideways at her, not used to such directness from the self-effacing girls of the island, but what has she to lose, Henny having left her?

– Are you from Portrona? –

– Damn right, I'm not! Betsack from The Broch at yir service, Madame. Ah've worked frae the Isle of Man to Yarmouth, richt roond the hale sea coast o' Britain! I can gut and I can pack and I can spin a full barrel on a saxpence! –

Madame is won over, because she needs a foreperson, because she senses that it will be best in the circumstances for that overseer to be someone from outside and because she admires Betsack's gallusness.

– Okay, Betsack Broch, I vill tak your word. Now go and recruit plenty knife ladies for Madame Wolkova's company! –

– Ah'm yir very man, Madame! And never mind the arlish, just slip us a few quid every Setterday nicht! –

Betsack hesitates for half a second but Madame's portemonnaie stays hidden in her skirt. Betsack may be foreperson but Madame holds the purse strings and will pay the advance to each girl personally and she will sign or touch Madame's pen.

Now is the time for all good coves (and blones) to stand up for old PA [Portrona], grab all the pride they can from the truth of the seas beyond the sullen Beasts where myriad full fat fish will brim. Portrona's own bounty, sought by Sassenach, Bucach, Roosian, but at the end of the day, our skeds, 'God's providence is our inheritance', let us never forget, let High Church, Martins, Low Church, Evangelicals, preachers, even the rebel Frees all join in petition and prayer to the Good Lord, so He will send the big silver matfulls down the Minch once more this summer, even if I rarely go to church on Sunday and never through the week.

Invocations such as these run through MacAllan's bullet head as he turns deliberately his back upon Madame, and speaks to his forelady:

– I want young Anna with you, you two will need to show the rest. They'll soon pick it up. I've a lot of smart girls coming in and you won't wait for the good fish, start learning them right away, filling up rates paid on Saturday night. There's bound to be some wee ones for practice, the East Coasters are arriving wholesale now –

And he was off chalking barrels, telling Henny that he had sent over a crony with a message to Anna at the castle to meet Henny on the pier.

Cheek! Henny looks in the direction of the castle across the water but she cannot see it; it will not become visible until the stacks of cane-hooped white barrels are filled and shipped out. I don't for a minute believe Anna will be daft enough to leave that cushy place for the bloody stramash of the farlanes, but you can never tell, she's a deep one.

Another one in the town (which would surprise Henny and even make her jealous?) writes of Anna in his Minute to the Disaster Fund Treasurer (no less than the ubiquitous

MacRoe. He may be difficult but he's trusted to account for other people's money). Odd to send a letter to someone whom you talk to every day, but until something was in writing it did not have credibility. Roddy Banker, flaunting his charitable credentials, writes to MacRoe to inform him of the peculiar circumstance of a girl mother widowed by the sea, refusing money when it is offered and asking him to keep an eye out for her during his dealings with the estate, Lady Emily inexplicably having granted Anna Flett a position as some kind of lady's companion at Portrona Castle, whilst her son is milk-nursed by the wife of the squatter on your list for an example. A small world we all appear to inhabit, MacRoe, is it not?

Madame discerns her first, tentatively heeling in new-shod boots between the heaped up ranks of naked soldiers at the top of the pier, the child widow of weird allure who interests so many. Why cannot they leave me alone, Anna is to say and soon. She comes through the tall tiers now and approaches the little group, hears the rival curers make wary arrangements about the placing of the farlanes in their respective curing stations.

Uncannily, does Norman Daft not emerge now from a dim trench among the barrels, beating his side drum to the tune of Anna's steps upon the planks of Number One. She senses him closing on her, turns, waits, he marches up to her, executes a halt! as trim as a soldier and crossing his rattling drum-sticks in front of his face, he salutes this fey girl, friend of his mother.

This salaam is a new one. He is staring at her from pale eyes that alter as you look into them, one second grave and wise, then with the open joy of a child. He knows so much, he knows nothing of this world's pain, a man with God or an Augur of Doom, why does he stop in front of me to give his strange salute, what is he seeking? She makes a great effort at a positive response, her torso visibly shakes, her new soled boots stamp lightly, Norman tattoos in unison, they start into a queer tap dance for a moment. Anna turns, runs to the women, not seeing MacAllan, although her original purpose is with him. He may help me decide, him with the influence at the castle? Whether to go back to the gutting, the world of work so hard it dulls out all else, or maybe turn my back on castle and quay and be buried in a curtained closet in my father's house in the country and there nurse my own child, imagine myself mad.

The bard told Anna of the ardour of the bond between foster mother and foster child, the power of the link made by the tie of the milk that in Gaelic culture is five times more potent than that of blood.

The power of the muime, her milk taking over the mind of the child as well as building the boy's body, the relation between foster mother and son partakes of the magic of the milk of the right breast. Did a hero once seize a feminine supernatural and taking the nipple of her right breast to his lips, call to Heaven and earth to witness his exalted state? What he does is symbolical, like it or not she has suckled him, become his all-powerful foster mother, put him in touch with her magick. What has such Buisneachd got to do with us today, educated people, yet even Lady Emily, when you think of Her and Him, if she admits his claim, she is bound by the tie of breast fostering to assist him in all his undertaking. Speaking of muimes, Fionn had sixteen of them, Rob says.

Relief to speak to Henny and Madame Wolkova of the simple hard work of the quays, the pleasure of finding that Madame thinks kindly of her still, though she had not approved her early marriage a year since, is it only a year?

Norman had taken the meek coin from his mother's skirt pocket and gone to buy his morning roll from Shonnie Baker's, changed from terrible soothsayer to wee boy at the simple thought of hot white bread on his tongue. That weird boy-man will be the death of me yet, I wish we were not brought up to the superstition and the scary stories in the Bible, rauts to keep us in awe of those over us, told us loud by black ministers to make us obedient. We need those who will tell us different. And there are those in the Bible too, who foretell?

Is there any way they might have known in advance that the unspeakable tragedy of the *Iolaire* may be waiting for them down the years? Not unless they believed in prophecy, as more than would admit it did, although if the seer foretells a deed as awful as a disaster that will drown two hundred of your men on the shore of home port in ninety minutes, then you have all leave to disbelieve him or her. Her in our case, our crone has guarded the terrible picture for many years, at first not believing, coming slowly to accept, but fearful to divulge.

It breaks into her mental landscape sometimes when she is near sleep. She prays that the augury might be mere nightmare; the heaving seaweed slimy backs of the Beasts at the harbour mouth crawl with heaps of frantic men in dark uniforms, their gaping mouths spilling water and soundless sound.

And so the crone who scutters around the farlanes and along the lines of barrels during the high herring days unnoticed by the very men and women whose unborn grandsons may perish dreadfully at the spot so near them now, cherishes a terrible secret she tries not to credit. Maybe it is for some other place, maybe it has already happened way back in forgotten history, maybe it is a punishment on me to have such terrors visited because I have been cursed with the second sight. Some other things I have seen are nothing like, a woman in a shroud on Dempster Street at noon, a fishing boat cowped over by a squall, a sail covering drowned men, worst to see, a pale baby buried in a barrel of herring. Why do I never see full life or hear a cry of pleasure?

Brown Skins and White

U NLIKE A TEUCHTER TO mutiny, forby the uprisings
of landless men when the potatoes stunk to heaven and
the fish went to better boats from elsewhere, the absence of
capital at last bit home, the end of a way of life that had gone
on for aeons, just wee rebellions to raise some publicity.

Jim Morrison in his *Bounty* hammock, then, no idea of
becoming a mutineer, mind you he had no time for Captain
Bligh, having seen his conduct over the coconuts. (Why? the
brown girls of course.) Fancy the most famous mutiny of
all time ignited by a bunch of bloody coconuts! Allied to
the fragile temperament and supersensitivity of your man,
Christian, his wife left behind on Tahiti, he couldn't take
his captain's nagging.

Who did our Portrona man leave behind? He says nothing
personal about the women, except to praise their bodies, hair,
dancing, enough you may say to conclude he enjoyed them,
but only as a sailor, no promises, no responsibility.

– Tell my friends I am in the South Seas –

It's what Jim shouted to the near-sinking boat with Bligh and
the rest cast away by Christian and the mutineers, those words
were nearly to cost Jim Morrison his very neck, only he talked
(wrote) his way out of it, the beauty. Our lack of self-belief and
need for famous men make us want to broadcast worldwide
our Jim's journal, now only meat for every academic or film

director, who has his own tuppence to spend on Cap'n Bligh, good or bad. They cannot leave the teuchter's tale out of it, try as they might, a lesson to us all on the peripheries, ignored or sneered at down through time. Think of Jim Morrison on that wet green mountain chopping trees down for his schooner, if it was today?

What about a taste of himself, then, discover the Portrona tongue (lightly disguised) that a unique man of the *Bounty* time came up with. Writing must have been compulsive with him. How in heaven he kept a journal during his years away, the mutiny less than half way through his journey which ended with him at Spithead, giving spiritual comfort to his condemned friends as they stood beneath the rope over the yardarm, before the drop? Takes a good and complex man.

Most deeply and cathartically though. How on earth did James Morrison feel, as he searched the Portrona Bible for words of comfort for the two unfortunates who were to bear punishment for all the rest, murder and maddening on Pitcairn, drowned on the Barrier Reef, released back to the Royal Navy for further (honourable) service? We shall never know, or how would writers make their people speak?

Listen to Morrison tell of their work of building their schooner in order to escape from the paradise island of Tahiti after one year:

'Norman & Millward to make Plank, McIntosh & Myself to put them on, & Coleman and Heildbrandt to make the Ironwork, and by Easter Sunday we completed Six Strakes on the Starboard side, our manner of proceeding was this, after MacIntosh had fitted one plank, and placed it, he left me to bore it off, and prepared an other, when it was bored off he secured it by driving one nail, and one Irennail in each timber, and three Nails in each butt. As we were like to be soon out of Plank it being now a whole week's work to make one of 30 feet.'

The *Bounty* had sailed for England twelve months previously and the party of Morrison, refusing a life on Pitcairn and remaining on Tahiti, were now so set on sailing themselves, they were attempting to build a schooner practically with their bare hands. Perchance it was the local politics:

'In the Meantime The Morea people harving [sic] rebell'd against Mottooarro, Chief of the Island & Brother-in law to Matte, he sent to us to know if He should send his arms over to quell them, to which We agreed, but told Him to send His own people to use them; and Heete-heete being present was appointed to the Command. The arms being brought to us we Cleand them and put them in order when they set off and Arriving at Moria soon brought them to subjection, Heete-heete having himself killed the Inspired Priest of the Rebels and their Chief forced to fly to Attahooroo, leaving the Island in possession of Mottooarro whose right it was, but from which he had been kept by Maheine his Uncle and His party, till the *Bounty* had sailed in April 1789.'

The South Sea paradise is growing serpents, naturally enough, only they chew cartridge and spit bullets now. Inspired priests they always had, of course, like everywhere else.

Meanwhile, the few steady men left among the *Bounty* mutineers get on with constructing the schooner they hope will take them back to England, home and beauty. Led by James Morrison, shellback from Portrona, the first(?) of a myriad of island men, whose Gaelic non-conformity takes them far, an over-developed sense of responsibility coming in handy. He is here, lucky, as one may be. McIntosh is a skilled ship's carpenter, wanting only a leader and our Jim is that man. One wonders at the peculiar qualities of James Morrison, good enough to make a midshipman without friends in high naval places, later, a mere bosun's mate when he should have been a lieutenant, a master gunner at the top of an Admiral's list, yet wielding the cat for Bligh on the naked backs of his errant mates. (To bosun's mate, traditionally, fell the task of carrying out the navy's cruel discipline of the lash.)

– Lay on well, Morrison! –

A mere piece of Hollywood scriptwriting, but it is also true.

Poor Katie Babie, of habit and repute a thief, whipped in Portrona, five stripes upon her naked back by the hands of the executioner at Custom House, South Beach, Dempster Street and Point Street, having during the whole procession a bottle, a piece of beef and a cheese hanging about her neck. This done when our Jim was an urchin of the quays (although judging by his education in English and mathematics, he spent well, considerable time with the brilliant schoolmaster Anderson, but he was a boy too). The lads run after anguished Katie, keeping clear of the forbidding grace and favour citizen remunerated for bearing the town lash (and hangman's rope?) see those much older and wiser convene to suffer vicariously some of the pain bequeathed them by Cromwell's men. Did they ever have the gratification of a hanging on Gallows Hill? There is no legal record found yet of such. Are we to assume only the wild MacLeods used the noose hanging high above the town and the island executioner was merely a whipper-in?

If they lashed women legally on their naked backs for petty theft, then less shame is discovered in disciplining men in the service of their country in the same barbarous manner?

– Can you wield the lash with sufficient art for it to flick round under the armpit and catch the breast, Morrison? –

– A twist of the wrist, merely, Sir –

Give him his due, to be fair, he was highly praised for the accuracy of his gunnery, never for his cunning with the lash. And he was a gunner not a bosun's mate, except on *Bounty*.

A native of Tahiti, the Tormod Daft of the place, purloins the box that is most precious to James Morrison, containing his 'writing utencils', as he named them. A Tahitian at the top of a tree discovers the precious casket and returns it to his friend, who decrees a swift whipping of the thief, a punishment accepted by all as natural and just. There is no record of the feelings of the victim, innocent or guilty.

Morrison as the mould for many a subsequent successful Gael. Overseas of course, Jim's qualities were hidden until they could do him no good, but we shall gain something strange from his strenuous representation of the good in us and the bad.

Rather than speculate upon whether James Morrison felt guilty or not about tearing the flesh off the backs of his shipmates, we should think of the fortune (or lack of it) that had him volunteering for bosun's mate on the *Bounty* in the first place, a man who had previously served as a midshipman, a junior officer, who could lay and fire naval guns with consistent accuracy, had fought in at least one sea battle (the musket ball in the arm), who could write better reports than many superior to him in rank. Modern tabloid notions would name him as some kind of sadist, reneging on a good career in the navy in order to indulge his peculiar taste in flagellation, but this argument dissolves after a little thought.

There was great competition to get aboard the *Bounty* and to go on such an exciting voyage, and Morrison did the only thing he could do to help himself, take a decrease in rank. Unfortunately, amongst all his writings, he never alludes to his difficulties in obtaining employment but we can be quite certain that he desperately wanted to go on the *Bounty* voyage and that his main purpose was to discover the exotic life of the South Seas in order to have original material to write about. The news of the soft life and malleable women in the exotic new world on the opposite side of the earth being the antipode to the hard cold world of Portrona puritanism he had left to join the navy at 18 in 1779.

The Cromwellian puritan ethic still pertained in the town for a few decades after James Morrison stepped off Portrona quay for the last time, bent on making up for his mistake by serving faithfully as master gunner in His Majesty's Royal Navy, famous sea battles still to see from a sweating gunport, trying to prove that he was really as good a gunner as the admiral insisted. The admiral's admiration would see him drowned one day.

Yet we may be sure that Portrona had its own share of sticks of ministers, men of the cloth whom Hector could demolish in argument between shaping a sole and heel (given the chance, which he was not). The days of staunch Free Church rigour, men who saw the sin in landlordism, these days were around the corner of time for the island as western history creaked into a gear that would begin the movement for change in mind set and body circumstances for all God's children instead of the few. The rule of money would grow relentlessly, giving simple morality a task it was to prove unequal to.

Although he is aware of the past history of the town, both political and economic, Roddy Banker seldom thinks about the past of the port, two or three generations before his own time, when the early curing industry were selling most of their salt herring production to feed plantation slaves in the West Indies, and it is unlikely he ever makes the connection (that we assume James Morrison did) between Minch herring from the North Atlantic and breadfruit from the South Seas as alternative foods for workers in the sugar cane and cotton fields. It is improbable however, that even our Jim, clever as he was, could have made the further connection that we can make today; the weird circumstance that thousands of black toilers in the tropical fields of the Caribbean were named by Gaelic names. A roll call of any kind there even today rings with Campbells, MacDonalds, MacKenzies, MacLeods and all the rest. We are everywhere and how we got there is its own story, just one of the many histories of forced and voluntary movements around the globe of the disempowered.

Now our banker glances around his office with its heavy table and iron cupboard safe secured in the thick gable wall of the old granite house he purchased in order to turn the ground floor into the first custom-built bank in Portrona. He lives on the two floors above with his family, the double bed placed above the safe, his mental mattress consisting of promissory notes, paper money and hard money, stashed on the shelves of his walk-in safe, where the fireplace had once been, enjoying the sense it gives him of being able to start things going in the town and beyond it. He can see, at three in the morning, the notes and coins being handed over, the boats hoisting sail, the myriad fishes boiling into the nets, the barrels rolling into the holds, the flushed faces of successful fishermen and curers as they return to him the spoils of the fishy harvest, with interest added, little extra chamois bags of glittering gold and silver coins, new minted in his head, placed in the safe within the safe. Not for Roddy Banker a mere separation in the ledgers, oh no, he wanted the monies belonging to him to be secured in a separate place, physically apart from the lucre that makes Portrona turn. Not that I'm a miser or greedy, but it is sensible to keep profit aside, away from risk capital. When the safe is open and fisherman or curer stands ayont my desk, looking over, they may glimpse a little of what money is available, given true loan and collateral conditions, but the profit, won and risked, is mine alone, Roderick Banker of this town, controller of so much. I am not truly a cautious man, but someone has to keep their feet on the ground, so many desperate men, keen to splurge others' hard won stoker.

How much does Roddy Banker, bluff for the townies, smooth (fairly) for his visits to the castle, know about the provenance of the enormous wealth that created estate, castle and its appurtenances, the quays and roads and exotic forests, greenhouses and gardens, all to the glory of the Scotch millionaire from the East. Perhaps also to please his English wife, although we cannot know if she was consulted in any detail of the developments (did she even like to eat the grapes or drink the wine grown on the Hebridean peat and seaweed with the aid of glass and coal-fired furnaces, the heat from the local peat deemed insufficient?).

Both knight and his lady now being dead, he is reduced to dealing with Lady Emily.

We do not know what people thought then about the exploitation of foreign lands and populations by the manufacture and shrewd distribution and sale there of substances such as opium. Someone like Roddy Banker might think nothing wrong of what we condemn as an evil trade, especially now that it has been transferred from paddyfield to council estate.

The honest shoemaker, Hector, may censure the drugs trade, given that he knows anything about it; on the other hand, as only unenlightened heathens are involved, it may not trouble his fundamentalist conscience one iota.

There was a possibility of acting blind to unpleasant realities then, that spread wider in society than today, when it is confined to those whose lives revolve around politics, economics and the law and their manifestations.

We must conclude that Roddy Banker knows little and cares less about the provenance of the millionaire's inexhaustible funds. He has no way of knowing through business dealings with the estate; they consist in the main of short missives from eminent bankers in London. They make him feel important and if the money from the East is cleared in London, why should an agent in Portrona query it? Also, a trembling thought at three in the morning: without the castle and the year round business it creates, can he continue as a banker?

And so Roddy Banker sits in his lair (as he likes sometimes to designate it) and admires his first visitor, on a day to be heavy with callers, a day for clearing up a number of outstanding business items, Roddy liking to bunch deals together satisfactorily.

Henny NicKenny sits primly on one of the soft-bottomed leather chairs in front of his banker's table, chairs imported by shrewd adjustment of orders for the castle library (nothing dishonest, he paid the net sale price for them, FOB Gravesend, the estate paid the carriage). Henny sits demurely in Sunday gown in front of the public banker's table, although she has privately lain willing in the past on the mahogany and leather desk in the provost's office in the town house, the brass door-key turned by herself.

Henny and Roddy go back a long way, in mutual respect and need, and the catalyst is thought by them both to be Roddy Banker's willingness to help Henny send Norman away to a private home on the mainland. An honest pretence. And Henny knows that Roddy's town house desk has supported many another pair of female buttocks over the years.

But this is not one of those times, this is a day for giving the business of Portrona another banker's dunt and Roddy is shrewd enough (and worldly enough, in a relaxed kind of way) to know that a talk with the honest Henny will give him the sort of information about doings on the quays that the like of MacAllan, for instance, or Madame Wolkova, will not.

First the banter, although there will be nothing to follow, time and place and mood not agreeing; strangely they both feel more relaxed in the constrained, public-place atmosphere:

– Oh, Roddy, famous, of course you're famous man –

– How am I famous, Henny? –

– Provost, banker, coal merchant, shipping agent, (lowering voice and eyelids) one for the blones, (quickly) and all that in one pair of Hector Campbell's best soft upper gents! –

– Ye aye flatter me, Henny. Aye. How's the boy –

– He's bigger nor you now Roddy –

– My offer's still on the table, Henny –

– Ah'll never send Poor Norman away, never! –

– I have to ask –

– Norman kens only here –

– Still following the funerals with his raut and silver spade? –

– Spends his time with Magumerad down at the graveyard by the shore. Digging –

– Are you not scared he'll take one of his turns? –

– Magumerad knows what to do –

– Dead or alive, Magumerad's your cove –

She looks piteously at him and he feels instantly for her, wishes fleetingly they were in his other office. Sometimes I just want to stroke the poor woman, feel the muscles of her back and shoulders move. Whatever made that stupid husband leave her for a brown hoor in a change house by a palm tree, the booze likely:

– MacAllan's coming here today, Henny. And Mister MacRoe –

– Him! –

– Little happens here without his sayso, Henny Rai –

– Glad he's nothing on me or my little house –

– You may be glad, Henny, but you'll not say I said so out of here –

A formality to say it, he trusts none more, strangely.

– I'll go the now, Roddy, you're so busy –

– No, no, I want you here to explain the curing to Lady Emily –

– She's coming here today! I'm away, Roddy, whit can I say to a leddy? –

– Sit tight, Henny, this is my bank office and you ken well I dinna give a wing meek whit people say –

– Roddy, I'm no used to this –

– You'll be fine, Henny, I need you here to keep MacAllan's rauts from getting right out of order. Oh and Madame may appear during the morning –

– My Goad, Roddy, a real convention you're planning today –

– Business, business, my dear Mistress MacKenny. You mean more in this town of Portrona than you ken, a Rai –

– If ah do, it's all due to you, Roddy dear –

Portrona's foremost manipulator of others' lucre rises and goes out into the passage, blinking. What is it about that lady, Henny, a child one minute and a mother the next?

The porch door opens and MacAllan comes in. His nose is up already, sniffing the metal money, trust a dooker from Havelock Close to enter the front door of a man's house without a knock even though it be a bank now. He signals to MacAllan to go into the office where Henny sits and himself turns along the passage to the back of the house, in search of a draught of cold water from the special drinking pail with the tight-fitting wooden lid in the scullery. He likes to quaff it from the tinker's tin mug, which adds iron to the taste and cools the water hauled by the servant girl from the Laxdale Spring, wholesome antidote to a morning thirst.

Meantime, in the office with the locked safe, Henny tells her new boss she has recruited several crews of fish girls, some with experience of fullgutting or very willing to learn it for the promised special rate. No, she does not know yet if Anna will be with them and is on the point of asking MacAllan (presently studying a red and blue map of the world stuck to the massive safe door with flour paste, a representation of the unresolved universal ambitions of Roddy Banker and many another Portronian, including MacAllan himself) why he is so anxious to have Anna with them, but she stops herself. Her feminine instinct hints it may have to do with Lady Emily and the chance that MacAllan's ambition has unhinged him to the extent of trying after an aristocratic Englishwoman. MacAllan's nose is but inches away from the South Seas; he turns to Henny but says nothing of her long-absent man. Neither does he remark upon clippers skippered by Portrona men, running opium to China and tea to the Thames, current drugs of East and West. The atmosphere in the room fills momentarily with a breath-stopping sexual charge brought by Roddy Banker, who now stands in the doorway.

He bustles forward to start the business of the day. Item

One's pages opening in his head, MacAllan's scheme for exporting special herring to the States, fullgutted for those unappreciative of caviar-like roes hard salted.

Roddy Banker (which he prefers to any other title) has heard pieces, dropped in change house and coffee shop, of the MacAllan plan; often greeted with that false hilarity by the other curers which betokens fear. They know Alistair has some advantage; the town and island women (they are the best and strongest) will work for him, take a chance on the local man, public opinion will ensure he deals them straight. By God, with his flash bugger's luck, it could well work, him with a clever cove of a cousin ashore in New York already and all.

– Got your ship, Alistair? –

MacAllan senses success, but he will not show it. The game between them must be played right, the joy of pretending you are not sure, that you are taking your opponent's words to heart, giving him a sight of your fear of failure (MacAllan), letting on you don't think much of his scheme (Roddy Banker). So they spar, words of business and Portrona slang mingle with the mild insults they sense in the dry moment they can get away with. Henny's intrigued face turns from one to the other, fearful of the figures (huge, unimaginable) that pass between the two most powerful men she knows (bar MacRoe, but she knows he has no lever to torture her with), Roddy showing her the side of him that attracts, leaning back in the armed carver chair, tilting it sometimes to prop against the now open door of the safe, his broadcloth suited stout body guarding the secretive canvas bags and thick pink ribboned papers lying spread within.

– Aeneas MacIver's new regular route from Liverpool to New York, Roddy. He only has to stop off here to pick up my consignments –

– It would never be worth his while! –

– There would be other, well, cargo, Roddy –

– What in heaven's name cargo else could go from here? –

For a long pause MacAllan beams at them both.

– People, Roddy, people boy! –

– People! –

Roddy Banker knows what this means but he pretends not and although MacAllan knows that he knows, he looks innocent and says:

– There's plenty dosh left in the emigration fund, Roddy? –

– The Special Emigration Scheme is defunct ever since the old man died –

– MacRoe's sick with crofters not paying the rent. Never mind the squatters, who pay nothing anyway. Some of the crofters are years behind, and no intention of cleaning up their arrears –

– A lot of the arrears is for meal, given out during the famine. When people were starving –

– I'm a businessman, no a deng philanthropher! –

– And I'm a deng banker, doesn't mean I doan give a deng! –

– I ken your heart is in the right part of you, Roderick. But I ask you this: who gave the top donation to the last fishermen's disaster fund –

– You did –

– Aye, a tidy wee slice of the dosh I cleared last season –

– And a tidy big headline in the *Highland News*! –

– A businessman needs to show himself to the town –

– So long as he doesn't make a geehow of himself, Alistair –

– The island needs to bleed off its surplus population, Roddy, to make it a healthier place –

– What surplus population! There's a million acres here, empty –

– Aye, black wet bog, most of it –

– Doesn't stop you stravaiging it, with Lady Percy. You'll need to watch yourself, MacAllan –

– And you'll need to watch yourself, with your tomarookie in your town house office, Mister Provost! –

Henny senses it is time for her to leave; she rises and glides out before either angry man is aware of her going.

The two proud Portrona crabs are now face to face; on the brink of breaking an acquaintance most valuable to person and town, a friendship even, with a *smeggan* in and the money having bred well. Between them, thinks Hector, even now, they have the making of one good man; could they but grasp religion, he has hopes of both souls being saved.

Now this long-lasting relationship of mutual benefit is going to be smashed, to everlasting regret on either side, just because Roddy Banker has a fulfilling sexual life and MacAllan does not. Or so the town thinks and as the town thinks, so does MacAllan, slightly ahead of them. For Roddy Banker, now it is not jealousy he feels, but fear, how often sick to his stomach, as he shows out one of his charitable lady cases (whether they have cohabited or not) under the eyes of his crabbit town clerk, whom he fancies puts his ear to the door, although it is very thick and of oak, reckoned soundproof enough?

Such a severing should not happen at this juncture in the ongoing story of Portrona and its two notorious ships and it does not. The scenario is saved by the most unlikely person of all, the one blackdyed villain of the piece.

Picture him standing in the doorway of the office (one day, soon, Roddy Banker will remove the thick coir deck matting in the passage behind the front door, so he can hear people approach), a heavily-built man with bent nose, cabbage ears, luxuriant moustache and mutton-chop whiskers, hairy brows, full lips and the giveaway, close-set eyes under a fore and aft black hat (yes!) with a broad creamy band. White high-collared shirt, black cravat neatly knotted, dark waistcoat dangling silver chain, grey trousers, all overlaid with a black frock coat. A dandy, or dressed today to impress and overbear those whom he senses his equals or superiors, and behind his back, his denigrators (even MacRoe must feel guilt, villains are only humans). Best of all, he carried in both hands a mighty walking stick, a clublike knout, held out in front of him like the weapon of the militia officer he likes to be, marching through the town on Royal days, ahead of a company of cowed men.

The factor's rap on the open door with the rhinoceros horn knob on the head of his strange stick, saves the situation. He sees the banker's face turn from rage to canniness at the sight of him, whilst MacAllan's pale countenance betrays only relief as he turns. MacRoe is familiar with the faces of men in their extremity, judging the depth and worth of the partial truth against the outright lie is part of what he enjoys of the position of unique power that he holds in the island. The old man did nothing to curb his dictatorial ways and nobody expects Lady Emily Percy to do any better. Meantime, even independent Portronians behave towards him with a wariness that depends on how they imagine he is able to affect them, through the use and abuse of any particular one of his varied powers.

He knows he has nipped a serious personal argument in the bud, in part because the two townies will instinctively ally themselves against him, the outsider, however deep their personal differences, but also because they too are, in common with crofters and squatters, wary of him and his ability to discover subtle new ways of making the law work against them.

Roddy Banker catches a pleading look in MacAllan's eyes, his anger recedes, he steps into the safe and reappears with a clay bottle and three small copper tankards, splashes the clear liquid into them, hands one to each man, MacRoe first, swallows his own in a single gulp, draws a choking breath after it, batting tears from his eyes.

– Gress – he says – best Gress tresstarick –

MacAllan swallows and coughs in his turn, yet MacRoe sips at his drink with no effect, something that no other that they know can do with tresstarick local whisky, legally distilled or not.

MacRoe speaks and snuffles at the same time:

– Tha e math –

It is one of his ways of throwing people off balance, to speak in his mainland Gaelic to those townies who do not have the language, but he reckons not with MacAllan's grandmother:

– Aye, MacRoe, it's the best. Thrice distilled –

– I know what treas tarraing means, MacAllan –

Roddy Banker indicates the chairs identical to those in the castle library (will Emily notice?); the two men sit and look at the bottle, wondering if this is the day for more than one morning drink. It is not. Roddy walks back into the safe and deposits the bottle out of sight. MacAllan wonders vaguely if there are any more in there. Does some struggling farmer or crofter pay off his interest charges with jars of home-made whisky? Such good stuff may be a likely export, although it will need watering, a cask or two to New York, my head's feeling it, why in the name did I say yon to Roddy about the dames he has in his office?

– You want to talk about the emigration fund –

MacRoe never wastes his time in preliminaries; MacAllan finds this disconcerting. Especially as he is not sure who MacRoe is addressing; another trick, throwing weighted remarks at the company and waiting to see who takes him up. Roddy Banker replies, as self-appointed chairman (who else would, in my own office?), working his buttocks back into the big chair, a joint of papers to carve in front of him.

– There's substantial sums left in the emigration fund but I am not sure why the subject is being raised the now? –

A quizzical look at MacAllan to which MacRoe adds the turn of a hairy eyebrow. MacAllan is caught between the two older, more experienced and better raised (softer, anyway) men. He stares at the open door of the safe, trying to visualise the map of the world on it, now hidden.

– I was looking at your map, Roddy, your map of the world.

A big place (inanely, but recovers well). Plenty room there! – (this to MacRoe).

Feeling he has gained some initiative, MacAllan sits up and looks at MacRoe, tries to meet his eye, realises he fears this man and wishes he had never thought of tying in his exports of special herring with the emigration fund, but Ally boy, it's a brilliant ploy! Who had said that? Himself, likely. To his astonishment, MacRoe says:

– Fine notion, MacAllan, kill two birds –

He is in favour of reactivating the emigration fund so as to relieve his ledgers of some of the entries in red ink and the estate of those who dare to defy MacRoe by not having money or even a cattle beast for him on rent collection day. His devious mind has tripped another cog, leaving the banker to fumble his papers, looking for the piece of information that will put him back in control of the meeting. Every deng thing he says, he puts a twist in it, Lawman and Factor both, I hope that gob of a club dissent scratch my good mahogany table.

Although MacAllan is unaware of it at the moment, events conspire to help him get a ship for his visionary notion of the export of peasant food to those who desperately seek to cease being peasants; yet they have to eat and they will want to cling to something familiar; what more familiar than the succulent skeds in piney salt-encrusted barrels that dulled the ache of hunger during dark North European winters? MacAllan does not think this through as we have done but he feels it in his flesh and that is stronger than reasoning?

MacRoe has had a preliminary meeting with the panjandrum sent from the South to enquire into the situation of the starving cottars of the island, following two autumns of rotten blue-black potatoes, with half the population now demanding registration as paupers in order to qualify for a few pounds of 'destitution meal' (cost of which is being added to the rents they are now quite unable to pay).

The cunning MacRoe has figured out for himself the eventual, unspoken, destination of the inquiry, after listening to those whom he does not regard as his superiors (although pretending to do so), with judicious remarks for himself inserted in the discussion at salient points (and he is the one who really knows the situation of the desperate lotters). In the way of visiting experts, they go cleverly at the business of picking the brains of the man on the ground, without revealing they are doing so but MacRoe is too smart for them; his bluff words, blind stare and well-chosen remarks lull them; he feeds them with what he knows they want to hear (only they're not honest enough to admit it), which is what he wants too; the chosen circumstances that will have to result in the eventual shipping away of those desperate men who make life difficult, who disturb his sense of being in control.

So I find myself in support of MacAllan's crazy scheme of exporting salted herrings to America. Does he think the Red Indians will eat them when the buffalo hunt is made unlawful? Aeneas MacIver will divert ships from Liverpool for emigrants to order, when he knows the fund has been reactivated.

Now he adumbrates, for the banker and MacAllan, the gist of what he wants them to hear of the words of the visiting government representative who is to report back on the state of the paupers in the islands, following on failed fishings and decayed crops:

– Sir Clarence adumbrated the Poor Act for Scotland for me, that no ablebodied person is entitled to relief, but if such a person is entirely destitute and without the means of support, then the Poor Board must decide if they will grant relief before the person is injured in his health by actual starvation –

– Or wait until he has a legal claim –

Roddy Banker makes clear he has a knowledge of the law as it pertains. He has often felt resentful at his exclusion from local bodies such as the Poor Relief Board, being called upon only to act for charitable funds as treasurer, now again reminded of the fact that MacRoe is chairman of the Disaster Fund, whilst he is only the treasurer (the fund that Anna Flett, young widow with small child, refuses to take money from, does MacRoe have any notion why?).

The same applies to the emigration fund and that is why they are meeting this morning and are awaiting Lady Emily, titular head of the business to hand.

Sir Clarence dined last night at the castle (to his credit, he demurred, at first) and Lady Emily has been apprised of the purpose of his visit; has been given a hand-written note of the questions that will be put to the members of the parochial boards and to the constables of the various villages he intends to visit:

1. Do you know of any person who died of want?

2. Do you think there will be destitution and is there a danger of persons suffering for want of food before the next crop?

3. Will the boards grant assistance to all destitute persons to prevent loss of life?

A few hours before reading this strange note, handed to her by the greying patrician across the white table, Emily had instructed Anna Flett and the housekeeper to fetch silver plate and bottles of wine from locked sideboards and the cellar, whilst the cooks in the kitchen roasted the beef and mutton that had come from the Yorkshire farmer who had the rich land at the harbour mouth, above the Beasts of Holm. I feel faint, I am away on the moor, the next time I shall ask Anna to accompany us, those girls I visited at the shielings, they are in danger of starvation, where is their hunger, with milk and curds and heat all around?

The clue which Emmeline cannot be aware of is in the reference to the next crop; grain ripens and potatoes mature in September (if not fogged and blighted) and it is yet only May. An empty stomach is just slightly more bearable in the heat of summer than in the cold of winter, but it is a tiny difference. Men starved to death in Canadian winters very quickly but they suffered in Australian summers almost as much during the depression years.

MacAllan sits quietly (which he can be capable of when his instinct tells him to) and thinks of the imminent arrival of Emily, a sense of proud excitement ebbing into anxiety. I'll keep my big mouth quiet and listen to the plans for the emigrant boats. If I can get a cargo space from Portrona, then Roddy Banker will give me credit, we're evens on the business of the blones we chase after, the cove is only a natural man.

Anna alone in her high room near the top of the castle looks down upon the cab and mare that Emily has decided upon to take her to the meeting in the town. I stare down as though I were someone else and the fear is on me, that I have done something wrong, yet I have done nothing that even Hector, never mind the black minister in the church up the hill nor Murdo Elder in the meeting house back in the village, none of them would surely say I have sinned, yet I am full of fear and feel like dirt, of no value or good. My son if he was here, or poor Jim Flett, his supple body to cling to, nothing maybe here for me but I must, I will stay, I will read and learn, and look, even go to England. I must keep to the castle here, let them laugh, let them mock, Gaelic or English let them speak, sneak, sneer, I am Anna MacLeod or Flett, mother of my poor boy, my proud son, mistress of my soul.

The castle coach scatters gravel in a haughty progress along Dempster Street, moving at a high trot, passing the deliberate carts, startling nervous country garrons unfamiliar with the traffic in the town now growing apace as the fishing season gets under way, and draws up outside Roddy Banker's, whose residence has yet to gain the title of The Bank.

The driver jumps down, the step flaps, Lady Emily alights, pauses, at the row of shop windows, turns to meet Roddy Banker who bobbles a little on his front step, goes to take her elbow, stops himself, guides her into his office and points at his grand carver chair.

Lady Emily takes the big chair and waits. Nobody speaks. MacAllan tries a relaxation of his lips at her but she turns to look at MacRoe, who stares back. How? Sardonically, now I know the very meaning of that word, I begin to sense how his every visit to the castle has the staff in a flutter of fear, even Anna, who is so brave. I must face him, straight:

– The Fishermen's Disaster Fund, Mr MacRoe, how does it stand now? –

– That is a matter only for the town and the island, Miss Percy –

Not a mention of a lady, honorary or not be the title:

– The estate gave one hundred guineas and also collected in London for the fund and therefore follows our interest in the proper distribution of monies to the widows –

– It pays the widows' rent, that is what they want and what the estate wants –

– They need money to feed their children. It appears to me you are obsessed with the payment of rentals to the exclusion of –

– That's what I am here for! –

– Among many other tasks, Mr MacRoe. Won't you adumbrate to Lady Emily the payments made to date? –

Roddy Banker feels it time to assert himself in his own office and is he not trustee for the money in the disaster fund?

MacAllan studies them all, feels pride for Emily Percy.

– My clerk has a book she's welcome to inspect –

– Has Anna, Anna Flett, ever been assisted by the fund? –

– Mistress Flett has no croft and no rent to pay. My understanding is she wants no help –

– She has a child to feed! –

– My understanding is she leaves the feeding of her brat to some other body –

A silence as Alistair and Roddy wait for Emily to reply. She cannot. MacRoe closes the subject of the disaster fund:

– The account is open to inspection and the money, I take it, is lying in that safe behind you, Madam –

Alistair MacAllan's bowels flood with compassion at the sight of the unfamiliar hurt on Lady Emily's face. He minds his Granny and her directness, I may be here to mooch moolah from Roddy Banker but I'm not going to let that Damn Shah walk over us:

– What I came here to find out, MacRoe, was not about your shenanigans with the disaster widows' rent money, but about the cash to take away them as wants a new life in America –

Better say America, port of New York, so nobody brings up the Canada option or God forbid, Australia.

– I ken fine what's leaving you here, MacAllan, after cash advances to sink in your smart schemes, and sink's the word, never you mind my shenanigans. I can say there is every chance of further emigration, given the growing number of desperate men here, who think the estate owes them a free life, never mind the squatters who are nothing but parasites on friend and foe alike –

Roddy Banker declares himself, once more:

– There will be ships sent here then, able to carry away excess cargo? –

Time for Emily to speak, poise recovered, ready with icy voice, to remind these squabbling men, That I represent everything that makes their little lives possible here, although Alistair would tell me that herring in the sea is nature free and naught to do with the power of the landlord.

– The emigration fund is there to allow those who wish to emigrate to do so in such reasonable conditions as can be arranged by the estate –

MacRoe bridles, that's the very word, thinks Roddy Banker, like a bad-tempered stallion, greying on the flanks. Before he can say anything, or Roddy or MacAllan either, wanting both to support her, Emily speaks her final word:

– The full original emigration file is at the castle. You may peruse it there at my convenience –

With that Lady Emily Percy rises to her feet, sweeps out of the office (imperiously, I think), fully conscious she is playing a dramatic role, that of the distinguished lady dismissing her underlings. The life on this strange island is not real, as though I were involved in playacting, how easy to show one's power, should I turn at the door with a haughty stare?

She is gone and the men do not move at first; then MacRoe rises ponderously, clattering his knout against the table, venting a grunting noise full of malice, thinks MacAllan, still lost in admiration at Emmeline's performance; Roddy Banker turns and dives into the safe for the jar of tresstarrick. All stand and drink, and then Roddy dismisses them and locks first the safe, then the outer door.

Portrona turns its attention again towards the hoyle, still sniffing, Alistair for that first landing of full-formed early summer skeds. It is what we are here for, thinks MacAllan, tipping his hat at random as he strolls the narrows: peopled streets and quays.

Meantime, Roddy Banker dons his provost's gown to take a meeting in the town house, whilst MacRoe blows the dust off certain pink-tied rolls of paper on the back shelf in his main office. It may be at about the same time that Henny discovers a cylinder of paper, tied with twine, sepia-sooted with age, carefully concealed between rafter and roof, surely the writings her husband had once spoken of, the journal of James Morrison, boatswain of this town? She has no way of knowing, being unable to read. But Anna Flett can:

'Since my return to Portrona, following upon my taking by Providence away from the awful fate of the unfortunate three found guilty of Mutiny and hanged from the yards at Spithead, I am glad to think that at least I had strength granted me by the Almighty to be able to Pray with the poor creatures before the gun was fired and their souls took their flight in a cloud.

'The guilt will remain; I was not sentenced to the same and only God and good advocacy and true friends enabled me to escape. Why should my prayers be answered and John Millward's be spurned? He bore arms on the *Bounty*; I was accused of the same; it was not true, I spent the Mutiny time hurrying along the boat for Captain Bligh and his companions to sail away, but that story is for another place, how it did not sink is truly a Miracle of our days.

'Also since my return to Portrona, I have contemplated long upon the particulars provided us by the strange life lived by those happy people on Otaheite, to wit, the fact of their sheer lack of any feeling of Sin, that Feeling which preoccupies all who surround me in Portrona. That feeling of sin, so strong and daily experienced by all, though buried deep in sober minds, is occasioned I now believe above all by one circumstance, one desire, strong if not the strongest after hunger, that of the overriding felt need of all for close intercourse with another, generally of the opposite gender.

'On Tahiti, the currency is iron, that is nails of every size to every purpose. These nails were used, despite our officers' best intentions to stop us, to purchase one thing, and one thing only, before even food was bought, although food was also involved in buying and selling; fleshly congress, to many, was above food.

'Nails then, were the most important artefact that Europe took to the Pacific, and these nails were used to buy, first, intimate intercourse with the women and, only second, food, of excellent quality, hogs and fruit.

'OUR LORD SON OF OUR LADY PERISHED FROM NAILS DRIVEN THROUGH HIS BODY.

'This is the peculiar circumstance that bedevils my thought, here in Portrona, now.

'The people of the Pacific easily take to the notion that God was born of a Woman although Woman is inferior in their eyes.

'The Son of Woman was once nailed to a Cross.

'The price of a woman in Tahiti was first, a tenpenny nail, later a twentypenny nail, finally rising to a thirtypenny nail and even a spike for one reckoned specially comely and of pleasing shape and lighter colour. Some of the women are dark and others, reckoned superior, of the Chief's families, could pass for Europeans, at any rate, those from the Mediterranean, albeit with somewhat flat noses.

'Many people must have mingled through the centuries in the happy seas between America and Australia; I would take a Wager they sailed once there from South America, some of them.

'I have refrained from mentioning the life of the Islands to those in Portrona as regards their Religion; neither to churchman, elder nor even in those peculiar Portrona Schools of Theology, the workplace of the shoemakers of the town, each with his Bible among the tools of his trade, one in particular, able to terrorise those whose grasp of the Reformed Faith may be unsure, yet the people return to hear his powerful sayings; what would these Men say of the beliefs of the people of Tahiti, or especially of our conduct in that place, each of us living freely, fathering children upon suave savage women?

'Where infants are murdered to keep the population stable.

'The lives of our shoemakers and carpenters turn rather upon nails, and leather, and timber, and immutable Biblical Truths, their fleshy doings being hidden and Shameful to them.

'There is a subtle connection running through my thoughts here at home, where I shall stay for a few months, before departing never to return; a connection between the astonishing freedom of bodily expression we found in the Happy Islands and the lack in the people there of any notion of loyalty to one companion, the single love that cleaves for ever, that we hear preached in the West by Church and by Literature, both.

91

'There is no sense whatsoever in the Friendly Isles of the belief that overrides all others now in the European World, that each man and each woman has a partner preordained and set out for them, with whom a lifetime liaison of happiness will ensue.

'Our Western dream of True Love predestined, like unto that of the Predestination that is preached to consign each and every one of us to Heaven, or to Hell, is a false one.

'WE HAVE BEEN FED A LIE AND JEALOUSY WILL DESTROY US.

'In the Pacific Islands, love is not a metaphysical state, it is a game, and the people use the word game to mean congress between man and woman, they do not even have a word which conveys love as we mean it; to describe what we mean by love, they just use the word Here, which is to say, Unite.

'It was easier for me, with two languages, Home Gaelic and School English, to learn the speech of the Islands and I have made a word collection, now in the hands of others, that I hope will be of use to those who go forth to spread the Word; the Word of Atua/God, for use in their Ahu/Church, for the benefit of their Aitu/Spirit, to hear about Bokola/Sacrifice (one who was Eaten). You will see they do not lack a religion of their own.

'Their easy way of Life leaves them plenty time for contemplation; this leads to discoveries of sometime benefit to their souls, for they are very quick if not possessed of our patience, another consequence of our religion, which grows in hard circumstances, not in a Paradise where food is picked off the branch, where one breadfruit plant will feed a family for seventy years without work, apart from the picking and tramping for storing.

'But there is a darkness under the breadfruit tree and the coconut palm, meat and drink at your hand reach, but the Serpent lurks there too, and if you study it close, you will see it also is a part of religion. I would hope later to tell of their Arrioi Society, where a free licence reigns, in the most dramatic way, among certain of their young men and women.

'I speak of the Mutiny here but seldom and then only in the pot houses of Point Street, when the *treastarraing* whisky distilled at Coll, Ness, Gress and other places goes its rounds; were I like unto many of my Trade and occupation I should be maggotty each night on free grog, so much do the men of the quays wish to hear about my time on the Pacific Islands; some of them think I am lying, not those who know my family, God fearing and respected in the town and associated with Ministers of the Cloth.

'Many times am I asked to repeat my part in the Mutiny, so that I begin to feel there are those would want to prove for their satisfaction that I am guilty of that Sin but I say my piece at the same time; how Fryer the Ship's Master came to me and asked had I any hand in the Mutiny and I told him I had not and he then desired me to try what I could do to raise a party to rescue the *Bounty*, which I promised to do, in consequence of which John Millward swore he would stand by me but Alexr Smith told Churchill he had seen me and Millward shake hands and to look sharp after me and called to the other mutineers to stand to their arms.

'Despite hints and catches I say nothing even here, on the task of a bosun's mate to wield the lash, tho I think of poor Millward's shoulder springing scarlet after his foolish desertion on Tahiti on our first visit to that place of joy and despair to our men, their skins so much more tender than the Tahitian thief who took ninety-three before his back broke open and not a murmur of pain.

'The way the Word has gone around England and even into America and Europe about our Mutiny, I am bound to think and record that our story shall remain known, when many larger events are forgot. It is because of our connections, specially with some staying behind, with the wondrous ways and People of Otaheite, that Island which does deserve the name of a Paradise in this sorry World. A Paradise with its Serpent tho, a circumstance I have not noted mentioned by any of the others who write of the Pacific discoveries, tho there are many Journals wrote by men who were there before us, with more to come. On a walk along the Strand, you can see such for sale in the window of every Bookseller, MY TRAVELS INTO PARADISE, etc., etc.

'Like every person on *Bounty* able to read, that is all of the officers but maybe only myself and John Millward among the others able both to read and write easy, all perused the previous Journals of the Pacific Isles, it was this sent us to petition for a place on *Bounty*, also, no doubt, some of the Ungodly seamen who heard stories of the Women of that Place in pot houses of every Southron port, lascivious ways being a dream common to every messdeck.

'Such dreams are far from me here in Portrona. It being Winter now, no chance to walk on the burgeoning moor in Summer, admire the Lilies, floating wax cups on the warm surface of small lakes abounding beyond the town. These Lilies, of creamy White and serrated Yellow, akin to the myriad rich growth of Nature on the beautiful island of Tahiti. I can see them in my mind's eye, and they appear to belong there, and not to here at all. They remind me of the hibiscus flowers worn by the women of Tahiti as garlands on their breasts.

'Sometimes I think on where I should be now, had I decided to throw my lot in with Fletcher Christian, not bent over a smoking peat fire with pen and paper and warm toddy for companions, anyway.

'But I fear the life of ease in so-called Paradise would have palled, indeed, with the construction of our Schooner on Tahiti, were we not making our plans to leave, and was I not the initiator of the vessel's building, aided by McIntosh the Carpenter's Mate, poor Millward and a few others I got to work?

'It was too easy decided by those in authority what made a Mutineer and what not, saying if you refused to go with Bligh in the boat, then you are guilty of Mutiny against His Majesty's Navy. I could see clear as a Summer day how the boat was overloaded and like to sink. Tho Bligh was a Tyrant to his officers and men, yet he is a remarkable sailor tho Blessed by Providence, which I hope he gives thanks for, getting that boat safe ashore over 1,000 Leagues.

'William Cole the Boatswain swore on my behalf that he it was gave me orders to clear out the Boat for casting off Bligh and those who were not with Fletcher Christian. This I was very glad to do, finding hard work is the best way to deal with a situation that is causing shame. Mr Hayward saw me thus engaged and said to the Court I was glad of countenance, enjoying his discomfiture and that of Capn Bligh and the other castaways, which was untrue, just taking pleasure in using my Body.

'I know not if the further evidence of Mr Cole in answer to a question from the Court, to wit, did he think I was in Awe of the People under Arms hindered my chances in the eyes of the Court Martial. Mr Cole told the Court that he did not think I was in Awe of the people under Arms, neither was I, they had no reason to fear me or do me harm and I had no dread of them, always treated my shipmates with fairness and spoke up against the bigoted conduct of Mr Bligh when he was in one of his rages against us and the world, or when Mr Hayward slept thro his Watch on Deck at night.

'Yet me it was handed into Bligh's Boat, Cutlasses, pieces of Pork, Gourds of Water and a ball of Spunyarn to sling the mast alongside, as I saw would be needed when they was not under sail, the boat being very overcrowded. It was claimed I said chearfully to those in the Boat, to tell my friends I am to be found in the South Seas and I may have done so, was it not true and how would I say it gladly, if I said it?

'Something of Tahiti that is often remarked upon is the

Tattooing of the Body, which is done on everyone, but moreso the men, and has a powerful significance too deep to discover in a short Unscientific Paper. My own blue marks are not seen here, when always covered in the weight of clothes needed to keep warm in this place in Winter, after near on five years in the blessed heat in the Pacific. Maybe I should have waited until the Summer of 1793 to come Home, but that before then, I hope to have taken Ship to far lands; she may or may not receive orders to sail to the Warm seas, South of the Line.

'It would give the Puritans of Portrona to wonder, were they to view my own Tattoos, the Star on my left Breast, but especially the Order of the Garter Below my Knee, *Honi soît qui mal y pense*; many here, Elders and others, would consider me swollen-headed and full of Vanity to arrogate such an Order to myself, accusing me of being a Man who felt he was due much more from Providence than God was pleased to give me. It is a Sin I may confess to at certain times of the Month, the Moon appearing to bear upon my innermost thoughts and feelings, as She does on every person, tho the Scientists would dispute it and, most of the Time, so would I.

'The Tattooing operation gives rise to the most exquisite pain, which I doubt not is the worst experienced by the Happy People, yet even pubescent girls acquiesce to it, with cries and groans that reach your Heart, and make you want to interfere, until you understand they gladly Suffer for the sake of Public Propriety.

'It is not easy to avoid having to speak of the late great excitement in my life. As I go my daily round of the quays and alleys, I am hailed by all and sundry, there being no sense of Class or personal privacy in the town of Portrona. This freedom here from that sense of Class so Universal in England and the Navy, is one of the very few good aspects of Life in the North. When I recall Lieut Hayward's animosity towards me, my very Life at stake at the Court Martial, it gives me sometimes to feel a terrible hatred for such as he. This was because he knew I despised him for sleeping on watch and other weaknesses.

'Under remarks about the cold of the day, the state of a certain ship that's in, or even the pretence of boldness by certain ladies who serve in the pot houses, I sense the need of the people here to discover more, much more, of my strange experience. There is naught overt said to make me feel guilty of any wrongdoing, a circumstance most helpful to me, for my notions of guilt or innocence in the business of what may become the most famous of all Mutinies, travel from the extremes of happy Innocence to those of a dreadful and fearsome Guilt, when I wish to escape from my very Life and only prayer and the nearness of some person I know to be saved of God can help me, Yea, even unto the stubborn and stupid Shoemaker with his Tablets of Stone.

'Yet the only way I can reveal my story is on paper, sitting by the taisged peat fire with candle and pen and ink, a barrelhead for a desk across my knees.

'Jack Millward had a Son on Tahiti as did some of the others among us who left Fletcher Christian and remained on the Island, sons and daughters, Stewart marrying his Wife by the local Priest.

'My main interest being to get to North America or England, therefore concerning myself with building our schooner, *Resolution*, with the help of McIntosh and some of the others, who thought she was meant for cruising and fishing in the islands, McIntosh also marrying his female tyo, with a child to show, no doubt this was why he fled the Navy and Captain Edwards although not a Mutineer, where we gave ourselves up to that Cruel Man.

'Could it be that I have left someone of my Own Island strain on that other Island, although not married to any tyo, yet the women are compliant with natural behaviour not frowned upon as Here.

'A SON OF MINE MAY LIVE. FOREVER MORE, THE BLOOD
OF A PORTRONIAN AND BEFORE THAT A VIKING MAN AND
A GAELIC WOMAN ADDS TO THE WIDE STREAM THAT FLOWS
IN THE VEINS OF THAT BOLD PEOPLE, SPREADING LIKE A
SHOAL OVER THE VAST PACIFIC.

'They are very like the Rovers who first settled Portrona as
a haven in a storm, with a Harbour sheltered from all the airts,
better than any on Otaheite.

'Let it not be thought the sun always shines there, tho it is
ever warm, even oppressive; they have wind and heavy short
rains in their season, rivers rush off the steep green mountains
into the sea, giving Tahitians fresh water to bathe in at all times
and it must be said, they are the cleanest People on the face of
God's Earth, washing their entire Bodies three times each day.
This makes their wounds hard to cure but they would not hear
when I said they bind and keep them dry for healing.

'The Men wear their hair in different forms with their beards
neatly picked with a fish scale and on Tahiti a Painter might
take an excellent copy of a Hector or an Achilles.

'The Women are finely shaped and the natural colour is
Brunette, tho some who are more exposed to the Sun are very
dark, especially those who are fishers. Those not so exposed
are of fine bright colour and a glow of Blood may be seen in
their faces. They are handsome and engaging, their eyes full
and sparkling and black almost without exception, their noses
of different descriptions, their mouths small, lips thin and red,
teeth white and even, their Breath sweet and perfectly free from
taint. Many, with the help of a fashionable dress, would pass
for handsome women, even in England.

'The behaviour of the People to Strangers is such as to
declare their Humane disposition, which is as candid as
their Countenances indicate and their courteous, affable and
friendly behaviour to each other shews they have no tincture
of Barbarity, Cruelty, Suspicion or Revenge. They are ever of
an unruffled temper, slow to anger and soon appeased.

'When on Tahiti I was fortunate to have by me still my writing utencils and tho they were stolen one day from my Hut when absent helping McIntosh fit another board to the Resolution, yet one of the Natives returned the whole box to me the next day, My upset at this theft truly revealed to me, what I had oft thought before: I may be a Bosun, a Master Gunner, even a Middy, with a course set in the Royal Navy, but were it possible to live off it, I doubt not I would desire to be an Author.

'With regard to the safe return of my writing materials, it was because of two circumstance, fortunate for me, these being One, that many of the Natives at Matavai Bay where Millward and myself settled, knew we were Friends of the Chief Poeeno.

'Now the second and main circumstance ensuring the return of my precious papers, pens and inks was this: the One who took them away and hid them in the bushes was a Man who has the mind of a Child still, One who has never grown those canny faculties that God compels to the rest of us. The Tahitians treat such persons as Holy or at least Innocent, and they begged me not to punish him, for he knew not what he did and merely took my Writing Box and placed it under a Tree, where it was seen by a Friend when climbing high for Coconuts the day after.

'I wanted to accede and not to sentence the Thief, whom I was able to perceive at once was a *Duine le Dia*, a Man Belonging to God, for we have such a One here in Portrona, termed Iain Gòrach/Ian Daft, but not in any severe way. He goes where he lists, aye treated with Kindness.

'I have yet to speak of the Method of the people of Tahiti to obtain forgetfulness or freedom of action or such; as we do in the West use Alcohol, they have a plant named Yava which they chew the leaves of to obtain a grey liquid like dishwater to drink, which makes them fall into a Trance, when their minds are turned inwards to contemplate these Large Questions which exert all Mankind.

'The Yava is not used in those Religious Rites they perform on the Morai, their Holy Ground, where they infrequently make human Sacrafices, of someone deemed sinful, in order to placate the Anger of the Powers Above, yet I am of oppinion they use the Yava in order to Escape from the petty problems that distract them in this world and to connect them with deeper purposes pertaining to our time upon this Earth.

'I am also of strong oppinion that all use of Intoxicants is for this reason, to close out the petty world of Everyday, to let the mind grapple with the Deeper Purpose of God himself, who has placed us here on the Globe with, given one does not swallow all that is written by the Sects, little counsel as to our Conduct, except Conscience and she may often be a contrary Guide.

'Hence, home here in Portrona, when I see poor Chimsy a staggering home from the pot house in the afternoon, in the Season, late at night, in the poor times, muttering and gesticulating to his own Devils, I feel in my mind that he searches for some first Meaning and not for simple Oblivion.

'Study will discover that many of the Best of men, and women too, although they have a greater grip through giving Birth of what is meaningful here and below, many of these, the best of our Kind, when they indulge, even like the Arrioi, to excess in intoxicants and debauchery, they may be discovered to be the True Searchers for the Reality beyond our petty day's circumstance. There is a close Affinity between Intoxication and Spirituality.

'Proof here in Portrona is found in the great number of Men who Turn from Debauchery to belief and wave a Bible instead of a Bottle, a Conversion as Welcome as it is Quick to those nearest altho Time will Temper their enthusiasm.

'It may be that Art is the One mistress who can Point a Middle Way.

'As you would think, upon an Island with a population of about thirty thousand souls, in a generous climate, there is active pursuit of Fisheries. I have listed those Fish for which we had names, to the number of almost fifty, in my Account of the Islands of Tahiti, which I trust friends in the South will see through the press for me: the largest, the Whale, Turtle, Porpoise, Shark, Albicore and Dolphin, are Sacred and the Women must not eat them.

'Among all the bounty of the Pacific, I never saw a sign of that Fish which is most precious to us in Portrona, the Silver Herring, which in a certain light, when fresh caught, reveals collours as fine as any in the Tropics.

'The Women of Tahiti engage in shore fishing from their small outrigger canoes, and they would remind me of the Girls of the Island here, barefoot in the herring guts on the Quays of Portrona, cleaning the fat Skeds which are netted in myriads in the Summer, cured with Spanish salt in thousands of Barrels, and shipped across the Atlantic to feed the Slaves on the Plantations of the West India Islands; why do they need Breadfruit, unless to take the place of Potatoes? In addition, every household in these Islands has a barrel of salt herring standing for convenient Winter Food, eaten with Potatoes. I know of Scholars in Edinburgh, Aberdeen and Glasgow spending a year at their studies on such Food.

'My own education in Portrona, under Mister Anderson, was more congenial and when I took it upon myself to go off, my learning was such as to enable me to apply to the Navy in Leith for a position as Midshipman, which I obtained. Without preference, this situation could not continue and I elected then to pursue the Art of Gunnery, Mister Anderson's teaching being particular and accurate upon the subject of Mathematics, good geometry making for a good Gunner, yet it was the Seamanship imbued in me at Home that obtained for me a much sought berth on *Bounty*, as mate to Mr Cole the Boatswain. An illfated Voyage, yet one that will live in History when many greater have been forgot.

'The Tahitian Cloth is made from the Bark of Different

trees by the Women; they beat it out to its proper breadth with square beetles, all the time performing a Song given out by one and Chorused by the rest, much as the Women out in the Country here full their Cloth after weaving except they use their hands. I did not discover if their songs were sad, like ours, or happy, but suppose them to be glad, for they are not a Tragick people and take what life serves them without kicking. To see them shifting the Piece back and fore till it is all beaten out to a regular breadth and thickness, with as many as two hundred Women and Girls striking off together when making a large quantity, they make as much noise as so many Coopers barrelmaking in a Portrona Yard before the coming of the Herring, excepting that our Coopers do not sing at their work.

'Their language is Soft and Melodious, abounding in vowels; they have only seventeen letters, the same as Gaelic, yet they can express anything with ease.

'In another connection with us, they fix Collours Cloth as from Berries called Mattde, a beautiful red shade, which they obtain by painting the prepared Juice onto the Cloth. Beside this method of painting, they dye by soaking in several Collours, as Brown, like our Crottal Brown from Lichen, only it is got from Bark. Black is obtained from the Sap of the Mountain Plantain, or by soaking the Cloth under the root of some particular Cocoa nut trees which grow in Swampy Ground. The Yellow they extract from Tumeric and the roots of the Nonno. The Ora is a Grey strong Cloth made of the bark of the Sloe tree. Although generally seen as Women's work, the Arrioi Society are very excellent hands in every branch of the Art but especially Dying and Painting.

'During the two years I spent on Otaheite, it was the Society of the Arrioi that most caught my attention for its difference to our ways. Cropping and Fishing and Cloth-making are similar to Home, if much easier by the kind climate. I have not been able to find any Parralell, at Home, not in England or elsewhere in the World where I have travelled, the Indias West and East, etc., to the Antics of that Powerful Society, the Arrioi.

'We have our Secret Societies in Europe, one in Portrona recently set afloat under the auspices of the Island's Landlord, a Branch of an Order to be found Worldwide. But these are mature Men who support each other, with no harm done to their Fellows. The Arrioi are different and extreme and I shall give here a Picture of their Activities and the Power and Significance they have.

'Where these Activities remind us of Situations in our own Society, the Reader will Judge. The Arrioi Society is composed of a set of Young People of Wild, Amorous and Volatile disposition who devote the youthful part of their lives to Roving, Pleasure and Debauchery. They are continually going from one Island to another and one District to another, in companies of four or five hundred together, upon Partys of Pleasure.

'Nearly all the Chiefs are of the Society, so the Arrioi meet with the best entertainment from them when they visit their District. So greatly are they respected that if any of the Members take a liking to the Cloaths which they see any person wearing they are never refused them or any thing else they may chuse to demand, and are always sure to carry off the finest Women in the Country.

'The older members of this Society are distinguished by having a black Oval tattooed under their left Breast, their legs and thighs entirely blackened from ankle to the short ribs. They are always well dressed, with the best Cloth that can be made, their hair Scented and Adorned with various kinds of odoriferous Flowers.

'The Younger Members, and indeed all in general being fond of variety, seldom remain any length of time with one Woman, but are Constantly Changing, and if any of their Wives prove Pregnant, they go away and leave them immediately, that they may not be obstructed in their future persuit and enjoyment of Pleasure.

'As it is deemed highly reproachful for a Child not to know who his Father is (which would be almost impossible in that Society), when they are Pregnant with a Child of which they know not the True father, it is no sooner born than someone strangles the little Innocent and buries it.

'These Arrioi ladies of Pleasure easily agree to this as they think that Nursing Children spoils their Beauty in the Prime of Youth.

'There are many people who are not of this Society who kill their Children for this Reason: if a man takes a Wife of inferior rank to himself and has a child by her, it is strangled immediately it is born to prevent its bringing disgrace on the Blood of his Family. And it is the same if the Wife be superior in rank to the Husband, both of which frequently happens.

'If the Child should chance to Cry Out in Coming into the World, or should the Mother chance to see it before it is killed, Nature takes place of Custom and the Child is saved.'

Once again Anna raises her head to stare into Henny's eyes:

– They murder their babies, Henny –

– It happens much nearer to you than that, Anna Rai. Besides, it's far away and long ago –

– Hector was after sniffing out my dates, Henny –

– You never said, before –

– Never wanted to tell before –

– What did you say? –

– I played the hoor, Henny –

– Oh, Heng, Anna, you never! –

– Ah'm no going to tell ye, ah'm no goin' to gie ye the satisfaction, Hector Greusaich, work it oot for yersel', get the birth and marriage dates frae the Kirk session! –

– And him an Elder –

– Oh, Henny, something wild came over me, I feel bad since –

– No need, ah Rai, no need, ye spoke truth. What else? –

– Ah'll pey for my damn buits, Black Eachan, ye'll get yir siller when I earn mah gold frae the toffs ower the castle! –

Henny claps and hoots and slaps Anna's shoulders.

Anna feels better for an instant, but when Henny goes off to sign up more of MacAllan's full gutters, the memory of that scene, at night, in the Narrows, running into Hector on his way back from a Session meeting to his lair above the shop; was it like something experienced in a theatre, as relayed by Lady Emily Percy in full excitement?

HECT: Adorning the body. Cutting the hair. If a woman have long hair it is a glory to her for her hair is given her for a covering.

ANNA: What can follow from such sins?

HECT: Divine retribution. You should know, young as you are, have you not already felt the power of His hand?

ANNA: It was the sea. The sea took my man from me.

HECT: He rules the sea.

ANNA: What was my sin?

HECT: Your man drowned and your child not yet born?

ANNA: What was my sin?

HECT: You alone know that. Besides.

ANNA: Besides?

HECT: When were you married?

ANNA: How long was I married for. Before the birth.

HECT: You are saying this, Anna.

ANNA: I am saying what you are afraid to say. Did I sleep with my man before we were wed. Is that not it? Answer me!

HECT: You who have to answer. If the bonnet suits . . .

ANNA: I went with my man, I went with him! On his boat, covered by the new herring nets he sold his soul to the banker for.

HECT: You sinned to anticipate thus the married state. To fornicate. And He punishes those who sin against his ordinances.

Like a masque in my head, now, I can smell the cutch. I must talk to Emily about Jim Morrison's papers, a piece of history that joins Portrona to the wide world.

Lady Emily reluctantly agreed to let Anna work with Henny for a few weeks, after Anna took her on a tour of MacAllan's curing station on one of the best stances on the South Beach. Fresh material for Emmeline's diary, the station yet unused, the huge wooden box of the gutting farlane pristine white, scents of pine and tar and salt from the Balearic Islands. (Dear Diary, Does salt really have a scent?) Towers of empty barrels echo like drums under the hammers of scrambling coopers.

Henny has deputed Anna to oversee the selection of the herring; length, quality and fullness (unspawned) being of the essence of the American cure. There are many prayers offered in Portrona during these opening days pleading for the early arrival in the North Minch of the best fat fish to satisfy the Special Order, fullgutted and packed by MacAllan's Yankee volunteers, who cast their lot in with the brave local entrepreneur. If it fails to work for him, many women will go home in August without any money to show for two months' toil. On the other hand, if MacAllan succeeds, his girls will be aristocrats among the curing fraternity, their purses will bulge with coins every Saturday night.

I am recording, from my assistant, Mrs Anna Flett, notes towards the paper I hope to deliver to the Society upon my eventual return to London, pertaining to the way of life of the women who travel each year around the coast of Britain in order to prosecute one of the great industries of our time, one which in my view is ignored, that of the cured herring exports. Thousands of these women come from Portrona and its hinterland. The sight of the quays across the harbour from the conservatory window here now beggars belief. A forest of masts, thousands of men and women. The thought that some female must individually handle each herring of the millions that will be needed to fill the incalculable number of barrels stacked everywhere! (I am informed these are half-barrels.) And when they start burning flares at night! I shall have a theatre unrivalled anywhere. The head gamekeeper has granted me the use of one of his best spyglasses.

We wear a beannag, tied behind our heads, knotted under our ear, fixed with a tiepin, a piece of hair left showing on our forehead. The beannag tied like this will not shift with your head in the barrels all day packing. You take fifteen minutes to fill a half-barrel with the herring gutted by the other two. Three baskets to the half-barrel, six hundred full summer herring.

I was promoted gutter and special selector after, but they started me on the packing, I have a long back and legs and am supple for bending into the barrel. The fullsize barrels are much easier to pack, you have more time with a straight back; it is the half-barrels now, they are easier to roll, but heavier on the packers' backs, they are small to get into.

In our wooden kists, we take blankets, a pillow and bedcover, three cups, plates and cutlery and a palme for our bunk, that's a curtain. Three to a bed! The curer gives us a kettle, oiled aprons and the cuttag, that's the knife; we have our own boots.

In summer on the mainland you have five selections; matties, mattie fulls, fulls, deads, that's the wee ones you throw behind you, and matjes. Now in Portrona, in summer, the large matje, them that Mister MacAllan wants to fullgut, specials for America. The foreman coopers put big matjes aside for Saturday eating. You have to shake the milt and the roe out of them.

The herring names are Dutch, they started salting them first, about two hundred years ago, but the Scotch cure is the best in the world now, since the cuttag came in at the time of Napoleon's War. Before then, they gutted with their finger.

The worst thing is the wounds, when you cut your hand with knife or fin, the salt wears away the flesh. We tie bandages of yellow calico on every finger but the pinkie but it's not enough.

The skill of the cooper makes the cure, he is in charge of getting it to taste right to the German and Russian buyers. The buyers will open a barrel, dig out the herring, eat it back down to the belly. Some drink the pickle too. They check the cure is correct for taste and for lasting out. The poor people in Europe have nothing to eat through the winter but salt herring. At least, we have potatoes with it, unless they're blighted by the fog.

It is a happy place to be with the coopers, fishermen and girls. We are in another world at the gutting. Enjoying ourselves with the boys away at the summer fishing and keeping quiet as mice when we are at home. We were all at the gutting. Some make promises; a boy might give a girl a thin ring with gold beads. Then, a marriage in the winter, but we would still go back if we could.

The herring loads come up from the boats by horse lorry in big tubs, swells they call them in England. The men put them into the farlane, the foreman cooper scatters a little salt so we can easy catch hold of them. We take out the big gut with two stabs of the knife and throw them in the right basket, selecting as we go. I've seen a Portrona girl gut sixty-three in a minute, a fishery officer across the farlane with a timer. We all hoorayed but she just put down her head; I would not have.

Last year we came home from away at the gutting with a lot of money, ten pounds for four months in Shetland and Wick and Buckie, more if you went to England. It depends on the fish being in it. The crew is paid by the barrel, sixpence a barrel, tuppence each, and thruppence an hour for topping up. The pay is a wee bit less at home. The biggest herring are at Portrona and Barra, but the Minch season is only six weeks.

The Bible says the herring is a wholesome fish; has it not got seven fins? Can you not see the double of the meshes of the net on the body of the herring? The herring's head is the image of a fishing boat with mast lowered. Does the herring not gleam in the light with many colours? The herring is more marvellous even than the landlord's salmon.

I read that the appearance of the fisher girls after a few hours of work beggars all description, although they are said to be good looking creatures as I can well imagine from my own study of the local women. Their hands, their necks, their busts, their *dreadful* faces and fiery arms, every part of them, fore and aft, spotted and sprinkled with little scarlet clots of gill and guts. Bloody and wet with slime, the gutter stands up with knife in hand, and whilst the packer stoops with horrid head to fill her barrels, the gutter plunges her bare and brawny arms again and again into the trough, scatters her gills and guts as if no bowels of compassion existed any more in this watery world. Towards evening, the fisherlass carefully washes her face, arms and legs, slips on her better garments and goes sedately about her business. The imminent season across the harbour here will soon acquaint me with the reality whilst I shall continue to take notes from my Mrs Flett, who has personal experience of the work.

Three things to teach the coilers who have never been at the herring; how to handle a gutting knife, how to pack bellies up, how to tie their fingers with the strips of calico; this showed to the young girls before they go, but it takes real work to prove who is good at what and if they are fit for it. The new girls we name coilers, the same as the apprentice fishermen, the boys who begin by coiling the ropes as the nets are hauled aboard.

It is at some cost the herring are taken ashore to gut and to salt. I remember the Wick Drowning, ten boats lost. I was a little girl but I can see today the frightened faces of the wives when the first news came. They sent a boy into town, the women, to find out on the quays was it true, a boat from the district lost in Wick? He came back from Portrona with the story and one of the wrecked boats was from our village, the *Mairi Bhan*, but only part of the crew were drowned, two swam ashore, but they had not the names of the two live men, until another Eye boat beat along the Pentland and past Cape Wrath, down to Broad Bay, to tell who was lost and who was alive yet. No bodies for the funerals was the worst, three Portrona boats alone, smashed out of the ten lost, thirty-seven Scottish fishermen drowned one morning at Wick, trying to land the fish on the beach in an onshore gale, thirteen of them men from here. It should not be as high as three out of ten of our boats lost in a gale. Our boats are not as big as the bàta Bucachs, they have no decks.

It used to be the herring came ashore at other places, before the steam tug to tow in the boats in windless weather, Gress, Bayble, Cromore and at Holm, beyond the Beasts, there is a smooth beach. It is easier now, with everything done on Portrona quays.

We are nine to a room and pay two shillings each a week, it is crowded but we are too tired to bother, the three of us turn in bed at the same time, by numbers. I prefer the huts on the mainland, no landlady, the boys visit at weekends, we lay them on our beds if they have too much drink taken. We never work on Sunday, we go to the Mission and sing the Gaelic psalms, specially the women. On Saturday we dance reels, after the up-filling is done and we have splogged ourselves up.

Rob Am Bàrd says the Romans wrote the people here lived on fish and milk. Not much has changed since, but the coming of the potato; fish and potatoes are better food than fish and milk, with all three you have a meal for a prince. The fish may fail in the sea, the potatoes may rot in the ground, but if the factor does not impound your cow, you will have milk for as long as she has a calf to nurse.

The scaff is the boat our men have here, and the sgoth; the scaffs are built in Bernera and the sgoths in Ness. The men go away to fish after Portrona is done, the women go with them to the gutting in the East, stretched on the ballast in the bottom. The young boys say we need decks on our boats, for safety's sake, why are we behind the Buckie people? The talk is of money, island men are afraid to borrow, it is a great shame to be in debt, pride pays its way, there should be more like Alistair MacAllan. Bigger boats are bought from the East Coast, but they are second hand. Curers buy them and loan them to fishermen who must fish for them only.

The Portrona fishermen are mocked by the bucachs for they won't fish on Sunday and they want to save the young herring in the early summer, but catch them in winter for bait. Can't you make up your minds, you teuchters? The locals may have poor English, but they know fine the fish are not fit in the early season, they are different every year though. The fixing of dates is useless when you deal with nature. There is talk of a close time to give the early fish a chance but East and West will never agree, it is like religion to some of them, they have books and rules forever, they forget the power and charge of nature over men and women, never mind herring. The Buckiemen are go-ahead, my poor Jim was with one of them.

Men from the government came to find out about the Portrona herring and the time best caught, for the fat sweet-flavoured Portrona skeds get top Scottish price in Petersburg and Hamburg, all this you can hear from Mister MacAllan and Mistress Henny MacKenny. The curers working here want the very best for foreign, yet some of them plague the fishermen to start when the herring are poor. There is no pleasing them, they fight like religious people, Henny says, but she is not a member of any church, being a bit of a targe in the town.

Adventing to the previous history of Portrona; much is made of the original harbour having been colonised by Vikings. I have discovered snippets of past centuries, events that thrust up from the Sea of Time as do the rock skerries of the Beasts at the mouth of its harbour, the last century represented by the coming of the Pretender in 1746, to hide above the Beasts for days whilst his emissary discovered the good burghers here wanted nothing to do with him. No doubt Charles was of hope that this town, allied over the centuries with North Europe, might afford him the chance of escape. There was no comfort for him from the cautious townspeople of Portrona and this knowledge assists me in coming to terms with the like of MacAllan, and the banker, though not the cunning MacRoe. There are limits which are well kenned by these islanders. I must point out that the town people are different to what is termed the country folk, Gaelic speaking and mysterious, enveloped in their own ancient way.

Before Charles, one hundred years earlier, Cromwell's ships bombarded the original castle that now lies a heaped ruin at the outer limit of Number One Quay. I stare at it through the spyglass, when the scene on the North Beach palls and visualise the internecine broils that led to the downfall of the House of MacLeod and the advent in 1610 of the MacKenzie Clan who owned the island until the present incumbent bought it with money made in the East, from fast clipper ships, the swift despatch of tea and grain and, it is suggested, drugs, to keep the clever Chinese in thrall.

The above is a resumé of what I discover of the previous history of this town and it will be enough. My purpose is to put down notes for a talk on the Herring exports of the Western Islands to Europe and beyond, if a current plan to extend the trade to America proves fruitful.

It will be necessary to adumbrate happenings since the trade grew last century and this is what I have been told:

The inhabitants of Portrona have with great industry and perseverance followed the fishing since the Union in 1707, with what is said to be exemplary success. Their ancestors and also the Dutch had always taken advantage of the unbelievably rich herring shoals, but it was after the Union that the merchants of

Portrona had full scope for this laudable pursuit. Then it was that the herrings which they caught and cured might lawfully be sent to the British West India Islands, to feed the workers on the plantations, with the encouragement of a bounty from the state.

Early in the 1700s, this trade was carried away from the town by means of hired vessels but by the second half of the century they had obtained for themselves some thirty or more stout handsome vessels of up to seventy tons' burden. The town was said to be a pattern of neatness and cleanliness and when the stranger entered their convenient mansions, he would receive well-dressed Highland mutton, fish and a bottle of port. To the credit of the industrious fishers and merchants of Portrona, their pleasant hamlet was rising into view above the bay, with upwards of an hundred slated houses, besides the many inferior ones, which I take to be thatched, such as the cottages that still are found in the villages scattered throughout the island, housing, it is estimated up to fifteen thousand country Gaelic souls.

This back country is of great importance to the herring trade, for it supplies the most necessary part of the labour force: the women and girls who gut each herring. The work done in this way is the backbone of the industry; without it, there would be no herring trade, for it is unlikely that men are able to use their hands with such delicate skill. It astonishes me to see the numbers of women now appearing on the streets, ready to prepare the fish for salting in barrels. That is now the entire focus of the town. In addition to the hundreds of local women, there are many others who have arrived from the mainland. It becomes easy to tell them apart; the local women appear larger framed and more supple, due to the hard physical labour on their pieces of land, growing crops and potatoes, barley and oats, plus the work of the moors, cattle rearing, milking and the digging of the vast stacks of peat they burn in the fires of their cottages. Every village can first be

113

seen from a distance by the pall of blue smoke, seeping through the thatch of the houses, which contain several compartments of some size, with humans congregating in some and animals in others. The smoke may act to keep down disease; one can get a notion of its sooty scent off the clothes of certain passers by.

Tenderness

THERE IS A BETTER bard than me, Rob, he who hides his melting flesh in the country. I have found someone who has his words on his tongue, which I am transcribing and translating. They will be of value when the time is ripe.

First a word on our poet, who I fear will not be long with his people in Uig, although he is only thirty-three years of age, scarce older than myself, the versifier of the quays, which is all I am, but with enough Portrona Gaelic to translate to college English the words of the Bard of Uig. His name is one found Europe wide: John, Son of the Blacksmith, in Gaelic, Iain Mac a' Ghobhainn, neat John Smith in English.

He was taught in the small school near his home and proved sharp and quick to learn, as bards are when young. He was brought to Portrona at eighteen and after only two years in the new Free Church School, hied him to Edinburgh University to train for a doctor. And how we need doctors who belong to us! To cut a brave sad story short, having killed himself with study work over five years, he had to come home when he started putting up blood. He has lived for near seven years an invalid but I hear he has not long to go now. His poetic gift has flowered; it may be he has done more for us already than he would have done in a lifetime's service as a physician; it is time that will tell.

The poem I have chosen is entitled *Spiorad a' Charthannais*.

To add to its nobilities, it has a slow sad melody in G. This I will not attempt to transcribe but I am able to sing it.

How to translate a poetic word is always a matter of feeling. Here are the meanings of the root word *carthan*: charity, friendship, affection, tenderness. A second sense of the word is given as politeness. *Spiorad* is as you expect: spirit (but also ghost), mind, vigour, heart. These words in your head, pity in your soul, a prickle in your eyes, and you almost have it. *Carthannais* is a cardinal understanding of the people here.

The life of the translator is one of frustration (a small ditty on the subject for Portrona Drove Day?), a plethora of weird words we have here, that hang between the two speaks of the place, never mind the posh lingo spoken over the castle, easily, stumbled over up Goathill. But I avoid the hard work of meeting dear John half way, him taking them all to task without fear or favour, only clichés have nothing to do with him.

Would we only befriend you, spirit of tenderness, how it would ennoble the nature of man.

An old cry from someone who has experienced it. What effect would this have on MacRoe if I left it on his desk? Would he consider for a second that it might apply to him and his twisting of the windlass on the throats of the most poverty-stricken of pigs without earth to snout in, as he miscalls the cottars, wanting them to go, anywhere, so they can not be the cause of red chirography on his copperplate ledger. I've seen it, in my perusal of papers in his office in the Octagon when I copy out for him, over and over, the cold Notices of Removal he is forever serving. He likes to ride out with them, not write them out, summon the miscreants from their rough illegal bothans, or pursue them to the shore, splinter with his boot a board of their fragile boats, whatever enters his snuff-soaked brain. He prefers to deal with the men, the women he is a little afraid of, none has ever entered his padlocked rooms on Church Street, apart from the crone, who scrubs them out with germicide every month, without fail, on the due day and date and at the appointed hour.

He keeps a loaded revolver in his safe.

O Spiorad chaoimh na gràsalachd

Now there is a word for you who love language, *chaoimh.* and it meaning such as beloved object, feast, meek, handsome, seed-vessel, and poetry even, bedfellow, a kind female, how to translate *chaoimh* when I have merciful graciousness to add to it?

The gentle reader will understand.

Antithesis of poetry is how I describe my work for the factor, meaning the language. Taste it, the despairing attempt to ensure that nothing is left open to chance, that the law be immutable. Is this why Mister MacRoe is so hard and fast in his way? Does he truly believe that language can control pullulating life, can fix it, as in some fundamentalist's bible?

the Defender having failed to implement the last inter-
locutor by pulling down and demolishing the new dwelling mentioned

How many stones torn out of the new-broken field are in the walls, how many rocks from the shore to house site in a bending willow creel that wounds a woman's back, with the straps that lacerate the tender flesh of shoulders and breast?

grants Warrant to get the said demolition and removal
effected

Chan eil carthannas ri lorg, no tenderness to be found to lift the spirits of the widows familiar to us all here, their men lost at sea on board their often inadequate boats, though the fishing vessel has not been created that can withstand a screaming Minch North Easter.

You would lift the widows' hearts to sing with huge joy
Nor leave them forgotten in dark sorrow of want

117

So sings our proud and desperate poet, knowing full well life is not benign to widows or others, but censuring the cruelty of men for the darkness in this island world. These terrible papers I have to copy bear him out in his pessimism. Yet his passion is to believe that the spirit of tenderness would smoor the fires of enmity, smooth out the brutal dark brows of such as Black Donald, Devil Factor.

> You would raise the cloud of wickedness
> from the face of the furious tyrant lord

How to apply these lines to the latitudinarian Lady Percy? Poetic licence is allowable to bards but is this taking it too far? No! We have our tyrants here, their regulations are yet in place, the feared factor ready, willing and able to enact them. And more. My understanding of Lady Emmeline's position is that she has not got the power to override MacRoe, even if she wished to. And sentimental as she seems, she has yet to show any inclination to change the harsh rules of the estate, by jot or tittle. As to her standing in the view of those who bother themselves about such, the up and coming ambitious of the town of Portrona, there is only her championing the ladies' school and the unusual interest she has taken in young Anna Flett to boast for her vaunted tolerance towards the poor teuchters of our island abode. So far. I yet harbour a hope that the decent and determined man o' parts, Alistair MacAllan, with his flair and unbended knee, will enable slow change to begin in the way we are governed here.

> Hairy hide of scowling selfishness clothing you around

The commonplace cry against greed from fattened cohorts of complacent churchmen we are used to hearing but seldom do poets cry out against selfishness, a *fremd* voice among a people who live from hand to mouth, with that hand empty for half the year. For is Feed Thy Neighbour not engraved on their pagan hearts?

Were a vicious world to come to a clean
   understanding of you
Consoling all our people, fraud and force to cease
The cloud of lies dispersed

Oh, Iain dear, is your optimism overcoming your common sense, but No!, a bard but feels what we all feel, he speaks out, they do not, out of fear, as well as lack of surety in their own words. If Iain feels able of such return to passionate honesty and clarity are not all men and women capable of the same?

Who now is the optimist? Maybe it is the curse of bards to imagine men and women finer than they are, but if we cannot envision them better, then they never better shall be. He answers me:

Ah, but World you are far awry
from that hour you rejected your noble loving-kindness
And took to Hate and Lies

Put the bardic equation in human terms, understandable to even Norman Daft of the silver spade, bring it down to earth, as Magumerad queerly says of the regular customers for his never-ending trade. Compare our poet's words with those of MacRoe's black law, as I have done before, or with the sermons thundered on Church Street on Sunday, then re-loaded and fusilladed each weekday in Crippled Hector's Island Boot Emporium. Where is Loving Kindness, where is Hate and Lies?

A musical instrument sans music
No string in smooth order
Not a regular note
Refusing to be tuned

A rampart of fiddles, their bird bones crackling, burned in Ness in the year of the coming of the men, but we have still the big pipe, making great solo sonatas sound from long before they were ranked in marches with loud tartan ribbons.

The bard's own words may reflect his own black mental state, tiny fish swimming on his lungs, eating his flesh, choking him in bright blood. Mister Ruskin, I believe, makes his theories of men and art fit his current bodily sentiments and it may be that John Blacksmith strikes the same note in his big song?

> You stroke the calm
> And strike the sore
> Bounteous to him that has
> Grim to them without

At the same time, does he not equalise the cruelty of the world about him with the tyranny of those who make it so? The laws of landlordism, and its bailiffs, puffed up with a little brief authority, who blindly enforce strange rules on people unable to withstand them?

In other words, my very own occasional master, MacRoe, with his bidden myrmidons, although he has not asked me to set foot outside this office of his in the Octagon on Number One Quay, because he knows I would refuse to carry a summons of any kind, far less put my hands and shoulders to pushing over an illegal house or, God forbid it, set a match to a thin thatch of straw on a cottage raised without authority.

There is a book to be made of the work of the factor here, proclaiming the many offices he is empowered with, an unlawful list of public appointments, that makes him into a dictator, in part of a nation that prides itself on bringing democracy to the world! And how he does enjoy the dominion his position brings him? I do believe it is this power over the people gives him his greatest gratification. Nobody can feel free from his influence, and were he to ally himself with certain of the religious, then Devil's Island would be preferable to this place. MacRoe, thank God, shows no inclination to religion apart from the usual lip service. He is a creature of the law of the land and this it is that gives him his cloak of invincibility. Black Donald himself in the eyes of the poor, powerless and unprotected ones that make up the bulk of the people here, whose sufferings fire the wrath and pity of the brave bard I am translating.

To just decode his key words may be enough? A long list of negatives, wakened by a world both wicked and weak.

Wakening a love of corruption and hatred of sacred things, his litany sings on, filling with fear his listener's ears. He then turns to religious belief of the inflammatory kind:

> Tenets of divines with appetite for strife
> In their hands Christianity grows
> The beast of many heads

The town of Portrona has its full portion of those with appetites for religious strife, many of them divines self-appointed. One I'm thinking of leavens his rigid dogma with blows on boot soles preaching

> The creed that does not make us meek

It is the work of men, always this crying out of powerful words and twisting of elaborate texts. The women listen, what they feel or think a mystery. Like unto belief.

We are smothered by laws and wily words. Yet the right words can save us.

Iain Bard has never met Hector Greusaiche, nor his powerful pulpit instructor, but he need not. The influence of the men who came over the sea from Skye a generation or two ago is endemic.

Yon preacher with praise, shrieking from his diaphragm. Power of the voice taken from the intestinal cavity, lungs blown up and disinsufflated to propel the wuthering words in a chant of such sonorousness it takes you along like a throbbing drum. The blind soldier, the

keening of the lovely psalms the bagpipe lilt to lift
you into the bloody trenches of the Foe. The Sinners
unrepentant, full of drink, looking out for a blanket and
her willing to slide under it with you to fornicate with
the abandon only alcohol brings, though there are drugs
if you ken the druggist well, elegant purple-glass phials in
his locked press below the shelf with the blown amphoras
of coloured water, the light shining through promising a
Paradise more voluptuous than the bare board counter
in the shebeens and change houses of Point Street, the
clay spirit bottles, greasy tin mugs, odoriferous barrels,
stale beer and worse beneath your sticking boots.

> Cursed you are do you not hear
> My creed which is the Right one

Yet give the men their due, they care not a jot for factors,
nor a tittle for landlords of the earth here below.

The black scowlers of Christendom, hard chewing their
dogmas, like unto seers in trances, promising slayings dreadful
as Napoleon, the bard compares with those who rise calmly
heavenward on the pinions of charity, whose humane hearts
nurse love, who acknowledge no named denomination nor
church. Such, we may be sure, is the bard at this minute,
seeing his early death each day that passes, advancing on
his red-stained napkin. Acknowledging neither bishop nor
presbyter, Greek nor Roman, as he says.

> But now he hails Her, Spirit of Tenderness:
> Lovely you are
> Grace of highest worth

He turns away from darkness to feast his eyes on the
highest of which Man is capable, but does not stay with
his bright spirit, taken down by the sable reality all around;
a poverty-struck people held in thrall by the cold-blooded use
of blind unfeeling LAW. His courage is up to naming the agent

of misery. MacRoe. And he calls him poor Donald! Yes, poor Donald. I sense mercy lurking, for the worst man this island has ever had. That we ken of. I cannot work for him more. This at least I can lay at the feet of Iain Blacksmith, an offering, though most humble. One cannot use the need to eat as an exculpation for selling one's soul surely, with shining torrents of skeds due to pour ashore in Portrona? It is not mercy for Black Donald, it is contempt.

We must pursue our brave bard to the last of his poems, which is the one he would want to be remembered by. As one of the guild, I must confess a suppressed desire for immortality, in a piece of work that the people will have in their minds generations forward. Such feelings make me guilty but on a moorland walk, when I espy on hillocks and loch islands those cairns raised by individuals over many years, a stone a walk laid down, the same as I pile up my heaps of words to be remembered by, I am comforted.

What is it that makes for the urge for immortality among men? Could it be that Mister MacRoe's arrogant cruelty is engendered by a deep need of which he is but partly aware, a compulsion to be remembered into the far future, if only as a villain? There are examples of this in history and more will follow. Does he maybe think God has rejected him already and he can live only in the minds of men?

Am fear bu rògaich' a' Ghoill.

Even with the help of such as Hector Shoemaker, who has the Bible on his tongue in Gaelic and can read it in English also; even with his dour advice, having shuffled brown notes and printed papers from the books-drawer beneath his shop counter, asking for the meaning and spelling of the poet's words, with Hector thinking that I had got the cùram and was eager to join his theological class, until he found out by smart questions I was still unregenerate; even with the subtle bootmaker's help, I am unable to decipher and truly translate all the bard's words and phrases. He has laid down many stones too hard for me to shape. But I persevere and where the word is only partly understood, then will it not beguile me into sweet machairs where multi-coloured seastones thrust through the sandy soil; smooth round ollags from a broken pile raised upon some Viking raider who died in a foray here centuries ago to be incarcerated in a cell of firm sand, trued as if Magumerad himself had dug it, with Norman Daft patting down the lid of turf with his silver spade?

Sand, even if salt, does not preserve flesh like peat does. That is why we do not bury our dead in the miles of peat around us, choosing instead for our graveyards the slivers of sand ramparts built up over aeons by the constant roar of the mighty Western Ocean. Also peat is black and sand is white.

Not often enough do we skalds put physical descriptions like this into our works:

> You of the hanging lip, shapeless mouth
> Face distorted by sullenness or grief (?)
> Blubber lipped and swollen cheeked

A caricature of the wicked villain of Portrona and its circumjacencies is the only way to explain this violent description of MacRoe. Our bard has learned from scrutinising those political cartoons, where the faces of famous men are bloated to embellish their extremes. He does it with words instead of black pen and white paper, seeking them in his home village among those who still retain a Gaelic vocabulary vast and true, words that have never yet seen the page of a dictionary, nor never will, now.

> You thought that every islander
> Should be banished to the forest

The big emigration of some years ago still upsets. It has not made a whit of difference; the population has grown apace, despite the predictions, yet we would never starve, so long as the shiny shoals seek out our coast every summer. We can send a million barrels of herring to feed the myriads of Europe, how can we not fill a few thousand more mouths on the islands? It needs only the proper direction of lucre and raising of perceptions of the poor, so they are seen as much worthy of consideration as the rich, who have pillaged much more than their fair share of the world's goods here and in the colonies. Shifting opium to poison innocent people is just the worst of it. Such profit should be cursed, yet I have not heard any voices raised against it here, in church or shop of Portrona town, that benefits from it and the castle it raised.

It is not possible that MacRoe has heard this flyting in his travels. Who would dare repeat it to him, unless one of his own creatures? No! They fear him too much, his power is absolute over every soul. There is no person here has not got a vulnerable spot to be pricked and prodded by one who bears the staff of all law in his name.

My atonement for my people is that I write down part of God's gift to Iain Blacksmith, his rhythmic fierce language flowing forth in subtle vituperation that I cannot translate fully but merely suggest. It is not harder to accept MacRoe's injustice because he knows our language? He is one of us! Why is it that those who oppress their own resort to the Draconian style more often than the outside person? Deep feelings are here found, to do with guilt and hatred of self and neighbour. Herein lies our poet's choice of title. Which can confuse but, taken to be ironical, does also describe the best of which his confraternity here is capable. The poem has this doubleness, of evil against good, in extremis both, whilst the foregrounded figure of Black Donald has always at his rear the one who holds the reins. He of the Portrona castle and the London money. There is a lesson here in the successful application of oppression? Does it operate full stretch when two are involved, master and actor, dancing partners to a baneful port? The ballroom at the castle is big enough for the both of them, I hear, plus the gentry of the town and the hunters and fishermen too, when he comes North and Lady Emily sets off the Autumn Ball.

As to Black Donald, he is to learn that kindliness is to be preferred to treachery and that vice has to be paid for.

Addressing his spirit of kindliness, which quality he finds Donald Black without, he develops his theme:

> In your nature is not
> In the hard iron breasts
> Of the baillies and landlords
> Put down the northlands

And compares the humble cottage to the grand castle:

> Charitable were the dwellings
> Dry and warm there once
> The land of the virtuous
> A poor and dreadful desert

Earth created from sweat and seaweed and broken spades, turned back to scrub, its only crop the whispering snipe rising and falling at eve. No sign left of the people whom he characterises as suairc, i.e. civil, kind, affable, polite, meek, gentle, urbane, courtly, generous.

Men and women in city tweeds, with slinking dogs and flashing guns move line abreast over the blasted heath. Take it from me, they will break your potato shaws and trample your barley crop to ground one more bundle of bloody feathers.

> You're not allowed to drown them
> So rout them across the ocean
> Worse than by the Beast
> Of Babylon their usage

He makes compare between the thousands from the North who fought well at Waterloo, whilst unknown to them, at the same time, their grey-locked parents were sent naked into the glens, their warm homes burnt to ashes. The irony that had Napoleon conquered Britain, the Gaels may have been better off, able to stay in sight of their beloved bens. The bard's thoughts here range much further than his own island. Many places are suffering and have suffered more than we. Yet a paid passage enforced on a poor squatter's family with the present of a tin dish to eat brochan from en route, makes of little comfort for those who do not want to leave. Were the estate here to confine their emigration to sending away only those who want to go, on the other hand, my fear is that the very able would desert us and only the poor and mean-spirited remain. The Americas and colonies would benefit from our best blood and we should sink under the feet of the squandering, amoral hunters who turn the land of heroes into a sports field.

> Would the grouse
> Manure a field for them
> They would prefer it
> To gold paths in heaven

But at the end of the day, it is the visible personification of the landlord's dominion, the unmerciful hairy hulk of Black Donald, one pocket lined with snuff, the other holding a loaded pistol (for it has gone from the safe) that concerns a bard who speaks from the core of his people.

How on earth did the authorities in Edinburgh and beyond give leave to one man to take into his own hands the reins and power of judge, jury and executioner? It is because they seldom think about us, and when they do, it is with contempt, as a lesser breed, white natives with no English, redshanked.

> The mourning sighs of widows
> Do puff up your opulence
> Each cup of wine you drink
> The tears of the wretched poor

There is no fear in the young poet's heart as he faces up to his own imminent ending. Now he calls dour death to his aid, now the only arbiter who can pay back the unfeeling landlords and their worse creatures, who vaunt the law and coldly abuse their power, with especial reference to Black Donald MacRoe:

> You order a large Estate
> The people cower under you
> Yet Death has shrewd Laws
> Yield power to you must
> He is a Landlord who orders
> Just deserts to each
> Your Freehold linen shirt
> Two strides of grey Earth

When the silent estate of death provides the mean ending for you, who tumbles the sheltering walls of the poor, sets light to their covering thatch, there will be no more removals from warm rooms to wet cold sitigs, no broken beds and smashed walls, no shout of anger to be heard from officers of the law, you can no more twist your ugly face;

> Then shall the creeping worm praise
> How sweet will be your flesh
> When she finds you well prepared
> So silent on the board:
> He's a fat rich sappy one
> Good for the beast of the cave
> He emaciated the hundreds
> To fatten himself for me.

Among the summonses I have been ordered to copy, one that grieves even more than any of the removals, concerns the young wife of an absent skipper, one of the Portrona captains who reside in the new white houses in Newton. The case concerns a debt, alleged to be standing against Captain Stephen for some years, which he disputes, and which grows apace for each time MacRoe and his legal cohorts take action on it, a further sum is added to the total. The captain is on the China Seas and quite unable to fight his case. I fear that there are moves afoot, emanating from the heartless application of law, that will cause summary action to be taken against the captain's young wife, Catherine Stephen or Morrison, whom I understand is enceinte and therefore not in any condition to meet a determined attack from the all powerful legal authorities here. Should action be taken to summon Cathie Morrison and to lock her up in the clink, I will inform Donald MacRoe instanter, that he must find himself another penman, though they are few in the town. Those who have any smattering of education or business consider themselves a mite above such humble work, but a poet must pick up what crumbs he can.

Another of the documents I have seen concerns the order to demolish a temporary shelter or bothan raised in the district of Eye, by the recently married son of a crofter, preparatory to the building of a cottage more substantial. There is nothing new in the legal pursuit of those who, without authority, landless men, attempt to raise houses illegally, on the occasion of the arrival of their first born child. What else are they to do? Until the law is altered to enable so-called squatters to obtain a piece of land on which to build, and grow, there will always be those who will act without authority from the estate. Thank God for the rich fishing of Broad Bay that enables them to feed their families for they are not permitted an inch of ground on which to grow cereals or even potatoes.

Now this order to demolish that has been sought against a Murdo MacDonald, concerns, if I am not mistaken, the husband of her who is nursing the male child of Anna Flett, the lassie Miss Percy at the castle has taken such an interest in.

There are nights when if I have not taken a tumbler of hot whisky in Chimmy's grog shop on North Beach, I lie awake in fear and trembling at the actions of men to other men and deploring my own part, albeit small, in the same. Yet, did I not pen the papers, would not someone else be found to do the work and would not the effect be the same?

What can be said of Hector the man, as opposed to Hector the symbol of narrow religion? What does that mean, narrow religion? It means something different to everyone who thinks it. Something personal. I was dealt with in such a fashion by men of my culture in the name of religion; I did not like it, ergo what they did and said to me comes under the rubric of narrow religion.

Hector represents multitudes; in Portrona, in Scotland, in Europe, in America, even in the paradise discovered by James Morrison; cultures destroyed by bigots of all persuasions. Cast your mind over the effects of missionary zeal wherever Europeans penetrated, and Hector's small intolerances fade like the grey smoke seeping through the thatch of the cottages of Laxdale, one of his regular mission patrols.

Aztecs, Amerindians, Aborigines, women, folk cultures everywhere, all have felt the sting of the words of his kind, so why place our Hector at the forefront?

Because he is a strong man, with a lot to say in our story of Portrona, full of righteousness which he cannot separate from self-righteousness, a most interesting character. That the fount from which he sips drops of soured theology has fed the springs of erosion flowing from civilisation over the world during five hundred years is not our concern. What matters is that Hector is a man with an appetite for the use of words, yet suffering an inability to translate them into successful living. The time which he inhabits does not give him the chance, but then, would he not have searched for and found a source of rigid law to suit him, regardless of when he was placed here below, in the timescale?

The muscles on Hector's arms squirm under his silken white skin in the light of his workshop window, his eye through it at the passerby like a ray, avoiding none. Nobody in Portrona can stare Hector down, not even Rob the Bard, specially since he became penman in MacRoe's office in the Octagon on the quay. Herein lies Hector's power, his words and glances prod at those places in your mind you prefer to keep aside.

Early she taught me another world was there for my winning, young I was and open to her teaching, wise in the ways of Our Lord. Does he not take care of His own here below, the veil gone from her soul, the Lord her Shepherd, *Is e Dia fhèin is buachaille dhomh, cha bhi mi ann an dìth,* I shall not want, yet we wanted Mother, not spiritual food, food of earth and sea was not always in it but you told us He would provide. The day I found a big beast of a coalfish in a tidepool, and nothing in the house for Sabbath dinner, Lord Thy Mysteries Thee perform as my bent foot made me unfit for sea, so it got me to be a shoemaker's coiler, now I own the shop and the house it's in, room to hold a prayer meeting or debate His holy word with saint or sinner.

She had spiritual certainty even before my father was lost, from the invisible no reason can show, no fear of death, heaven waiting as home, where the royal line perfect and elevated minister to their king, victory over the Grave, Death Thy Sting Drawn, as the Marys tasted of their feelings, seeking the sepulchre with spices in hand, finding only Angels.

The Gaelic church has ministers and men of power and vision; the master improves, and refines, and specialises His own instruments to a wonderful pitch of perfection and yet the highest of us fall short of so much that we would need to know, and we need the English tongue to spread His word afar.

The lives of our Portrona men, even on the far deeps, show forth the gospel they got from ministers and elders here. As the wings of the bright tropic birds they see flash, and close, and flash again, so is the sunlight of the divine love that floods the world and into which our mariners go, in the sure knowledge that His law is unerring. The joy and glory shines from Portrona faces over the sea and is a centre of sunlight and blessing to all who can see.

Seafaring men, Portrona and island bred, tell me how, influenced by Highland blood, after much travel, they undergo a transformation, making them brim with the love of living, yet still they keep the picture of our old guard religious ones fresh, as they try to turn away from the world and its temptation to flesh and to spirit.

I see her firm face, with broad brow of marble purity, her slightest wish my law, her way to me so tender and true, I saw it warm and bring light to many eyes that seemed dead before. She never counted God's ways strange, her whole being was in harmony with all. Her voice rose in Gaelic psalm-praise, the minister said it was like reeds near pure hill-streams, pure and quivering, symbols of a spotless heart, rebounding from widow's bondage, at family worship in our humble house.

I remember a little boy handing her a Gaelic psalm-book, she catches his hand to her lips and blesses him. He now sleeps in the garden of the Pacific, the seething waters over him, they sound the sighing psalm.

She had, like so many, a retreat in a sandy nook by the rocky shore near the Beasts, where she wrestled with God in prayer, and felt the unity of His love and in all and over all, how He worked, this all God, in bud and flower, in breeze and calm and sun on our lovely island, after the gale, the wondrous peace. She said in Gaelic:

– I meet my Master on the rocky-point shores, where the sea remembers nothing, where it licks our feet at times, and then it mocks our heart's thirst, after its jaws have taken our fairest from us, the ancient waters that lick our Beasts, with fascinating, treacherous kiss –

On a Communion Friday Question Day, I heard one of the men pouring out his secrets from that workshop of the mind, furnished with decades of bible reading and hard discussion. The pictures and sonorous words bewitched me and from then until now, I have sought out the means of grace, with meetings and tough mind-chewing of mysterious meanings, alongside those whose eyes have been opened, the men of our own day, spiritual giants like unto those who have gone before, mayhap not, yet together we are able to bring to conclusion many of the needs and problems of the town in the light of our understanding of His Holy Word, able to question those who sin and stray, that they mend their ways and one day save their souls. These men I speak of carried a keen eye, could see everything distinctive in a young minister, men who sat in brooding contemplation of things unseen by the natural eye. They have entered within the veil but their fragrance is still with us.

The first Free Gaelic Church was burnt down, a time of trying men's faith, but Morrison's ropeworks gave sanctuary for worship. The fire developed loyalty among the people and a new church grew and with it a vestry. There my mother drank in life and power from a well-spring of joy and blessing and passed it to me. They had a precentor who had been a shepherd in Kintail, which made him a deep-breathing, strong Gaelic singer. Oh, the sonorous psalms, the sonorous psalms. If you have Gaelic, you will be carried above by them. They have replaced the profane songs of old, driving their message of worldly flesh out of the hearts and bodies of those who strive for purity.

How often I have heard how the good news come here from Waternish in the hands and heart of John MacLeod, come to teach how to read the Gaelic Bible, his work overcoming the deadness of the established minister.

And the folk flocking across the moor from all over the island to gather in their thousands on the top of *Mùirneag*, the Beloved Woman, to hear the teaching of the great Finlay

Munro, Highland evangelist. Did he not preach to the hungry and thirsty from the text:

> And in this mountain shall the Lord of hosts make unto all people a feast of fat things, a feast of wines on the lees, of fat things full of marrow, of wines well refined! (*Isa. 25, 6*)

The carpenters trying who would build the best wooden pulpit box to shelter our gospel men and their jewelled book when they preached in the wind and rain to the thirsty and hungry souls of our forsaken Gaelic people.

How dark was our island then, spirits and tobacco sold by smugglers at the sanctuary on the Lord's day, a vessel wrecked on the coast welcomed as a great prize, with prayers offered by elders for such a disaster to happen. We know the bitter truth of tragedies at sea for ourselves now, young widows left with young to feed, to get sustenance from where they can, or live off the charity of the few who can afford to tender alms.

One thing I have learned from reading and hearing of holy scripture and holy men is the importance of the question that we must always be putting to sinners in order to steer them and resolve if they are on the road to glory. The asking of the right question is above all else in the work of salvation.

Many were the signs of his work among us in those days when the secret of the Lord was granted as a boon to those whose labours for Him were not in vain. We try to continue the efforts though it is not easy in a sinful town, where much is hidden from us; not as life is led in the country villages where all is known to all them who may wish to know the goings out and comings in of their fellow men and women. Yet there is always a question pertaining, to be discovered in scripture itself, which speaks to those who can hear.

Strong ministers we had and one who possessed the gift of hearing, although he would deny it. Did he not sense a promised evil in a heathered gully one night and travelling there, find a young man and woman of this parish in the act of digging a hole in the ground, the girl with a newborn babe wrapped in her shawl. Grasping the man's shoulder he put the girl on his back and took them to the manse, sat them down, put the babe to the maiden's breast and married them in the very minute. That was a man and a minister of power. The sinful two did not even have to stand in the church on Sunday under the sackcloth though it may be the elders called out for it, for had they not indulged in carnal fornication?

Another time a newborn babe was left at the manse door and brought in and cared for. The child remained unclaimed for months and Satan began to whisper in the ears of parishioners, even elders, that the minister himself was the father of the foundling. The elders were asked to accompany the minister, the babe and its nurse to deliver the child to the real parents. Nobody knew who they were, but the minister led them for miles, till they stopped at a peatbank where men were cutting peats. He called one of the men to him and said to him, Take your child. To the amazement of all except the good minister, the man said, Thank you, Minister, my wife died giving birth and I am poor, with no near woman who could give him to drink of her milk. That was a man and a minister of power who could see and hear in his silences things that are hidden from the rest of us. Sometimes, I think that strange power lies on Norman Daft, when he utters words that may have come from some source like the Book itself.

These stories of babes and young mothers are from across the Minch and from a time before, nearly back to the Popish Pretender who was refused a ship by the good folk of this town to their honour. The minister of whom these tales was from the island here, of a race well known over the centuries, first for Brehon law, then the church, later for worldly music and poetry and last for their skills at the sailing, including one drowned off the Shiants on his way to marry a girl from Scalpay who made an idle song on it, the last, I am thankful to say, of these heathen laments sung by women for dead lovers, instead of turning to Him who can heal all wounds. This Allan had some cousin in this well kent Portrona, whom I decline to name, their pride is high enough, the one sailor from here who ever got off a mutiny death sentence, after being king on a Pacific Ocean island, so the family used to boast.

The hearing of the answers to questions put in prayer and wrestling, the getting of texts from holy writ to enter your mind in travail, for one familiar with His word on tongue and brain, the thousands of texts, how does one answering sentence jump out and seize your mind and ask you to grapple an answer from it? These are mysteries. One day, coming through the town from Bayhead to Cromwell's fortwalls, did I not meet a Christian friend from the country who asked what ailed me, though I felt naught in my body then, yet was my heart weary and I bethought the pain in my breast sometimes, which I meant to trouble the physician with when he ordered new boots and bethought maybe it is serious, so I unburdened to my Christian friend:

– I have a pain sometimes and fear my life may not be long on the land –

– I have prayed for you, Hector, many times –

– Oh, that is very Christian of you, and what did you get for me? –

– I got Job 5.26, my good friend, Hector, for you. Thou shalt come to thy grave in full age, like a shock of corn cometh in its season –

I went to South Beach and arranged with Roddy Banker to put in train my purchase of this place and wrote away a full order for leather, nails and rosin, a new lapstone, that very day and here I hammer still, whole-hearted in His work. They that sow in tears, shall reap in joy.

Our Shadow?

MRS FLETT TELLS ME of the Son of Stronach, a figure of fear used by the island mothers now to frighten their children away from the dangers pertaining to lonely places, as seacliffs and moorland lakes.

The story originates with a real person who is said to have lived on the island as an outlaw for seven years, yet the number seven denotes a story with folk origins. Yet, also, so Mr MacRoe informs me, seven is the number of years pertaining to legal statutes of limitations, beyond which time no charges may be pressed upon an accused person (apart from a charge of murder). I infer that the Stronach who roamed here to the terror of the lieges as recently as the thirties of this century was wanted by the law of the land for some serious crime, but a crime less than murder. Yet, according to the people's story as relayed by Anna Flett, the Stronach was responsible for no fewer than twenty murders, the last of them the very hangman who was to hang him on the scaffold that frowns, a splintered ancient pine, on Gallows Hill behind the castle. Much telling has gone into the tale but the fact that it originates from a real person and so very recently adds much to its fascination and the tale will make a most valuable addendum to my report to the Society. It falls to be noted that although Anna Flett relays the local stories about Stronach to me fully, it is not at all certain that she believes all of it, or even a part of it.

It may be that the Gaelic Church frowns on such idle fables. Anxious as she is to be seen as capable of less cognisance to Gaelic beliefs, the smoother the path ahead for her ambitions. Which is a pity, although understandable. There is yet still a part of Anna that fiercely wills to believe in the riches of her culture, a circumstance which renders her situation piquant if not poignant, in my eyes.

The Son of Stronach, we may safely infer, stayed hidden in the wildest parts of the island from 1835 to 1842, the time it took to have his name removed from the charge sheet for his crimes: seven years. But what was that crime? There is some evidence it may have been in the nature of a venereal assault upon a woman, a traveller, a servant maid with the family, or it may even be, his own sister, a most shocking circumstance if true, but one that could well lead to such a terrible self-punishing exile, to live like a hunted animal for seven long years. After all is said and done, folk tales are meant to shock, that is what gives them their power over us. And they always start from a truth.

– He was afraid of dogs and ghosts but not of men, Emily –

– Imagine him, Anna, afraid of ghosts, creeping to the back of his cave and staring all night at the dim light in the entrance –

– People were frightened to walk the moors when he was here –

– Did he ever hurt the milkmaids on the shielings? –

– One day he came to a shieling and sat down on the ceap. I know that the girls would give him milk to drink and crowdie and cream to eat; he was always hungry –

– Were they not afraid? –

– They talked together, but one girl said something that made him very angry, maybe she sported with him and made him wild –

– Heavens above, Anna, did he assault her? –

– Oh, no, Emily, he just went off across the moors brundalling under his breath –

– Simply went off muttering, how very strange –

– They did not know who he was until he was gone –

The name Mac an t-Srònaich has made a place for itself in our folk history so large and so secure that no thought is ever given to questioning it. Stories heard down through the years; places named after him: his bed, his cave, where he killed, robbed, fought, committed his myriad crimes. According to the mouth history of the people of the island, the Stronach was a major criminal, the first serial killer. Significantly, the motive most often imputed to him was hunger; he ravened about the lonely places for seven long years seeking what, not whom, to devour. The hunger made him totally ruthless and any man, woman or child who stood between him and its relief he killed without a thought. The significance lies in the fact that the crimes of the Stronach reached their acme during the time of the great potato famine when the emaciated spectre of starvation roamed the fouled reannags of stinking tubers and a sack of meal was more than a sack of gold dust.

The hungrier grew the people, the more ravenous became the fearful outlaw of the moors; the more desperate the folk, the more dreadful the crimes of Mac an t-Srònaich.

Came the day he murdered an innocent child for the blanched bone he sucked.

That is what they say.

The Son of Stronach, a man who appeared to folk, now and then, here and there about the island, lonely places or familiar, disturbing stock, stealing and eating sheep, taking advantage of travellers, robbing them of their goods. And sometimes killing them. A turbulent and cunning man, when he had to be. And, had it not been so, he would not have done all the deeds that his story tells us he did. He provided the foundation for the expansion of his own story, but a sure foundation, that proves such a man existed. And there is more, not mouth words merely, but writing.

Has not Lady Emily ordered MacRoe to bring certain files from the fiscal's office to the castle library and has she not found proof of the Stronach's existence, although not named as the folk name him. There can be no doubt that someone prevailed upon the procurator, not so many years before, to issue the warrant that Emmeline will probably incorporate into her addendum to the paper for the learned society she wishes to impress upon her return to the civil South:

Procurator Fiscal v. Bodach na Mòndach or fantom
(*sic*) A Moor Stalker

Unto The Honourable The
Sheriff or his Substitute
The petition of Proc. Fiscal of Court

Humbly Sheweth

That the petitioner has received information of there being a man lurking about the island who is suspected of having committed some serious crime but for the present has evaded being brought to justice, and as he puts the Inhabitants of the Island in fear of their lives (he being armed with dangerous weapons) besides, as their sheep and other cattle may be destroyed and their goods seized & carried off by that person who at present can have no lawful means of procuring subsistence, and hence the Petitioner suspects him either to be a criminal escaped from justice, Vagabond, or Plunderer, which renders the present application necessary. May it therefore please your Lordship to consider what is above set forth, and in respect of the peculiar circumstances of the Case, grant warrant to Officers of Court, Constables, their Concurrents, and to any of the natives of the Island to pass, search for &

apprehend the person before referred to, and to bring him before you for examination, and thereafter, upon again advising this application with the declaration of the accused and other evidence that may be adduced, do and determine in the premises as to your Lordship shall deem proper.

Further in the Meantime grant warrant for citing witnesses to be precognosced in the cause.

> According to justice.
> Sgd. Tho. B. Drummond
>
> > Proc. Fiscal

The Sheriff Substitute having considered the foregoing petition grants warrant to Officers of Court and other executors of the Law to pass, search for, seize and apprehend the Man or person referred to in this petition and bring him before me for examination anent the facts stated in the petition and grants warrant for citing witnesses and in a precognition as craved.

Does the use of the word fantom give us a clue as to the possibility of doubt of the Bodach's existence on the part of the fiscal, albeit even unconscious? And who petitioned for the warrant? This knowledge would clarify the fiscal's attitude, for were it some person in a superior position, such as a minister of the Kirk, or the landlord, he would feel constrained upon to act though he were sceptical?

Even the principal folk story of our island is tainted by law.

– If I keep to the hills of Uig, the hills of Uig will keep me, what he used to say, Emily, the grey hills you see over the moor, where Mac an t-Srònaich had his cave, the one nobody knows where it was. There's one of his dens at the mouth of the river near the castle. I'll take you, or maybe Mister MacAllan. It was in Uig he was seen in the company of a woman, on the moor, in the dawning of the day. Just the one time. I never heard who she was or where she came from. One abominable act he is said to have done is ask a child in a cradle for the bone he was sucking, saying, Put out your hand and when the babe did not give him the bone, he hurt the child so he died. Oh, Emmeline, can we even think any man would kill an infant in his cradle? –

– It may be part of the folk tale element, Anna –

– It never truly happened? –

– Very likely, but one cannot be sure –

There is truth in the stories about our fantom, however, in the sense that such deeds as are attached to his name really happened. Happened, somewhere, sometime, in history or tale or myth. Buried in the unconscious of the folk are incidents that recur through the ages and this is how the tales of the Stronach's evil acts (for nothing good is imputed to him; is this because of the particular place where he developed his existence?) became his. Or is it only some of them, but which ones?

He was created in the ceilidh house of the island during the days of fireside entertainment, made by those who could tell a yarn. Yet, there has to be a grain of genuine history to irritate the creative juices into play, and a main character upon which to hang those strange events, actual or imagined, that take place on an island where there is much silence, much space and no person about, except him, the one whom we do not recognise he who goes about on the periphery of our attention, seeking whom he may devour. For we are all guilty of something, and could you not argue, that Mac an t-Srònaich was going about punishing selected secret sinners, some with the ultimate penalty? May he not have been a natural disaster, sent to punish, like unto the terrible indiscriminate tragedy which history is secretly storing up. A specific event, one day, will scourge the thousands by drowning of hundreds? After this, the Stronach will fade from our ken.

– The children enjoy tales, Emmeline, they scare them, but as we know now the Stronach was hanged behind here on the hill above, Hanging Hill or maybe Inverness. The children listen at the ceilidhs, the religious folk like them to, stories of a big sinner who hung and if there are any untruths told about him, they say even the lie is none the worse for a good polish! I will speak slow in English, so you can write them. The poem he made on the scaffold for the child he put to death:

> The look my child gave me
> In the wooden cradle
> I would give my soul
> To have him on my knee.

He could not have been all evil to say that, nor all powerful. He showed repentance when facing his own death on Gallows Hill, for killing the babe.

The women did better against the Stronach. The minister's maid in Uig, when he came into the kitchen, she gave him the best in the house, plenty you may be sure. The people took fish and potatoes and milk and eggs to the manse when they had anything. After Mac an t-Srònaich ate his belly full, did he not take out his big knife, it was huge, Emily, and start to chase the maid around the table in the kitchen. But she knew the way and got out a hidden door and ran across to the barn and slipped around the back but he went into the barn, he thought she was inside. She ran round the barn and shut the door and he was locked in there until the men came to take him away, but he must have escaped, because he was going around for long after, for seven years he roamed. I don't know where the minister himself was at the time, maybe on some poverty committee over in Portrona.

It is like a fairy tale from the brothers in Scandinavia, Anna, and you must not speak ill of those who serve on committees and who have the welfare of the deserving poor at heart.

143

There are strange truths hidden in the ancient stories for our enlightenment!

There was another woman coming back from the Eye shielings with a big island dog, maybe they came down from the Lochlanns. This one was faithful only to the maid, for he was with her on the moor always. They met Mac an t-Srònaich and he said: Stad, a bhean, air neo bidh do bheath' às d' aonais. Stop, woman, or you will be without your life. She asked what he wanted and he said money. She said, Not a brown penny on my journey. Then have you food? I have not, said she and do you see how the dog wants to lay hold of you? The Stronach was very afraid of dogs and the maid had heard. He caught her by the arm but she shook free and ran, leaving the struggle to the dog. She was near Portrona town before the animal caught up with her. She had been hearing the man swearing and the dog snarling. He never managed to put in the knife that time either.

There are strong men too, they pride themselves on it, Emily, lifting big stones, near bursting their veins, to show the power in the corn they grow and the mutton they take from the moor. It is not just cows and calves out there, sheep too, you can smell them in the hollows. The old men eat the mutton in the winter and one will say, That sheep summered on such a place. They can tell where a lamb was grazing by the taste of the meat. Someone tried to put a fix on it for one bodach and he got very angry but yet insisted he could taste the grass and heather from a certain part of the moor on his lamb's flesh.

Gourmets here!

They fight among themselves, there is one who is the best, he gets asked out on Saturday night to prove himself against the young men. But he has been champion for a long time, he is old now, though yet to be beat in a fair fight. His name here is Cooligan; someday soon, he will bow his head, my father says. He sails on the clippers and learned to stand up on Custom Quay in London. It was not just the women who got the better of the Stronach in his time. I told you of the big boy from the West who took his knife off him. You can see the knife today, if you go to the right house across the moor.

And clever wee men, Emily, this for your book. Wee Red Donald, he was small but he was brash, and he frightened Mac an t-Srònaich. Donald was going home from Portrona to Uig with a pole for a mast for his boat and he refused to wait for the horse and cart because it was too slow, although the others said, Wait for us, Donald, or the Stronach will get you. Did Wee Donald not just set off by himself with the pole and crosstree on his shoulders, over the moor, miles and miles. In the middle of the moorland, did he not see Mac an t-Srònaich up ahead, coming to him, no way of escape, but the robber did not see him yet. Wee Donald jumped down into a hollow, took off his trousers and his coat, put the sleeves of the coat over the crosstree and tied his trousers, filled with heather, on the pole. The Stronach was coming closer and closer all this time, when suddenly he sees the Devil leaping the tussocks towards him! Who was this but Wee Red Donald in his drawers, with the effigy flying above him and this is how the smallest man in Uig scared off Mac an t-Srònaich –

– How exciting and theatrical, Anna! But what about all the murders the Stronach is said to have committed? You make him sound more like a character from a fairy story than the wicked and evil man who is supposed to have killed twenty people –

– It is said he killed others as well as the babe, Emily, but it is him putting his hand in the life of the child that makes him dreadful. There is another murder they say he did, killing a man who came into Portrona to get the pig of whisky for a wedding, leaving his body on the road, drinking the whisky and breaking the pig, sticking the pieces in the dead man, to make people think the man had fallen with drink under his load and the broken clay pieces stabbed him when he fell.

But nobody believed it, they knew it was Mac an t-Sròaich did it –

– There is no proof that the Stronach committed that crime, Anna, indeed, I would suggest to you that he did not. It does not ring true to me, out of character in fact, and I shall make this point in my paper. It may even have been an accident, given the undisciplined way in which some of the men here take spirits when they get the opportunity. When I told Alistair MacAllan of the quantities of whisky appearing on the bills of lading that pass through my hands here, he was shocked. He shall raise the subject of limiting the licences to sell spirits in the town at the next meeting of the excise –

– The men must learn to drink with care, that is the best way, Emily. I do not think Mister MacAllan will lose sleep over those who are not capable of looking after themselves. He is more like to say, Let life teach them, if they can –

– Some ladies of the town, Anna, at my recent levee, were able to cast some light on the subject of this outlaw. It appears he had island connections, including relatives who belong to the cloth. That in a certain house, in Portrona, a lady left food out on the window-sill for him, although how she would be aware of his presence baffles them, when he was given to roaming the vast miles of the island and avoiding the town, knowing there was a warrant for him. As he would know. If food was being left out, why not messages? It is on Kenneth Street, I was given the actual house, but prefer to avoid exactitude; I do not wish the estate to gain a reputation for prying, certainly not from my point of view. The virtuous and omnipresent MacRoe is sufficient in that quarter.

Most interesting is what I was able to discover of the crime that the Stronach is said to have committed. It is generally agreed that this happened on the mainland; that the family had an inn where travellers put up and sometimes, as is the way of such places, guests were robbed in their sleep. The name of the inn is also repeated but again I shall not be too specific for reasons of slander. I can reveal it was in Ross and still is, for the events we talk about took place not so many years ago. It would appear to me, on deliberation of the various pieces of lore attached to the circumstances, that the Stronach committed the crime of forcing himself upon women, willing or unwilling, travellers or servant maids, at various times over a period, taking advantage of the darkness of night. There is also talk that he robbed the guests while they slept. Indeed, Anna, it is interesting to speculate about those who tell the tales; the difference between the ladies who say the Stronach was a thief and those who say he was a lecher can be marked, so I conclude that talk of theft is but a symbolic statement of the stealing of a woman's virtue. It would appear this is one way in which simple folk stories are transmitted through time. It would be interesting to discover more of the mind workings of those who symbolise against those who declare the facts, sordid as they may sound. What have I concluded?

Well, Anna, there is often mention of the Stronach's sister, and her befriending one of the servants. This servant owns a precious necklace, which she wears in her sleep to keep it safe. One night, the Stronach's sister pleads for the necklace to wear when the girls share a bed, perhaps because the inn is full. In any case, this is the night the Stronach decides to steal the necklace. He goes into the room where the girls are sleeping together. In the darkness he fumbles for the necklace, finds it as he thinks around the maid's neck, strangles her and steals the necklace. He has strangled his own sister by mistake and must flee!

You may well gasp, Anna, but in some views, it is worse than this, my dear. You see, he has not actually strangled the lady in question, this is what the tale makes of it. The truth is, he has violated the woman wearing the necklace. His own sister. This is the awful crime that had Mac Ant Ronnick hiding here for seven years, Anna! Incest and rape of his own dear sister, mistaken in the dark curtained bed for someone else. I feel sure

I have hit upon the truth of it. Had he murdered someone, the Statute of Limitations would not apply and he would have been an outlaw for all of his life, not a mere seven years, long as it appeared to him and to the people of Portrona and beyond. But why did she not cry out to him, Anna? Do you believe my tale? Surely they would know each other, even in the dark, a brother and sister together? –

– It may be they came to know each other after a time Emmeline, but by then it would be too late for them –

– How, late? –

– They could not stop, Emmeline –

– Oh! –

God's Acre

MAGUMERAD SURVEYS HIS GROWING crop, measuring lairs with his joiner's eye; making calculations as though the rough sward around him could be sawed and chamfered into uniform boxes. His watchword in the change-house after a funeral, the exact same measured out to each customer, nobody never complained about room to me yet. The regulation as to depth of grave, and the volume to give space for the loving spouse to be placed above, rules for the planting of headstones that grow larger in weight and inscription by the year, the job of getting the bottom of the hole exactly level.

Magumerad the master carpenter brings his skill along with the biggest spirit-level from the slip to his chosen trades of coffin-maker and gravedigger. In small towns were men of more trades than one, who led a satisfying working life, balancing tasks, changing when bored with one to another. For myself, the boss calls without warning, there is the need of a new grave when you least expect, makes life interesting never kenning, thought Norman Daft, now.

Magumerad lifts his bird-like head to the proximate beat of the burst side drum cast out by MacRoe's militia, patched by Henny with glue and labels bearing Russian words, as it makes its death-rattle way up Oliver's Brae; Norman Daft is sounding another death in the community. At once, our worthy tradesman throws open the wooden cover on his list of earth tools and casts his eye to the slanting incline where the new lairs are laid out. Levels are going to be difficult to find here. Norman, now, is not able to get a grip of the idea at all, that a grave dug on a slope must be deeper at one end than the other. To him, Magumerad's shipwright's spirit-level is just another of life's mysteries to be ignored. Maybe we should name him Tormod Glic, Norman Wise; you never can tell if he knew before it took place or chust after?

Magumerad awaits his detailed instructions, climbs to the highest point:

HERE LIE THE REMAINS

OF

CHARLES CALDER MA

LATE TEACHER OF GRAMMAR

SCHOOL OF PORTRONA HIS

UNCOMMON HEART AND ASSIDUITY

LAMENTED YOUTH CUT OFF IN

EARLY DAWN

Now Norman vaults the wrought iron gate of the cemetery one-handed, his other holding the drum to his side, drumsticks held between fingers like chopsticks, thinks Magumerad, whose eye has lit upon a flat stone:

SACRED TO THE MEMORY OF

CAPT. D MACLEOD AND HIS

WIFE CATHERINE MACIVER

WHO SLEEP NEATH THE CHINA

SEAS

Norman's drum is unbeaten as he wends towards his self-chosen master, the other side of the meek to Norman's mother. Magumerad sees him tittup between the graves, dancing, one would say, stepping side to side, never treads upon a mound. Light step and silenced drum in deference to those who sleep forty two inches beneath his feet, those who had the attentions of Magumerad. Anyway, Norman thinks all time before Magumerad never happened.

Funny how I never think of him as daft in the graveyard.

The surgeon has placed a piece of paper with a name and address scrawled upon it in the side pocket of Norman's greeny coat, alongside the poke with Magumerad's dinner piece. Fat meat today, surely, Monday, cold mutton from yesterday.

– Not a sudden death, someone from the infirmary, easy for Norman to foresee, eh, son? Here's your share while I look for the lair. Come along, I'll tell you the famous folk of Portrona town, lying here with chust the Beasts of Holm to look upon, could they but see son, could they but see.

Masters, both ship and school, get slabs for sure but not many ordinary folk. See the tulachans you hop around there, covering the forgotten:

IN MEMORY OF

NORMAN MACKENNY

&

JOHN MAGUMERAD

GRAVEDIGGERS

I'll have one done for us two, never fear, Norman dear, get it from the masons special rate

TO LIVE IN MINDS

WE LEAVE BEHIND

IS NOT TO DIE

Might borrow that one for us, Norman Rai, now there's history here, yours and mine but mebbe not, chust the toffs, tho many a likely lad, here now:

SACRED TO THE MEMORY
OF
RODERICK MACKEEVER
UNIVERSALLY REGRETTED
AS
AGENT OF THE FISHCURERS
BANK AND OTHER
INSTITUTIONS HE WAS MARKED
FOR ZEAL AND PROBITY
AS MERCHANT AND
SHIP-OWNER GREAT INTELLIGENCE
WELL JUDGED ENTERPRISE
AND HONOURABLE DEALINGS

There a payan o praise for ye, Norman dear! The original Roddy Banker. Ma tha thu ag iarraidh do mholadh, bàsaich. If you want to be praised you must die in Portrona town but we need not concern ourselves –

Magumerad falls silent and Norman chews the last crust carefully, departs to fetch water in the blackened can from the spring that runs by the cemetery edge and that causes Magumerad to ponder where the water for his tea has travelled, his mind making scenes of seepages into long-lost lairs. Could I be drinking of my ancestors? Anyway it's well boiled, plenty driftwood on the shore, so long as new schooners rise on the slip, peaty tan tea from one of thon China clippers with captains from Portrona town. Norman will be wanting his piece of sugar lump to suck with it.

– While the water boils we'll take a walk and see the memorials of those who went before, a chosen few:

RIPE FOR THE SICKLE, Norman, so it says here, ready for the cuttag dè do bheachd? No use asking innocents what they think about it, eh son?

Here's one of the oldest I can read for you:

God's Acre

the Year of Charlie, who stood above the Beasts and we refused him a ship, a sin of our omission, not the first nor the last. We are good at standing on the fence, we have been watched for a long time here; King James, Oliver Cromwell, Prince Charlie, the Customs and now the Church.

Here a sad piece of Portrona history, Norman:

DONALD MACGREGOR
LOST AT SEA ROUNDING
CAPE HORN HOMEWARD
BOUND AND ALEXANDER
MACGREGOR LOST AT SEA
HOMEWARD BOUND EX
NEW YORK

Homeward bound, them's the words, Norman, homeward bound, all of us and you're the cove to beat our drum.

CAPT DD MACDONALD
LOST IN THE CHINA
SEA AND HIS DAU.
MARGARET DIED AGED
13

Wonder who went first, the dates are not etched proper, but it helps to imagine better if you haveny a date.

Homeward bound, they can't wait to get away and they can't wait to get back again, what a push-pull of a place we stay in.

Chust as well you have nothing to say, Norman Rai. The noisy person above standing changing into the silent person lying below is all you ken, innocent big lump that you are, but I'd prefer your salute to the Thin Red Line's when I go.

153

Now Norman, has it entered your poor head why there is no Gaelic on them memorials and it all around, even the Portronians with a good smatter to speak it yet never write it? I tell a lie, here's some, I'll need to spell it out, I only ken *GUS AM BRIS AN LATA*, Till the day breaks, here it is, at the bottom of this slab: *AN DOCHAS NA BEATHA MAIREANNAICH A GHEALL DIA DHOMH DO NEACH LOMAS BREUG DHEANAMH.* If I sound it out slow I see what it means, In hope of eternal life that God promised who cannot lie. Here endeth the first and last Gaelic lesson, Norman.

Shoemakers now, we have many of this most necessary craft buried here, and we are not short of them in the town, the Lord be praised, for how would a man keep his feet dry else? Coopers and shoemakers are the men of the moment, barrels and boots our emblems in Portrona, summer and winter. And coffins.

The hammer our instrument, carpenter, cooper, bootmaker, all. And yourself, Norman, you have your drumstick to beat us with into eternity, a procession to be proud of in Portrona town.

Here another one, now you chopped them deantags away:

HERE LIES INTERRED

DONALD MCKENZIE

LATE SHIPMASTER PORTRONA

DEPARTED THIS LIFE

1798

Before my time, and well before yours, Norman Rai.

The funeral procession in Portrona, now, the stately grace of the men, pacing two by two, up to the feet, nod your head, take your lift, four handles, step aside, then rejoin the end of the line when it comes up to you. All work stopped for the day, no wages, but that's the price of death or is it sin, Norman? Won't trouble you either way, bhalaich. And yourself tapping the pace right at the end of it.

And I am not forgetting the most gracious and final instrument of all, the mighty spade, special to you and to me, you with a silver one, made in London town!

And the women, ah the women, left behind to spend our tears for us.

IN MEMORY OF
ANN MCRITCHIE
WIFE OF JAMES
MCASKEL SEAMAN
PORTRONA WHO
DIED AGED 19

Plenty drumbeats due there, Norman, but before your time again. Another here, one of my own craft!

SACRED TO THE MEMORY
OF MASTER CARPENTER
GEORGE MACROE
ACCIDENTALLY KILLED
AT PORTRONA UNLOADING
A CARGO OF TIMBER
ERECTED BY HIS EMPLOYERS
SIR ANGUS AND LADY AND
FELLOW WORKERS AND
SORROWING WIDOW MAY.

I was on the quay myself that day, they were finishing the castle.

This one will agree with you, bhalaich, neither of us can fathom it:

HER UNDER LIVILER
STOVIT AI CAPT
JOHANNES JOHANSSEN

Some foreign Skipper handed in his ticket here, unexpected? Others wanting to be unknown:

J M D June 1801

K M D Aug 1823

D M L Dec 1843

Locals, you can tell, the M stands for Mac, but who? Made sure of the date of expiry but no the full name. I should ken the 1843, the Church disruption year. I took over the digging when the cladhan's siatag got too bad. Soon I'll be a martyr myself. Do you think you could, Norman? No, of course you couldn't.

Speaking of innocents, the ones who break your heart, the wee white boxes for those with money, the linen cloth for those without, the short ceremony, the tiny hole I dig, I'll never show you one of these. I never hear you drumming when a child dies? See this plinth erected for the mother of so many, she can stand for all of them:

ANNA MACLEOD

MOTHER

WHO DIED AGE 49

AND

SEVEN CHILDREN

WHO DIED IN INFANCY

What a tragedy, Norman dear, carved on that slab:

SUFFER THE LITTLE

CHILDREN TO COME UNTO ME

What's the use? You can't read, or write, or speak proper, and we can never know if you understand. Or think even?

Moonraking

THE CHAMBERMAID PLACES THE ewer of hot water on the wash stand and turns uncertainly to look at the coils of knotted hair lying on the pillows of the brass bed; all that is visible in the semi-darkness of its occupant. Making up her mind, she steps to the wall by the window, winds open the drapes, bringing a flood of white early summer light to sweep the room and also the first stirring from under the cream coloured sheets. Emily's face now appears above the bedclothes, like a wee girl waking up, to find the usual routine altering. Instead of noiselessly leaving, the maid stands at the foot of the bed, her fingers entwining in front of her, backlit as if on a stage, thinks Emmeline, stupidly.

– Sorry, my lady, there is no sgeul of Anna MacLeod! –

Emily sits up straight and, discarding decorum, kicks off the light covering, swings on smart buttocks to the side of the bed, and still nightgowned and barefoot, runs out into the corridor and into Anna's room, followed by the girl, flustered by such an immediate reaction to her news, fearful. A girl leaves her room at night and goes to the seashore, it could betoken tragedy, a suicide. It is not unknown on the island for unhappy persons to take their own lives and drowning is the preferred option. The maid is now frightened as never before, the way you are when you suddenly find yourself, for the first time, in a central role in some terrifying and worrying circumstance. Why was I the one picked?

Emily is fingering Anna's daygown, laid out upon the unbroken bed, lengthwise, not across, as though lying on her back she had been magically spirited out of it, without disturbing it, leaving it spread where it sank down to rest, empty, empty.

– Fetch Chrissie! –

The chambermaid carefully yet swiftly runs down the wide stairs, not familiar completely with the buoyant carpet held down by long yellow rods that glister like gold in her eyes, each time she makes her way between the floors of the castle. Now though, she does not see the broad steps, she fathoms cold grey water sloshing tirelessly against fronded brown rocks, peers down to make out the vague shape that floats beneath the surface, altering endlessly its contours, always returning for a split second to that of a slack bundle with pale face turning, rising up and falling back, the remains of one who could no longer gain the fortitude to go on living in the close and closed community, where even secret thoughts are known.

Lady Emily stares out of the window in Anna's room. It overlooks, as does her own, the lawn in front of the castle, sloping down to the inner harbour, beyond which the barrel ranked quays and old buildings of the port stand out against the waters of the outer harbour, whose entrance is framed by the white tower of the lighthouse to the right and the unquiet Beasts to the left.

Daily sighting of the eternally changing intercourse between rock and sea in all weathers has given Emmeline a sense of fearful mystery; the opaque depths fascinate and repel, both. What if?

A finger wags from a college lectern and remembered musty smells of books and leather fetch her away from thoughts of a drowning. A deliberate act of such a nature could never be expected of Anna, her courage and integrity are vindicated for

Emily, yet the cold fear of the chambermaid has penetrated to her and she feels her flesh creep with the chill draught from the open window. Who had opened it? The weight of the sash was such that a man was required to do so.

Chrissie appears in the doorway, the alarm on her face doing nothing to reinforce Emily's faltering courage. Action is required.

– Fetch the big spyglass and stand and then help me to get dressed –

She looks out again with the feeling that something is different today; the boats tilting and straining towards the harbour entrance are more numerous than she has seen them. But that is not the only change she now realises; each sail carries a tail; a moving white cloud, a froth of seabirds attracted by the sliding shining mounds of herring that fill and overspill from the fishholds. She remembers tales from Anna of the times when the fleet strikes the first swarming shoals boiling down the Minch and the sea comes ashore as a myriad of fishes.

Despite her anxiety about Anna, she has a fleeting thought of Alistair MacAllan and the majestic herring he wants for New York.

Back in her own room, Emily pours hot water into the basin, adds a practised splash of cold and makes a swift toilet whilst stepping out of her nightgown. She is fumbling with the ribbons of her petticoats when Chrissie arrives, panting, carrying a heavy brass telescope and a three-legged stand. Without being told, she sets it up by the window and turns to help Emily, whilst that lady hauls a gown off a shelf, shakes it unceremoniously out, before stepping into it, turning to the telescope, Chrissie behind her, doing her up.

– Leave my hair! –

She sits on the chair Chrissie places beneath her and swings the spyglass around.

– Get someone to raise this window sash –

She starts by focusing on the broken walls of the tower of the old clan stronghold that stands in the inner harbour, just beyond Number One, and despite her dread, her imagination is fed with images of the wild clansmen who once roistered there, that time before government power and intrigue replaced independent island folk with those who understood the ways of politics and the need to face always towards the centre of Edinburgh and later Westminster.

– The rocks, Lady Emily, the rocks! –

Chrissie is back at her side, craning anxiously, as though she could see with the naked eye any strange bundle left by the ebbing waters.

Full of misgiving and by now infected with the fear of the local girls, their conviction that something dreadful happened down by the sea during the short summer night just gone, Emily obediently turns the telescope on the wrack-line below the castle.

Mild and low summer tides have deposited little to alarm her, broken barrel staves, fragments of brown netting, a few black bottles, a burst buoy of dogskin which puzzles her for a minute. Certainly nothing resembling a ... She refuses to form the word, even in her head.

– Nothing down there, Chrissie –

She hears the maid's long exhalation and feels Chrissie's warm breath on her bare neck.

The head carpenter, he who made the cradle for Anna, knocks on the open door, enters to Emily's signal, heaves up the lower sash, places a wedge, nods politely at them, and departs. She notices that he has left his boots downstairs and this oddness of a man in his stockings in her bedroom tries to blot out more vital thoughts. Her mind is desiring of trivialities in order to avoid facing an awful possibility.

Now a rush of love and pity blurs Emmeline's sight and she chokes. Chrissie lays her face by her and presses her hand on her shoulder. Emily is undone, her own word, I am undone, undone, but silently.

In a little while all is well; Chrissie snatches two handkerchiefs from a drawer and both girls wipe and blow and smile at each other:

– Cha dèanadh Anna a leithid. Anna would never, my lady –

– I am sure you are right, Chrissie, such a brave, beautiful, no never, and young Iain, how did I forget the child! –

– The child, yes –

Chrissie goes but Emily turns back to the spyglass. She now becomes aware of the feverish activity on the other side of the inner harbour. From the boats tied up on all sides of the piers, carts are hauling baskets of herring towards the farlanes into which they are emptied out in front of the gutters whose gut-speckled arms and hands make bloody knives to flick, flick, at each fish for a second before tossing it into the packer's basket behind without looking. The best girls can make as many as seven selections, even as they nip out the top gut, although it is unlikely that any one catch would include such a variety. The packing women, they of the long backs and generous hands, take the filled baskets of gutted herring a short distance to the barrels, into which they are swiftly packed in salt, supervised by the coopers, then rolled to the stacks.

Emily can feel the animation and excitement of the hundreds of men and women busy at their work, although they are nearly half a mile away. Even the horses and seagulls sense it, are a part of the out-pouring of energies repressed for a whole winter, the silver time here at last, with hot sun, a light easterly and the waters beyond Portrona teeming with blind fish eager to spawn, but there are no spent fish in Portrona today, not yet a while.

The trig MacAllan hovers above his own farlane, exhorting his special ladies to select and fullgut extra large fat herring, wondering just where he can draw the line, for length and girth. Indeed, today, first full day of the season, he is not at all sure if any of the fish landed by his hired skippers will qualify as large Portrona matjes and goes to confer with the fishery officer and borrow, if possible, his measuring stick. So that when Emily's magnified circle moves over Alistair's farlane she does not see him and does not therefore pause to find out if Anna is with the crews there.

Emily swings the glass back to the tideline beyond the lawn and studies again the rug of hair tangled there. She concludes it is the corpse of a drowned dog and moves on. Only someone like MacAllan, well kent in the ways of East Coast fishermen, could have told her what she was looking at was indeed a dogskin but one that had been pumped up and used as a net buoy. It would not have made her feel any better; she finds the congruence of hair and water disturbing and she will return to it.

Now she travels with the telescope round the harbour, following the line of the path that swings away from the castle and runs above the rocks, fearful of seeing a dark head bobbing in the water or a white body stranded by the tide, which her newly acquired local knowledge tells her is about two hours into the ebb of a full moon. Full moon! She shivers and, muttering aloud of superstition, rises and pulls at the kitchen bell twice to alert them to bring her tea and buttered rolls. From the first batch of the morning, that same baking that provides Norman Daft's. Portrona, despite its small snobberies, is yet that sort of town.

Restored, Emily returns to her survey of the port, sure now that her anxieties about Anna's possible fate have been raised by the superstitious fears of Chrissie and the top-floor chambermaid, whose name she always forgets, it being Gaelic and hard to pronounce. The mispronunciation of Gaelic words when talking to Anna does not perturb Emily, but she finds it unacceptable to make any kind of error when addressing the staff and therefore insists upon anglicised names being used at all times among the locally recruited employees who are the most menial. Anna's position at the castle, on the other hand, had never been made clear, in the way that so many ladies' companions of the time never quite knew where they stood.

Suddenly she sees a grey bowler hat at a familiar angle swimming through the press of men, horses and carts at the near end of Number One where several boats are being unloaded by means of full baskets swung ashore to be dumped into the carts and then returned aboard to be filled again and again. The scene looks chaotic but every actor in it knows precisely what to do, down to the small boys and the seagulls, both intent upon snatching up any fallen fish, before they are crushed to pink pulp under foot. With a sense of relief, Emily watches Alistair MacAllan weave his way back towards the esplanade where many of the farlanes stand, each surrounded by its congregation of gutting women, immobile apart from the swift movements of their knives, hands and arms absorbed in some silent rite. Is Anna among them?

MacAllan's farlane is situated in a favourable position; nothing between it and the inner harbour but tiers of barrels, one thousand of which are already marked by MacAllan's cooper for New York, although the special herring that are supposed to fill them are still swimming past Cape Wrath and what if they do not fit the parameters of the fishery officer's measuring stick in any case? Many a malicious remark has passed in the howffs of Point Street, in the Long Island Bar on North Beach, and especially in the Temperance Coffee House up town, about the heathen ways of Alistair MacAllan and his un-godly presumption that his empty barrels are certain to be filled with special full extra large! To mark up your barrels before they are packed is seen as tempting fate to the extreme and likely to attract bad luck to all involved in both fishing and curing, be they godly or un-godly. Already, some NY stencillings have been brushed over with tar.

Rob the Bard thinks Alistair MacAllan is the only genuine atheist on the island. He has little evidence for this and may be using his view of MacAllan as sustenance to help him digest his own response to the preponderance of religious performance in Portrona, projecting pagan thoughts onto the successful, elegant and fearless impresario of whom many local people in town and island are secretly proud. This year, is he not hazarding against the sea and New York, a double throw? And if he prays for success, nobody has ever seen him do it. Oh let him get one over all the East Coast and Sassenach fishcurers!

An avalanche of glittering herring slides into the farlane and MacAllan's head cooper nods satisfaction, scattering salt. Henny and Anna stand at the side nearest the water surrounded by the women MacAllan has recruited. Henny talks them through the fullgutting process, whilst Anna shows how: only one flick at the neck, followed by a thrust with the very tip of the knife to open the belly, making it easy to take out the milt or the roe. You have to use the knife hand for this and may lose your hold on the fish in the other hand unless you fix it with a special grip using the thumb and pinkie finger. The clumsiness of the operation will result in frequent cut hands. It will be very slow in comparison to the usual procedure and already MacAllan realises there are reasons other than simple economic ones, why the fullgutting process has never caught on. Yet top prices in New York with payment received in US dollars should make the business pay well. Alistair joshes with the girls, Any càirdean in New York may eat the fish you gut, eh? A few days of these bràmairs and your money's sure for Saturday night.

Something to look forward to is all a blone needs.

Now Anna shows how the fullgutted fish are tossed into tubs of fresh sea water to swill out the blood before being packed in salt in the barrels. The washing in sea water is an added refinement of MacAllan's, another sign of his attention to detail. He knows that the belly is where decay starts, and also the peculiar, unmistakable odour which any person who has anything to do with fish can both smell and taste. One tainted barrel and his New York ship is dead in the water. MacAllan, sleeves rolled up, swishes proud fish in a tub, delicately thumbing red clots out of fat bellies. Bheir do chorragan a-mach à sin. Take your fingers out of there, Mister MacAllan, from one of the bold ones, raises a gale of laughter, leaving MacAllan delighted with his world. He departs to seek a trestarrig from Roddy Banker. He knows when to leave, trusts them to work with a will behind his back.

Anna now steps to the very edge of the quay, out from behind the barrels, to talk to the crony who is handing up buckets of sea water from a small boat.

She swims into Emily's ken and a whoop of relief echoes along the corridors of the third floor of the castle.

– Bheil am bùrn sin glan? –

Is that water clean is what Anna says to the bodach in the wee boat, getting rum and tombac' money from MacAllan to be sure his New York majesties are free of blood and guts. Never heard of such killieorums at the curing but Alistair MacAllan's a true cove with an open hand.

– I been out the Beasts to get it, clean as a whussle –

She turns back to the farlane with a Glayva over her shoulder and bumps into Rob Am Bard, his cheek clay-coloured but his eye red.

– What in the name of Fortune? –

– Anna, they done it, the law of Portrona has surpassed itself at last. Oh my God, they'll never get away with this one, Anna! –

– Take it slow, Rob –

– You know Cathie Morison was chailed for her man's debts? –

– Everyone knows –

– You know she had twins? –

– Yes –

– That she was nursing them kids at home –

– Rob, please don't keep on –

– I am sorry, Anna Rai, but I'm very upset –

– Now tell me what has happened –

– MacRoe got Cathie Morison locked in a cell for debt and her twins only a few weeks old –

– Lady Emily made representations, Rob, I asked her myself –

– I ken you would do all you could, a mother understands –

– Rob, will you in Heaven's name tell me what's gone wrong. Is Mrs Morison still in the gaol? –

– Yes, Anna, Cathie Morison is still locked up. But there's worse, far worse, Anna –

– Oh, I should have spoken to Emily again. But I was planning to come here –

– Too late, Anna dear, too late. The worst has happened. The twins are dead

– Oh no, a Chruithir Ghràsmhoir, dead, her babies dead. Oh My God in Heaven, no, no, no! –

– Yes, Anna dear, yes, the mother in gaol and the twins left at home to die of thirst and hunger –

– It's murder, Rob, murder! What are you going to do about it? –

– I walked out on MacRoe and I'm going to tell Hector Greusaiche what I suspected for a long time, there is no God and he's a bloody fool –

– Oh, I must tell Henny. Henny, Henny, Cathie Morison's twins are dead –

– What a crying shame, poor woman, I knew something was bothering Norman, last night –

The word spreads like a buzzing fly around MacAllan's farlane's gutters, then his packers, then the next farlane and the next, and the next, right along South Beach and you could see, had you Emily's spyglass on the top of Gallows Hill, you would see the break in the rhythm, the way the lines of women ceased weaving to the ancient tune of communal work and stuttered in their movements, as though some unbearable dissonance had suddenly erupted in the music of the first day's celebration of the cure.

– I hope to God, I mean damn it all, I hope Norman leaves that bloody drum at home, it never seems right that racket –

– Don't be so dreary, Rob –

– Any scribing going with MacAllan, Henny? –

– Don't think so, try Madame Kupper –

– She's got yon Betsack Broch who kens everything –

– Rab, don't say I told you, but poor Betsack never got to go to school –

– She's illiterate? –

– She cannot write or even read, just the stencils on the barrels, she learns them by drawing them in chalk on the quay –

– Does Madame know? –

– Madame doesny care, Betsack's worth top money for her work. You could ask the Englishman? –

– I'll ask them both. I'll be back for a fry of they beauties –

– It's the females you'll be after, Rob –

– What else –

Some equilibrium restored, life takes over again, as it always does, thinks Anna, plunging both hands into the sliding silver mounds.

For the first time in many months; unaccountably, Rob feels his spirits rise to that state of euphoria he always seeks and seldom gains. He moves carefully among the frantic throng, breathing the pungent oily ozone from millions of fresh caught herring.

The bard's head worries at words, as is the way of poets. The sight of the hundreds of men and women, frantic about fish, hungry as the gulls that swoop to steal from your very hands, has him going thus; the philosophers of money are the bankers, Roddy Banker, with damsels squatting on his desks, the men who crave power, fool themselves that the dominance that comes with money will help them to change the world about them for the better, which is to say, the way they want it. Money needs to make it work though, clever men who take a chance, follow a dream, and who am I, a dreamer born, to denigrate any man's dream? Or woman's, what's Anna MacLeod or Flett's dream?

The Town House, where they get together, and Roddy Banker's office, with the money bags behind him in the walk-in safe; but he needs the gambler to take his siller and make it breed, or die. Roddy Banker, philosopher of this town.

All of us, we believe in Fate. Some call it luck, Lady Luck. We think we can do something to change her. See them here, the curers and fishermen, the business folk of the town, the shopkeepers, shebeen owners, descend today on the quays to gloat over the silver harvest that will produce the money to be spent in their emporiums and in the howffs and dens of darkness on liquor interfered with and overpriced.

Some think we can do something to change our luck. Others speak of the will of God, which nothing can change, or discover. But can you discover what can change your luck? Many believe this. A flutter, a gamble, a venture, a hazard, my life on it! And so it is, each time he goes to sea, for the fisherman. Fishermen are superstitious, because fishing is a daily gamble, a casting of lots rather then nets. Gambling makes one superstitious in turn, so it becomes a vicious circle.

So while the religious man sings his psalms and hymns and mouths his prayers while his nets drift and bob around him, the gambler has his own secret way of trying to change his luck. He puts his life on it, not chust a wee flutter, my very life on it, depending on some uncanny trick, like nailing a horseshoe to his boat in a hidden place below the waterline.

In a place of religious power like Portrona, it takes huge courage to put your fate into the hands of the Lady, rather than the hands of God.

Mind you, he's human enough, Roddy the gambler's friend, more than say some ladies, fine and friendly with our Henny and kind to that poor boy with the drum and the silver spade. Wants to bury us all, weird, he never sounded for the twins, makes me shiver. MacRoe now, will he be waiting for Norman's drum to beat about the town? Will he visit the quays today, to catch out those who owe rent or put up bothans without permission, creeping around in his big furry coat in the middle of summer, like it was armour, with his knobby stick in front of him, pushing his way along the quay. Knows well when to step aside can smell a squatter from a distance, or a crofter owes him rent. *Cuiridh mi às an fhearann thu.* I'll put you out of your land, what's the sense of that, will he create even more squatters?

On the edge of the anxious fury of the curing stations, some boys line up to play Timmaree, the leader keeping time with his fists pounding on the back of the boy 'below':

> Timmaree-ro-me-raddy O!
> Lay on her, Braggimore.
> Timmaree-ro-me-raddy O!
> Lay on her, Singidore.

and so forth, with significant parts, arbitrarily chosen, like 'everyman', 'not a man', 'harder', or 'softer if you can'.

> Fists pummel a hollow tattoo
> On the back of the boy 'below'
> His hollow chest resonates.

The leader stands with his back to the wall; the boy 'below', generally Norman Daft, goes down with his head up against the leader's stomach; and the rest, who are assigned such names as Braggimore (Breug Mhòr?), Big Liar, Singidore,

Pots-and-Pans, range themselves ready for action. The first transgressor, who lays on when his name has not been called, or does not begin in time, or stop, or mitigate or accentuate his drumming when he should, has to offer his back to the smiter in his turn.

– Bury you with spade of gold, Norman sings, Henny –

– It's silver, Anna, Norman's spade. He found it in yon new forest in the castle grounds, left by some toff after plantin one o them exotics –

– How long Norman sing spade song, Henny –

– Ever since his father, altho he was mebbe no right before –

Her two best girls have left her, yet Madame finds time to talk to them and travel about the quays, offering a judicious cheroot, chatting to the women more than the men. Nothing stuck up about Madame; they say the blone is a Rooshion princess, knows her skeds, where to find the best fish in the West. Nobody mentions the dead twins.

The bard ceases his self-pitying ruminations and rescues Norman Daft for his lesson in mathematics. This town is noted for its maths and navigation, and righteousness will surely follow these, Norman Boy.

The boys resume their diving contest with the seagulls for the fallen herring; a fry sold is a poke of pogo eyes to suck for days.

– Total number of boats this year? –

– Six –

– Six what? –

– Six with two nothings –

– Six hundred, there's more, but we'll stick with round figures. Norman, now, what fishing town has the most boats here? –

– Portrona town –

– Unfortunately, Norman Rai, that's no right, Proud Portrona town must take second place behind the Bees.

– Bee Effs –

– Dinna mak it sound like a swearword, or them hymn singing Bucachs will heave you in the hoyle, daft or no –

– Bee Eff three with two nothings, Bard? –

– You are a genius today, Norman, here a wing for a sugary roll –

Chust think, near four hundred fishing boats from one small East Coast port. What riches and ambition can be found in Banff; all the brown breeks of Buckie tweed, blue knitted ganseys, and ringing hymns.

Henny moves quietly but firmly into a flurry of spilling baskets and circling girls and Madame takes Anna aside, intrigued:

– For what you go to the castle and now you leave, Anna? –

A spilling of words to the neutral, understanding foreigner:

– The people of my village are all related to each other; ties of blood are strong in a time of want. You have to share, Madame, to give to those with less or nothing. Have you ever been hungry – it takes a day or more for the ache to ebb. There is another side to the closeness of the folk, they need to know all about each other, they search without favour into local happenings, the troubles of others, their meat. Regardless of the privacy of the person you talk about, which I wish for too, they keep after the affairs that take their fancy with endless questions. You are obliged to tell; it makes me sad when they find out all they want, they go and assail the ears of all about with the details. Why is it so, that people who will give you their last cup of milk will go and talk badly of you behind your back? –

– You should be angry, not sad, Anna –

– Do not worry, Madame, I am that, too –

– Steer it well, no? –

– How is Madame W –

– Anna all she say, the Portrona girls, afraid of Betsag but respect her, she can gut and she can pack –

– And roll a full barrel on a sixpence! –

Thanks be to God for laughter.

Now a tall leonine figure with black hair and flashing
eyes and a kingly neck above a barrel chested navy blue
gansey comes under the attention of Anna MacLeod or Flett,
her thought coloured by daily commerce with Lady Emily's
Hebridean diary.

– It's only me, Anna, come to see MacAllan –

– Hoh, hoh, Tonald – says Henny – And whit have you in
the basket? –

The large wicker basket is clamped to his hip by one long
arm. In the bottom lie several full herring of a size seldom
seen anywhere, never mind Portrona Quay.

– A sample to show MacAllan –

– You're not signed to Alistair MacAllan, so far as I know –

– I'm not signed to nobody yet –

– My but we are shure of ourselves, isn't he, Anna –

Remembering the diary, Anna replies, with a straight look
at him:

– Is he no from Eye and a fisherman of the lion type,
Henny? –

The two women poke gently at the fat fish in Donald's
basket:

– By Goad, MacAllan wouldn't half like his farlane filled
with yon for the next few weeks –

– Extra large maidens, Donald –

– That's what I thought –

– Can ye get more? –

– Plan to follow the shoal from Upper Minch to Lower as
far as Barra Head. I've got its marks –

– Barra Heid! And how in the Name will you get back here
in time against the wind? –

– I can land at Castlebay when they go far enough south –

– MacAllan's no at Barra, if he's your man for the New
York ploy –

– He could send you or Anna down –

– Hoh, listen to the entry prenoor speaking here, Anna Rai. Ye should keep a wather eye on this cove, if I was you! –

The two are standing with the basket between them. One each of their hands is in the bottom of the basket, fondling the swollen fish.

– You can tell them apart by their belly shape, Donald –

– Hens and cock, Anna –

– Ah'll fetch MacAllan to ye. He's away for a morning nip at Roddy Banker but he'll want to see this –

Henny goes but the two are oblivious. Anna feels the shoals swim in the minches of her body for the first time for many, many months. Donald is leaning at her over the basket with his fine sample, pleading without words.

Eviction

A T THE END OF the day, let us face it, the practicalities of a death in Portrona during our time is in the hands of Magumerad. The twins draw no drumming from Norman, so the thoughtful lone gravedigger now selects a small sharp spade from his kist and preoccupies himself with the protocols of death. Will I make it straight so the two can lie side by side or chust straight down only shorter than usual, with the wee coffins lying one on top of the other, the first born below (or above). Better make it so they lie side by side, three foot square, flicking open the brass and parana-pine ruler to fix the exact dimensions on the earth in the captain's recently purchased lair.

The grind and snort of a vehicle stopping at the fence beside him. Heaven's Name, the cortège is no here already. Be chust a carriage or two, no a double line of men in black and white, those who can buy a sober suit, the rest in jackets and white scarfs, treading quiet, with silent signals as they pass the bier from hand to hand.

A second glance tells the watchful digger that he is seeing the smart trap borrowed from the castle by MacRoe for his abrupt visits to the far reaches of his dominion. He is heading today for Eye, but why does he stop at the roadside to watch me start this grave? The twins, that's it! Cruel factotum ah Hell, denying babies their mother's breasts, you will never be forgiven; Suffer the Little Children. Magumerad fetches a pick and plunges it into the leaden clay; his anger recedes with each grunt.

He can hear behind him now sounds of snuffling ingestion as the factor refreshes himself for the work to come. Unusually, notes the keen-eyed grave-shaper, he has three men squeezed into the vehicle along with him. Must be some hellish work on foot in Eye; likely an eviction with demolition. Hell's sake, he's sharing his snuff with his bruisers!

MacRoe intercepts Magumerad's stare and vents a shout in Gaelic. The driver leans forward, thrashing the air with the reins. The carriage rolls away on the road to Eye. The town toughs scrape their noses and ogle the rum jar between MacRoe's feet; he, meantime, feels the hard thrust of the revolver in the side pocket of his coat – *my comfort in time of affliction.* He has never fired it in anger, but there is always a first time. *One day a squatter will break, but I have the law with me which no man can put asunder.*

Magumerad then experiences something he has never felt before in his sombre necropolis by the sea. As he stares out over the Beasts, baring their backs eternally, Magumerad shivers like an animal spooked.

The carriage grinds smartly along the shingle road over the isthmus where many generations of the Eye folk take their final rest. It may be his ruminations upon Magumerad and his angry digging that causes MacRoe to shout an order to the driver that takes them off the road and across the machair to the roofless ruin of the ancient Celtic church. MacRoe, to the annoyance of his now thirsty companions, alights, tightens his coat belt, pushes his way through the rank weeds around the chapel and ducks inside the doorway.

He studies the ancient carvings on the inside wall; medieval Hebridean knights whose history is lost, whose bones sometimes appear on the beach below as the sea currents of Broad Bay eat their way into their sandy graves. Despite Magumerad's preference for machair land as a burial place, it may be clay has its own advantages?

At MacRoe's feet, covered in cattle muck and broken weeds, lie grave slabs with ancient heraldic markings. I better warn Samson to keep his cows out of here, any excuse will do the squatters to raise trouble.

MacRoe settles his sealskin coat under his buttocks on top of an ancient flat gravestone that pokes through the plethora of nettles and dockens now choking the ancient Lewis MacLeods' place of worship. He puts the clay rum jar beside him alongside a quart tinker's mug taken from the water bucket on the way out from a long forgotten foray into a smoky interior, in lieu of an overdue rental again non-forthcoming, the red figures forming a mist in the ledger of his mind.

He yells loudly, a Gaelic word with a mainland accent, quite unintelligible to hard coves from the closes of Portrona town, yet to them it means one very intelligible message; black rum, the emollient necessary to ease the dark work of an eviction allied with demolition. They appear in the nave with eager eyes and stand in front of MacRoe. He glugs a pint of dark liquid into the tin jug and hands it to the one who thrusts himself to the front at such times.

The powerful samh of the rum released from the prison of clay rises as the men quaff, each in turn and turn again, then hand the empty tin back to MacRoe, whose own nostrils twitch wetly, tickled by the liquor scent mixed with wildflower and rank weeds and maybe, who ever kens, that of death.

Better not.

He slops a half pint more into the mug, hands it to the least of the men, who bobs in gratitude before quaffing judiciously.

– Wait now in the trap for me –

Give the alcohol time to work a bit. MacRoe squints out of one of the gaping side window embrasures, across the sands, at the Aird settled with those decanted from the Harris Deer

Forest, as it is now referred to, always in capital letters. A report of the time which almost upset the arrangements, the worst situation ever seen in these islands, worse than Ireland. The cottars of the Aird, crouched for the winter in stone and turf bothies, the roof timbers broken, no way to take advantage of the riches of the bay, apart from the shellfish bared by the tide, source of much skitter sickness.

Even as he looks a bare generation since their coming, one of their sharp-prowed fishing boats is nosing out of the Faoghla mouth, the brown sail hanging ready. The new-generation lads row with powerful strokes, their fishing baskets neatly coiled at their feet, the shellfish now baiting sharp hooks from Portrona town on barked lines with horsehair knots, sure of a catch of Bay haddock, whose bellies bulged with creamy livers to mix with oatmeal from the bolls bought in to last until the harvest of their own fields in September.

The Aird people are the best payers of rent in the entire island, even the sea-bereft widows pay on time and on the appropriate rent collection day, sometimes coming to the office in town even, to get a receipt from the clerk before the due date. Give good men the means, in this case loans for boats, and you can be sure of your money back.

He needs a new clerk since that insolent Bard . . .

It does not occur to MacRoe that the rich sea and the poor land is the key. Landsmen and seamen are a totally different breed; sometimes they even eat around the same table, yet they will never understand each other.

His fingers trace a carving on the slab, a man covered in a suit of mail, wearing a heavy sword and holding a spear, a chief of the quarrelsome tribe of the MacLeods, whose combative ways will ensure their demise within a century or two. Another inscription: *Hic jacet Margareta filia Roderici meic Leoyd*, widow of Lachlan MacKinnon, 1503.

They have such a history yet live crowded in hovels on land which they think should be theirs by right . . .

MacRoe heaves himself up, his gorge rising once more at the arrogance of mere peasants.

Now to work on the unkeyed walls of Murdo MacDonald's temporary dwelling, himself away at the East Coast fishing, supernumerary Heilanman in a Bucach crew.

First though a piss; having seen his three new garrulous minions out the door of the roofless ruin, MacRoe goes to the wall below the large east-looking opening that once held stained glass (what story?), gaping out to Broad Bay.

Loose the buttons of the sealskin coat, then those of the jacket, followed by the flies of the tweed trousers; a dragging out of a tail of woollen shirt; finally with a surreptitious look around and up into the sky, the most prepotent man in Portrona pulls out a tiny penis, no bigger than a child's thumb. He stands with whistling breath for a few seconds, then watches the yellow stream wet the ancient wall in front of him, percolate through nettle, docken and moss under the grave slab beneath his boots, unknown, unmarked, but he is aware of it, yes he is. He flicks and finishes off and rebuttons item after item, turns to the door and back to the horse and gig, with merry men and dour driver hiding his impatience, feeling the aura of fear from this bulky man who carries it around, you can smell it.

Whilst MacRoe and his well-oiled hirelings grind towards the village of Shader Big and the rough stone lean-to raised hurriedly by Murdo MacDonald in a few days before the herring started to move south from Shetland, we may take a minute to think about the occupant of the grave that MacRoe has been wetting his boots on.

Must be that of a woman, as there is no way of identifying it now; someone's relict or spouse. So we may as well talk of the stone placed above Roderick Morrison not too long ago. Indeed when MacRoe stepped on it this morning it had been there much less than a century, with the words clear cut and readable once you pushed the heavy grasses (sickly and weak and too tall from overfeeding), and you could read Roderick Morrison's details.

Familiar as he is with the rolls of papers in office and castle pertaining to the island, and forever in search of some forgotten legal quirk or useful circumstance, MacRoe could fill in the family story in his mind. So we are able to give it now, for it encapsulates some fascinating history, which ends for our present purposes, winds back as it were, to the redoubtable midshipman cum bosun's mate and master gunner who made his name on Tahiti. Although nobody will know about it until one of his descendants, another compulsive penman and historian, will bring it to light long after our present history comes to its tragic end.

Seventeen Ninety One. Here lies the body of Roderick Morrison. These Morrisons go back forever in the story of the island; Irishmen or Norsemen or both, swordsmen, sailors, poets, musicians and merchants, seers and churchmen, journalists even. Follow the Morrison or Morison (one Ess, same clan) story and you have a brilliant tale, brighter than this one.

Hereditary lawmen established by the Norse (when? say 900 AD), with one thousand years of kenning their fellow islanders should be wise now? And they were (are?). Our Roderick's elder brother, none other than that Allan Morrison, lost in the Minch, subject of that heart-tearing lament by Anna Campbell of Scalpay Isle, Allan drowning off the Shiants about the same time as his cousin James supervised the building of the wee schooner that was meant to take him away home from the paradise isle of Tahiti. There is more, according to our Harris genealogist: was not the same Roderick's brother John the grandfather of the near-mythical 'serial killer' Mac ant Ronnick, as he is named by our Lady Emmeline (the romantic side of her). Yet another brother was the father of that John Morrison who stood beside Nelson at Trafalgar. We could go on but it gets too much to take in. However, mention must be made of that Morrison who was both a minister of the church and a seer, a beautiful example of the island predilection for accepting religion and superstition, both, together (not quite at the same time of course). If you do not believe in the wisdom of the gene, you may find all this anathema. Hallelujah!

Much as we love our graveyards, some of us, only repositories almost to date of our history, we shall leave them now, at least as far as earth burials are concerned.

Sea burials another story, death in the living element a different tale.

Chust afore we go, let us travel back to glimpse Magumerad, tidying the tiny resting place of the twins that died of thirst, as he straightens his sore back in time to catch a glimmer of the long jerking figure of Norman Daft speeding along the Eye road, silent drum for once against his back.

Where on earth? Intimations of a cradle beneath sliding boulders, smoking straw thatch pass through Norman's mind as scudding clouds. We can be fairly sure of that.

Magumerad washes his hands in the summer trickle in the burn, locks the cemetery gate and treads to the top of the hill overlooking the town. What he expected to see is visible: ramparts of white barrels, from this end of Iomair Sligeach right along to the concrete piers of Numbers One and Two. He cannot see the quays but can follow their contours from two miles away by the sheaves of tall masts sprouting around them. In between the trenches formed by the stacks, women crawl from board to barrel and back again; Magumerad is reminded of ant-hills. Showers of seabirds pass and repass over the distant silent scene.

It is a sight that never fails to give him joy and he extrudes his tongue in anticipation of a pint of porter at the Long Bar in North Beach in the company of garrulous Bucachs and sombre islanders, drinking to the arrival of the shoals.

Nobody should die at such a gossar of a time, the grinning bodach should take time off, far less children . . .

Someone is coming out of the town in a hurry towards him, a woman, with pauses to cast off clothing piece by piece, even her over-skirt, now running clumsily till she kicks off her boots, then with an athlete's ease, the balance of one who is young and has worked physically and kens her body and what it can do.

Magumerad prepares himself, this sight he has never seen and it betokens dreadful news. Now he sees a man following at a clumsy half-run and makes it out to be that late clerk of MacRoe's, who goes about delivering himself of words that sometimes make sense and songs when it's late in the shebeen and spirits are decanted by sailors home after long trips. The girl is harder to recognise, strangely, without her normal coverings. She is very close to him and he can hear her rasping breath, before he knows who she is. He grasps her shoulder and stops her:

– Anna Flett! –

She cannot speak, looks at him without recognising him. The bard comes up to them:

– Anna, wait, it's miles to go. Lady Emily! –

She stares without seeing, her harsh breath slowing.

– Lady Emily is bringing a gig from the castle to take you down –

Sure enough, a gig has appeared and approaches them at a smart pace, Lady Emily at the reins. A true emergency unfolds itself on the road from Portrona to Eye, as the gravedigger watches impassively.

Lady Emily's gig arrives and stops in a shower of stones. The mare's eyes stare whitely at him when the bard catches her look for a second; his peculiar mind starts to compare her with the long-legged woman who leaps down from the carriage and clasps the limp Anna to her breast.

– Help me –

The bard pushes at the two women and they settle on the leather seat. Emily takes up the reins, shouts at Rob, startling him:

– Get in! I need a witness! –

He climbs into the vehicle just in time as Emily unhooks the thin whip and cracks it over the back of the mare, who moves into a fast trot, then into a near gallop.

Rob grasps the side of the vehicle; Emily now has one hand on Anna's shoulder, driving with the other, standing up.

– Bloody Boudicca! –

Bards are notoriously brave with lip and pen but many are physical cowards. Moral courage is what counts, must be due to brighter imagination, the symbolic workings of my mind. My God, this mad Englishwoman will kill us all.

Anna now shrugs herself free and looks at them clearly for the first time. There is blood on her bare feet.

Blood on Anna's bare feet and seeing it, Lady Emmeline loses sight of the road; her rush of love slackens the reins and drops her whip, slowing down the vehicle.

– I am eternally grateful – Rob says to someone.

When her vision clears, Emily sees the larger castle carriage move onto the Bràighe road in the distance, coming back into town. She knows MacRoe and his minions have completed the demolition.

Does Lady Emily also know, in this moment, that she signed the order? We cannot be sure; her kind sign so many papers without troubling to read them.

The two carriages approach each other on the narrow track at pace and one will have to give way. A shout from the larger vehicle and it appears to gather speed.

Lady Emily holds fast to her track, and begins again to wield the whip in the air, creating cracking sounds, the wheels spinning to the rhythm of the steel springs beneath. Rob begins to enjoy the spin, that's where the word comes from!

Nearer and nearer draw the two vehicles and neither is giving way and Emily's is moving the faster.

Near enough now to hear the swearwords from the rum-fuddled passengers in MacRoe's carriage.

Suddenly the factor's vehicle draws to a stop, the driver leaps down, takes the horse's head and leads him off the road onto the machair.

Triumphantly, it would seem to MacRoe, Emily and her passengers drive up to them. Curses from the men are put down by a lash of Emily's whip. The men cringe but MacRoe is immobile, staring out at Broad Bay. Is he sensing the start of the ending of his illegal autocracy? But it will need the people to do it; this stubborn bitch will be away back south in weeks, her love affair with Portrona forgotten.

Some women had shouted in hard-to-understand Eye Gaelic, as the men pushed over the walls of MacDonald's squatters' lean-to; the unmortared stones had been easy to shift and it took only a few minutes. To his astonishment, one hysterical woman threw a peat at him, and he had to show his revolver to the leader of the crew, who plainly thought this act gave leave to rape such a harridan.

Then the daftie from town came and they could see him heaving at the tumbled boulders as they drove smartly back along the gravel road to Garrabost. He was plainly insane and should be sent away.

Now this so-called lady was riding post haste to Eye with a half-dressed fishgutter and that ingrate clerk. A well thought out session of paper work was needed. Urgent covering work.

– Get on, man! –

The four-wheeler regained the road and rolled rapidly back to town.

The two-wheeler continued its spinning way deeper into Eye. They were pacing smartly along the level road between Garrabost and Shader when Anna cried out:

– There's Norman! And Mairi after him! –

She tries to get out of the vehicle but Emily stops her and holds her shoulder until they draw up in front of Norman, who they can see is clutching Iain's cradle, its canopy of cedar crushed flat, the rocker snapped, transformed to a dusty box, trailing soiled linen.

With a blood-freezing cry, Anna leaps from the carriage and struggles with Norman for the broken cradle. He withholds, braced like Atlas, her world at arm's length high above his head.

Why, why, why?

She leaps, Anna does, hangs from his powerful arm, his uncontrolled muscles like animals in her hands. Suddenly, then, the cradle is in front of her face, strong fingers rip off the canopy, a living (?) bundle is proffered to Anna. She holds her child, she licks away the dust from his eyes, from his nostrils, his mouth, feels his breath on her, warm. Now she can no longer see him but only feel him as she opens her shift; tearing at the cloth, puts him to the dry breast. Can tears replace milk, now Mairi is there, her familiar actions as she takes him makes the situation right. But that Emmeline has also torn her shift open and begs to offer her own milk. Mairi shouting angrily at the distraught Englishwoman in harsh Gaelic, so that she covers herself (in front of that arrogant clerk!) turns to her vehicle, takes the whip from its stand, lashes at the stupid poet's wondering face (he has witnessed a scene that will feed his mind for life and he knows it). Now he crouches at the roadside and feels the rising weal on his forehead (she missed my eye, thank the Lord), watches the castle gig fly off to town with Emily lashing at the mare, so fast she will soon catch up with Norman, running to Magumerad with the solution to the mystery of life and death in a broken cradle.

The Gaelic women hurry back along the Eye road, huddling round the child. Can you give suck whilst walking fast; why not, did I see a pearl drop appear on Anna's nipple after Iain?

Iain will grow and see land riots and much later, a grizzled navy veteran, will drown at the mouth of the harbour. The Beasts, yes.

Lady Emily will leave soon and never return. Her book will not be published, not in my lifetime and who will care for it after?

The Morning God Nodded

– CUIMHNICHIBH GUR E MISE Dia –
That was the minister's opening word to the sermon,
the Sunday morning after.
– Remember that I am God –

I stood across the road from the gate to the Free Church on
Kenneth Street from ten o'clock.

You can see the entrance door in the lower half of the huge
triangular end wall, one tall blind window above it. Higher
still, in the steeple that crowns the building, the brass bell
rocks with muffled sobs, swaddled in a bit of old sail canvas.
Now and then, the clapper breaks free and strikes true with a
single low wail.

The congregation are coming now, from both directions,
from the town and from the sea. Kenneth Street runs from
trees to water, the church in the middle.

My God, the words I have heard and said loud and silent,
ever since I stood gripping the stanchion, braced for the waters
cascading over the deck of the yacht, over us, trapped between
the rows of rock teeth, a rope to the shore our only chance but
there is no rope, not yet, the hero of the hour not appeared,
the saviour of some of us who will bear the cursed name of
survivor till the day we die.

My God, now the words respond to the colour of the clothes

186

of all who pass in front of my eyes to tread the gravel path up to the gaping church door; the blackness and bleakness of their gear, only the white shirts of the old men. The women's hats are soot black and cut the same, crowned with black crêpe and sinister veiling, the hand of the best milliner in town clearly to be seen. I heard of her overtime, the urgent order away for materials to make mourning hats, designed with an opening at the back to take the coiled-up bun of the widows' long hair. My God, my God, why hast thou forsaken the women here, with their thick long hair, never to be unplaited again or laid on a bed.

The scarlet underskirts are gone, burnt or buried or cast into the sea.

Just before eleven, I enter the church, passing sombre elders preparing to close the heavy doors. One of them looks out to see that there are no latecomers. An idle thought, the local people have a way of arriving very early at church and then sitting in hunched silence for what seems a very long time. I used to think this was a penance, fear of being seen to be taking the service lightly. Today, I discover why the folk of my home island make a habit of sitting for a long time in church, prior to the service; it gives them time to think, deeply, without interruption, with solemn mind and countenance, of the meaning of their placement here below, for an arbitrary time.

Maybe the habit only grew after the first telegrams from France in 1914?

The building was filled and I could not see a single space in a pew that would enable me to squeeze in at the end. Chairs had been laid in a line down the aisles to take the overflow and I found an empty one not far from the pulpit. I was surrounded on all sides by silent folk in their Sunday clothes and very aware of the hundreds who sat upstairs all around. How many does she hold, Portrona Free Church? One thousand? Two? On this morning the building is filled to overflowing.

I became aware of unusual sounds about me, soft noises

that one does not associate with church. There was no rustle of sweetie papers or the rare loud report of the falling of a pepper-mint onto the hollow wooden floor, the most embarrassing moment in many people's church attendance. The quiet noises I now realise are sobs, as the silent time brings home to the bereaved the reality of their loss for the first time.

I prayed for the service to begin and soon the first psalm rose around me, a ragged sound, then with succeeding verses, the power of the voices grew stronger, until they filled the huge hollow building as Fingal's Cave answers the rollers of the Western Ocean.

The singing took us over and we were triumphant as we rode the waves of the final two lines.

The precentor kept us at it until the music of our own chests and tongues and throats released us to sit and hear what God had done to us on New Year's Morning 1919.

Psalm Ex Ell Vee One; why pick that one today and why did the precentor keep on after the usual three verses? To give us time, or him? The Reverend in his pulpit, grey-faced, fumbling his notes. What on Earth can I say to them, whom shall I blame, maybe the psalm?

> God is our refuge and our strength
> In straits a present aid

It goes four lines in the Gaelic. Then:

> . . . though hills amidst the seas be cast;
> Though waters roaring make,
> And troubled be; yea, though the hills
> by swelling seas do shake.

Never took in the sense when singing, naturally, but now you can see why he took that particular psalm, God making the waters to roar on the Beasts of Holm. And the line he has chosen for a text for today, near the end:

> Be still and know that I am God.

He does not go on to give us the following line, Among the heathen I will be exalted, no.

– These words, Be still and know that I am God can be applied to times of unusual trial, dark and mysterious happenings in the providence of God. We seek to solve the mystery in some way that accords with our own mind. We assign the blame now to this party, now to the next –

The blame has been assigned in the pubs of the town already, I can testify, Reverend Minister; the blame is fully and wholly placed upon the British Admiralty, the Royal Navy.

The men in the bars may be satisfied with this simple answer but are you? Am I? Is God or the widow?

They say officers of the *Iolaire* were drunk but I was there and never saw a sign of drink. They say the officer's body glowed with alcohol as it lay on the shore, so says the know-all, never saw that particular body myself. Men took a drink out of a bottle on board at midnight, other men sang a psalm and read the Good Book.

It availed neither of them. Who can say who was saved, the man with the bottle in his bag or the man with the bible?

We shall return to the question of guilt again; we can never leave it alone.

Those men in the pubs, they were all out of their minds on New Year's Morning, useless, dead to the wide surge, when the *Iolaire* crashed on the Beasts.

When I got to the rocks on the crest of a seventh wave, landing in a hollow that gave me time to get a grip and some air in my lungs, which had taken no water, I realised that I was marked out for being saved. My luck was as good as the luck of the boys to my right, lined up on the quay at Kyle, turned away by the petty officer and marched aboard the *Sheila* to get a safe and dull sail across, their loved ones waiting on Portrona quay, along with the hundreds expecting the *Iolaire*.

I must have been thinking of not reporting back when I got to the top of the low cliffs and turned my back on the lights of the farmhouse where the other survivors were. I had no plan; I have nothing you could call a plan now, days after the disaster that turned out worse than I feared when I dived for the rope. That's another thing; that rope, taken ashore by the hero of the hour with the help of other brave men who kept the head that dreadful morning of darkness, sea and storm. That rope whipped across me in the water, just about fell into my hands. I kept warm in the middle of a haystack until early morning, then walked into Portrona.

I know a small shop in Inaclete that sells goods and groceries. It was open, despite the holiday and the early hour. I was the only customer. The young woman stared at me in horror, realising where I was from, thinking I was a ghost. The town had heard of the sinking, but I put her mind at rest; she sighed and blew her nose, then hunted out the items I asked for; a semmit, drawers, stockings, a gansey, dungarees and a tweed cap.

This was to be my uniform for now and forget college and away and especially the British Navy.

I asked her for a place to change my clothes and she led me to a small bedroom at the back of the shop. I took off my uniform, the blouse, collar and bell-bottoms, and put on the gear of the anonymous island man I now became.

Returning to the shop, I handed her the uniform items I had discarded and asked her to get rid of them. She made them quickly into a neat parcel with brown paper and string and handed it back to me. I took the parcel and offered her a large white bank note, still wet from the sea.

– If the Good Lord brought you safe ashore from that awful drowning, I cannot take your money –

I left her but yet I see her sorrowful face and her stillness, behind the scarred wooden counter. I dropped the parcel by the bin outside.

The carts from the various villages attend the Drill Hall at Battery Point each day. The old men and boys who search through the white faces of the dead laid out on the drilling floor often don't find who they are looking for; there are far too many still missing, the list is very long. I half expected to see my own name on it but how could this be? They never took our names as we boarded at Kyle on New Year's Eve; all they had was numbers. They can never be sure who was drowned, who was saved. The authorities depend on the goodwill of those who lived and the relatives of those who died to get their list into proper order, something which must make Their Lordships seethe down there in London. They'll be wanting to close the file as soon as possible.

They will never get their list balanced out, I am seeing to that, the unknown Lewis sailor, silent witness of their arrogant carelessness, if not worse.

My original plan to bear witness at every burial is not possible, for how can a person be in two or more places at once and the cemeteries scattered all over the island by the sea, east and west? I am choosing to follow home certain carts with drowned men, on impulse, or because I recognise the old man or one of his companions, or if the body of one of my chums has been recovered.

Last night I followed the first of the night interments down the steep path to the sloping graveyard in the most north-eastern village, a large community with many men on war service. The older men are in the naval reserve, recruited over the years since before the turn of the century. Some watches in the Royal Navy are composed entirely of islandmen. This village depends heavily upon the fishing, like many others; the island fishermen make splendid sailors, encouraging the Admiralty to enlist thousands of them into the reserve, ready for the next war.

The men in the army militias, on the other hand, are very young, as army recruiting began only just before the war. Thus, the casualties from the trenches during the past five years have been mainly young men, many still in their teens.

The navy libertymen on board *Iolaire*, however, ranged in age from eighteen to over fifty. Many veterans, familiar with the sea, were lost along with many of the youth.

The procession was led by a tall young man, wearing a university scarf over a black overcoat, probably his grandfather's. He held up a barn lantern, with well-polished globe and trimmed wick, to light us down the path. He paced proudly, at a measured rate, as the corse to the ramparts we carried. You could see in the light reflected on his cheek that he was weeping.

As one college man to another (not that I intend to return to my studies, after this), I talked to our beaconman afterwards. Speaking urgently and clearly, as though to impress it upon my mind, as if I were some lecturer he had to satisfy, he told me his story. I mind it almost to the word and give it here:

– Who would go with the mare and gig to meet Donald off the *Iolaire*, Donald who normally drove the wild brown mare, Donald who would take the reins himself on the way home? They decided I was too inexperienced to steer the mare into the town and another boy was sent. Donald was twenty-five, with yellow hair, gladness always in his face, a face you'd see in a painting or in a moving film. I was as a younger brother to him. He lived next door and that night it was my own mother was preparing his homecoming supper. She was ready and waiting for him; Donald was like a son to her, she having given him the milk as a baby when her sister Anna's breasts were inflamed. It was four days later that Donald came home in a narrow coffin and although my mother asked me to go and view his body, I did not have the courage. He told me on his last leave, hearing I was to go on in education, that he would fetch me history books he had seen in the window of a bookshop in Dover. The Beasts of Holm got them –

I have ceased to visit the Battery Drill Hall; I cannot bear to see any more, the lines of drowned matelots laid out with the white tickets tied to their wrists naming their village of origin. For some reason, the naval authorities think this enough in the way of identification, knowing well, perhaps, that a person from a certain village will be able to identify any man who belongs to that village, while names like MacLeod and MacDonald and MacKenzie and MacIver are so commonplace as to lead only to confusion. Let me be charitable.

Another consignment of coffins arrived last night on the mailboat. I saw them being swung ashore after the passengers and those meeting them had gone; little loads tied together, three or four long varnished boxes at a time, the wet brass fittings glinted in the harbour lights. The authorities are very anxious, now, to avoid transporting the dead in any other way, after the fury expressed by local men who saw our boys being landed on the quay in slings like so many dead cattle; plus the hysterics of women running after wagons and trying to climb onto them, to see if their loved one lay in the pile.

It is bad enough watching the women scouring the wrack line, picking up the toys the men were bringing home to their children and scanning with fear the names and numbers stencilled inside the navy caps lying all along the Holm shore. The bodies that landed near and early have all been moved but still the women search in small and silent groups.

By no means had all those expected home that night confirmed their coming by telegraph and one or two miracles have occurred, with men who were thought lost having stayed in Kyle. Never did missing the boat have more effect. But hopes have faded; there will be no more wonders connected with *Iolaire*.

There is the story I hear of the wife who found her man's cap in the seaweed, his very name and number inside it. Him still safe in Kyle although she does not know it. Who picked up the wrong bonnet on the train? It is easy done, and one sure thing; we'll never know, but surely someone with the same name?

His telegram arrives that very afternoon; we cannot conceive how she feels as mourning turns to happiness with a yellow envelope. For five years a yellow envelope bore only dreadful news; Killed in Action; Feared Drowned; Regrets. Now, for the one and only time, it says: I am Alive; Joy.

Having gone to reassure my family that I was safe (we live just a few miles out of town), I returned to Portrona, having told my mother I had to report to the Admiral, along with the other survivors, the numbers of whom were then unknown, but were expected to be few by we who had seen men washed off the decks into the boiling sea like flies off a carcase on a beach. The sheer rocks on the shore, although not high, gave no grip. The boys were drowning between wreck and rock, like unwanted kittens, scores of them, the heaving waters carpeted with bodies; I nearly said alive with bodies, but these men would never draw breath more.

When the tears burst from my head, there is at the same time a red rage which boils up in my chest; I fear I shall take a fatal turn unless the emotions of New Year's Morning's work ease a little in me. Are the authorities fully responsible for this awful tragic disaster or did God use the Royal Navy here for His own fell purpose?

I stood in the shelter of the sea wall and watched the door of the Waverley Hotel, naval headquarters since the beginning of the war. Every few minutes, a pale island navyman, hunched in his greatcoat against the cold that has chilled his bones, goes in to report. The local men are easy to pick out from the navymen from away who are stationed at *Iolaire* base. Do not ask me how but you can spot a Portrona man anywhere in the world, never mind on the streets of the town.

I kept watching for their return, looking out for someone I knew. They were not inside for long, just to register their name and number and ship of origin, Survivor off *Iolaire*, Sir!

No thanks to you!

– You will be ordered to report to the Board of Enquiry to give evidence. Home address? –

My chum and mentor, John, came out the door. He must have been inside longer than the others, for I did not see him go in. I knew he had made it ashore, hand over legs on the rope, a hardy fisherman in his prime. What is more, he comes from Lochs, and to these boys, born seamen, the entrance to Portrona harbour is their Saturday road into town; they have boats instead of carts. The very man to know something about the deadly error that took *Iolaire* off her proper course into the harbour mouth. Fortunately (for I did not want to lie to him, a brother who had also endured) he assumed I had already reported. He explained that his observations about the movements of *Iolaire* in relation to the land had caused the Admiral to question him at some length.

– I saw the land to starboard five minutes before she struck and at the same time the *Iolaire* began to turn to port –

– Was she too near the land? –

– Too near –

– What land was it? –

– Holm Island –

I grabbed a stanchion when the seas came over or I would have been over the side of her, I told him.

He never said he helped get the line ashore, then the heavy rope, before saving himself on it. And me, only God can say, how I never got flung off yon hawser, with only my hands holding it, my blouse round my neck, fit to strangle me. My couple of years in the Navy did not prepare me for this and the sight and sound of the men drowning below terrified me out of my mind, and when one of the drowning men got hold of my legs in a grip of death my fear was such that I screamed into the storm and kicked at him savagely with a foot that broke free from him, stamped his glimpsed white face and open mouth into the teeming waters below me until he let go. My grip still secure, my hands convulsed on the rope, I got a leg over it and dragged myself to the top of the rocks, leaving the boiling choking scene in the sea below me. I drowned that man, smashed him down into the seething surf, him or me, him or me, him or me.

– Are you all right? –

Shock, John, sea shock! Trying to make a joke of it, we had heard of shell shock among the boys in France and a lad from Eye was shot at dawn for sleeping on duty, though some said he was shocked after an attack.

– The naval enquiry is on Wednesday. Have you been called? –

I bluffed him with words about not having seen very much after he left me to help with getting the ropes ashore, leaving such important work to real sailors, real fishermen, which was true enough. I do not know who it was moved the rope up amidships later to gain some shelter from the storm, but that man saved my life, for I was not able to make my way down to the stern, along the shattered heaving deck, through the frantic men still on board.

– I'm off to the shipping agent on Point Street to find out any chance to get to Canada. This island is finished after this –

He left me and I went off the other way, my steps turning without thinking towards the beach at Holm Point.

It was strange, the first few days, how I wanted to go back to the scene (the scene of the crime?). I was the only one of all the survivors who ever went back to the wreck, so far as I know. Nothing else occupied my mind; night was nightmares, day was wanting to see the reality, to help ease away the pictures that kept coming back, lit up in the ghastly light of the flares.

So I sit on a rock and watch, the men in the fishing boats working offshore, dragging grapnels along the shallows. Every now and then, they connect with a body and a wet dark bundle will be dragged over the gunwale. I think of friends of mine.

In front of me, just yards from the low cliffs that frustrated and killed so many sailors, the broken masts of the *Iolaire* thrust up out of the water. Just beyond the sunken yacht are the backs of the Beasts, high or low, depending on the tide, surmounted by the jutting metal spike that is supposed to mark their presence for passing seafarers. This prod of steel is called a beacon, though how a dead iron shaft can be referred to as a beacon baffles me. Were it a proper beacon, with a light on it, the tragedy would never have happened; the officer of the watch would never have run her onto it. My belief is, having listened to John and others talking of the course taken, the officer, running down from Eye Peninsula, new to the area, steered straight for Arnish Light on the other side of the harbour mouth, forgetting all about the Beasts, or thinking he was further offshore than he was.

The crime was to take two hundred and sixty men on a yacht with lifebelts and boats for eighty, with half a crew (I heard nobody was on watch when she hit the Beasts). Every damned thing conspired to put me and the others in such a desperate state we fought each other for our lives. Believe me, there were struggles to the death in that cauldron below the cliffs, even between chums, must have been, though I heard of a boy who made it ashore and then went back into the maelstrom to find his younger brother. His mother had asked him to look after the youngster. She lost them both.

Talk of recurring funerals will lead to a sameness in my story; there is a great regularity about the obsequies in Portrona and environs, where we have adapted our own demi-military style of ceremony. The double line of bearers (always and only men) tread mutely forward to take their turn at the lift and carry, then drop back to the end of the lines, to start the ritual again. The nearest and dearest (always and only men) take their places at head and feet, holding onto the strong silken cords fastened to the casket that will later be used to lower the coffin into the final resting place. Personally, I want to hear a muffled drum beating, but then I am a believer in meeting the rhythms of life as they arise, unlike most here, some of whom would consider such a simple innovation a dreadful sin, imagining that our method of burial was ordained in Ancient Israel.

So I will not repeat the stories of each of the funerals I attend; they are all the same for those who act as bearers and in my own case as a witness. Each burial of the scores that have taken place and will go on until the sea gives up the last of our dead, each of them, I do not have to say, is unique to the nearest and dearest. I am going to speak of such a one at some length because it was unique in ways that nobody in their wildest imagining could have foreseen. It made public something of the private agony being suffered by our womenfolk.

Our obsessional dwelling on the subject of death is something outsiders accuse us of, but we have had a long acquaintance with the Bodach with the Scythe and have always faced him belly to belly. The past five years of trench slaughter, followed by the unspeakable tragedy of the *Iolaire* on the Beasts, ensures we will think of nothing much else for years to come.

Did one of the ministers state that the terrible drowning on New Year's Morn was like unto the Jewish Passover? We are familiar with the Old Testament stories on the island and need no elaboration on that one.

To the funeral that will now stand for all of them; bear with me whilst I describe what happened that shook us all and makes me rethink my place as an island man.

The house is new, two storeyed, chimney gables at each end, the old black house nearby, now used for the cattle and their feed storage. I join the men of the village, mostly old and very young, you notice, with a sprinkling of mature men, sucking on tickler tobacco cigarettes, hand made, ex-servicemen, survivors. We hunch against the lee walls of the house, listen to the faint ululation of the Gaelic psalm from inside. The old men puff pipes of black twist and spit with admirable accuracy.

The boys cluster together, holding onto the big brother's hat that is too big.

It is comforting to us to concentrate on tobacco, keep our hands and mouths occupied, cut down the need to speak to each other. Nods and shakes of the head suffice us as we wait for the house service to end and the funeral proper to begin.

The shining coffin with brass handles and brown silken ropes stands on a black bier (every village has its own) placed upon four chairs in the middle of the road. At least the Admiralty did not stint on the quality of coffins supplied, I find myself thinking, among less noble thoughts. The brass glints at me.

Inside the house, I know, each room is crammed with chairs borrowed from the homes round about. They are occupied mostly by women, who sit hunched in stillness, except when their pure voices play with the subtle grace notes of the Gaelic psalm, sung at beginning and end of the short service, led by one of the village elders. It is the minister himself who takes such worship as a rule, but how can even an eager evangelical minister be in more than one place at a time? Too many interments.

She had a mane of dark brown hair which had not been dressed for many days. It was the first thing you saw when she broke away from the cluster of women at the door of the house and went out on the road to stand over the head of the coffin. That and the imperious nose and nostrils, horselike. The old elder and the undertaker's carpenter looked uneasily at each other.

We waited for the widow to make her farewell gesture, a hand caressing the varnish, perhaps a kiss on the polished brass nameplate, then return to her place alongside the other women.

She had other plans; against all the unwritten rules of the island, the young widow appeared desirous of accompanying the cortège all the way to the burial place.

Not just desirous but determined; she pulled the silk cord at the head free and wound it tightly around the fingers and wrist of her left hand. I noticed that, my mind very acute in these moments, every detail to me then of pure clarity.

Neither Norse nor Celt, my mind said; she is strange to us, or half of her. She is going to show us grief, the public side of private passion revealing itself in her because that is what she feels in this solemn moment; the sheer waste of her husband, lost without cause or reason in the wash from the rocks and wreck when he deserved to get home to her whole. After her patient wait, they brought her a disfigured cadaver in a screwed down box which they did not let her see, but deep in the night had she seen?

Now she is going to the graveside and the women mutter uneasily; not one of them has the courage to accompany her, not that she expects it or looks for it, or wants it. She is alone as one is at such a time; who can share such unspeakable grief, the death of passion forever?

I heard a man cry out as she began to break up. Mo ghràidh chan fhaic mi chaoidh tuilleadh thu, Darling, I shall never see you again. I thought now maybe it was him and I could feel his despairing loss.

And hers.

Whoever he was cried out, Mistress MacLeod could not have known about his call. This was her name, I gathered, from hearing the pleas of the old elder for her to rejoin the womenfolk and leave the funeral procession to the men. She shook her head and wound the silk cord the tighter. He gave up and nodded to the first bearers to take the lift.

It was not a long walk to the local cemetery, less than three miles. All that road, as the rest of us moved up and down the line, took our lifts in turn, she walked with steady steps behind the casket. She looked steadfastly forward and as I passed I saw she had no tears on her face. Indeed her eyes

200

looked drained and dry as though her head had been emptied of its fluids.

When we arrived at the gate of the cemetery, the gravedigger met us and led us to a fresh mound of sandy soil that pointed out the grave. There were other mounds all over the place, waiting.

The bearers laid down the bier at the top end of the grave and retired. The elder quietly indicated men whom he knew were blood relations of the deceased and they stepped forward to take a cord apiece. She did not move until the men lifted the coffin from the bier and approached the open grave holding it up by the cords, when she stepped through the rances of the bier beneath her feet and holding up her end of the casket by the cord wound round her hands, she stood with the bearers the coffin poised over the final resting place.

The others lowered together at a murmured instruction and the casket went down neatly to the bottom of the pit.

But it went down at an awkward angle. This because Mrs MacLeod did not loosen her grip on the cord she held. It was therefore too short; as the kist bumped below, the weight of it pulled her into the open grave. She toppled face down on top of her man's coffin, landing with a hollow bump out of sight of those of us who were not standing at the lip of the opening.

To add to the horror, a young boy, on filling-in duty for the first time, now shovelled a heap of sand into the grave on top of the recumbent woman, lying face down on the coffin, not moving, eyes closed as if in sleep, I was later told.

Realising what he had done, the boy threw down the spade and ran with a strangled cry towards the rear of the cemetery, dodging round the gravestones like an athlete on an obstacle course, pursued by an old man, who failed to catch him.

Others tried to help the widow out of the grave but further frightfulness awaited. They could not lift the woman up at all. They saw she had become fastened to her husband's coffin by the cord and they climbed out of the grave in fear and trembling.

A frozen tableau like that in a picture film; we all stood there not moving, and the cliché about time stopping thudded repeatedly in my brain.

But there is always a hero appears in every difficult circumstance and we found him here too, thanks be to God. A fisherman, too old for war but too young to forgo a full life. He now knelt at the head of the grave, knife in hand fumbled with the woman's skirts, found the cord stretching tight beneath her to the casket handle and sawed through it. He nodded at a couple of men (his boat's crew?). They took an arm each of Mrs MacLeod's, gently hauled her to her feet. She stood for a long moment on top of her man's coffin, her uncertain shoes with their segs scratching his brass nameplate. Then they lifted her out and half-carried her to the gate where they commandeered a gig to take her home.

In hurried guilt we poured and shuffled sand into the grave, rolled out the turf covering and then scattered on the pretence of looking for the stones of our ancestors. This is very difficult; no matter how often you visit a cemetery, you have problems finding the grave you are looking for, and if you start from a strange grave instead of the gate it becomes a true puzzle.

A national newspaper has taken note of our awful state and a piece appears some days after our entrance into the slough of death; sympathetic words to be sure, rapped out in Edinburgh. The appalling catastrophe still monopolises all thoughts on the island, the villages like places of the dead, no-one going about except on duties that cannot be left undone, like feeding the sheep, fetching water from the well, burying the dead? The homes are full of lamentation and of a grief that cannot be comforted (the biblical cadences have their origins here I suspect and not in the capital).

Be fair, remember the duty of a witness is to state that he sees truly; here is a small part of it, when the reporter goes on: carts in little processions of two or three, each bearing its coffin (a separate cart for each drowned man, each polished casket – I feel queer not having noticed it myself, I congratulate the reporter, who must be the local man and not the man in the city).

The newspaper says, carts pass through the streets and all heads are bared as they pass. There is no mention of the agonised aftermath, the arrival at the door of lamentation, day or night, the prayer and psalm, the decision on holding the funeral today, or tomorrow or tonight, even where shall he lie until then, on his bed, in the porch, at the door?

Truth resides in these words: scarce a family in the island has escaped the loss of a near blood relative. Many have had sorrow heaped upon sorrow.

Our own newspaper has risen nobly to the task of telling the kind of dreadful story that I am sure a local reporter dreads, for how can he be impartial and emotionless in a circumstance that requires him to tell the tragedies of his friends and relatives? But there is the rub, newspapermen think they are impartial and without personal feeling. They speak the truth and the facts being sacred when the real truth is that they are just as emotional and partisan as the rest of us.

Be that as it may, it is time to cease from pontification, now I have put a scholar's state behind me and report what can be read in the *Portrona Gazette* on this unspeakable tragedy. I shall let the editor speak for all and merely choose some of what he said:

The terrible disaster at Holm on New Year's Morning has plunged every home and every heart into grief unutterable. Language cannot express the anguish, the desolation, the despair, which this awful catastrophe has inflicted. (There will be sorrowful songs, yet it remains to be heard if music can assuage where words can not.)

One thinks of the wide circle of blood relations affected by the loss of even one of the gallant lads and imagination sees these circles multiplied by the number of the dead, overlapping and overlapping (like the waves on the Beasts) till the whole island – every hearth and home in it – is shrouded in deepest gloom.

All the island's war losses of the past four cruel years – although these number fully four times the death roll of New Year's Morning – are not comparable to this unspeakable calamity. The black tragedy has not a redeeming feature. The surrounding circumstances but add to the horror of it. Some of these circumstances will form the subject of the searching and impartial inquiry which is being called for, and which must be held, though no amount of investigation can give the island back her dead.

Other circumstances having no relation to the cause of the disaster add poignancy to it. For over four years, on all the seven seas, many of the men so suddenly hurled to their doom had braved the elements in defence of liberty and right. And now, with all these perils past, they come home only to be cruelly done to death within twenty yards of the shore at the very entrance to the harbour.

The island, God knows, had already more than her fair share of losses of the war but hard as these were to bear, there was alleviation for the heart's pain in the thought that the men died fighting in a just and glorious cause and that they lost their lives consciously facing death.

What a sombre thought to think, that all of the ones who fell were aware of their impending death, or does the editor mean conscious of the possibility (in the trenches, the likelihood,) of being killed? We know that some men had premonitions, and, now and then, spoke of them. But many who later appeared on the roll as K.I.A. did not.

'Cruelly done to death.' These words will ring down the years as regards this awful event. They reveal how the minds of the people here are already furious to apportion blame, and even the impartial editor of the *Portrona Gazette* uses such emotional language. 'Cruelly done to death' by whom? By God or by the Royal Navy?

Another Sunday morning, another kirk in town. They (the ministers) are not able to leave the subject, as though they are afraid we will blame God for what has happened and they cannot decide how to apologise for Him. The parish church minister says he is struck dumb by the horror of the awful event which happened at our very doors.

Is this the true abomination, that it happened at our very doors and left us to clear up? Which melancholy work will take weeks and months; when will we find the last body? We shall never know when we come upon him; are we quite, quite certain sure exactly who is missing to a man and a name and a number?

And what has my disappearance done to the Balance of the account of the dead? Thrown it out forever, which may partly explain the agitation of the base accountant. I see him with his daily tallies of bodies and the list that never adds up. The lack of balance is carved on his face, as he makes his triangular path from the Waverley to the Base office, to the Battery temporary morgue, his untrustworthy files buried in a crowned navy briefcase. I try to feel sympathy for him but I do not succeed; my feelings are generally quiet, lying low like a beast in a lair, suddenly to jump out in anger, in a bar, say, when I see the balance of our young men staring into their greasy glasses.

The watchnight service took place at the same time as the wrecking on the Beasts: at the moment when the ill-fated boat was struggling with the elements, some of us were listening to words drawing a comparison between the brightness of this New Year and the darkness which shrouded the past New Years of the war.

And others were getting out of their minds on the whisky quota, making them unfit for any rescue attempt, giving that guilt after drink that begins now to turn away from themselves towards the Admiralty with mutterings outside and cries in the bars, that the crew of the *Iolaire* were not just short-handed but drunk.

When one person dies we feel guilt for being left but when scores die, hundreds, what is the agony that overcomes us all and how can we cope?

I was saved and I have the anger to help me.

The evening service, somewhere else. What is going wrong with me, that I spend my time following funerals and attending church services, unless the need to find an answer?

Thy way is in the sea and thy paths in the great waters and thy footsteps are not known; the opening remarks, most of them go to the psalms for texts, seeking the musical comfort, the rhyming commonplace, harder to dig meaning out of verse, words bent for sound rather than sense, my lecturer in theological questions might have steered me?

And he chose the same text as the Free Church minister, Be still and know that I am God. He said the truth, the whole island from end to end trembling with grief and sorrow and, like Rachel weeping for her children, refusing to be comforted.

My feeling grows that the men of the cloth here have given up trying either to comfort or explain and who can blame them?

God in His inscrutable providence, His way is in the sea, has visited us with fearful judgment (there it is!) but it is our place to be still and know that He is God. Our hearts going out in pity and sympathy to those who are stricken down with grief and who are rent with sorrow for fathers, husbands, sons and brothers (not sweethearts), who lost their lives so mysteriously within sight of their homes. Our desire and prayer that He who hath torn will heal, God's ways in providence as mysterious as the sea, yet done in love and wisdom according to His eternal purpose; our duty to humble ourselves under the mighty hand of God.

Naught for thy comfort, I repeat over and over, naught for thy comfort, as I wander the dead quays with blinded eyes and bethink myself of Job.

My walk turns towards the castle grounds, seeking the comfort of the exotic trees spread over many acres. Have they cedars of Lebanon, I find myself wondering, then I laugh loud in the wet avenue at my preoccupation with biblical matters as though religion was the only way to help make sense of what happened. A student of philosophy, even from a bastion of Calvinism, should be able to find answers to make a balance of the circumstances pertaining to this unspeakable event?

This fellow from Eye is looking at me through the trees and will surely conclude that I am mad, laughing alone at such a time. He bursts into laughter himself as he comes up to me and puts his arm over my shoulders. *B' fheàirrde sinn siud*, We needed that, in the name of God, must we cry forever? Donald tells me his own story:

– The New Year services were being held in the Eye main church and it was two o'clock in the afternoon before anyone heard of the loss. Three of us went up to Holm on New Year's afternoon and we saw the boats grappling for the bodies. When they recovered a number, they would land them and place them on a horse-lorry and go off with them to the Battery.

There was a big hall there, for drilling, and the bodies were lying on the floor with a tarpaulin over them.

You would move along the line of drowned, raising the

tarpaulin from each head until you saw someone you recognised; this, you reported. The naval people would then tie a ticket to the body and send for the undertaker to come with a coffin.

I recognised the face of the sixth man I looked at, a boy from our village. His hands were held up in front of his face, his fists clenched, as though he was trying to shield himself from something –

This proves again that the Navy did not have the slightest information about the passengers that they had piled on board the little yacht, but surely the men would have their paybooks on them?

The Navy's carelessness will only have made my disappearance from their ken the more easy.

I spoke to Donald of the identification procedures and he said, grimly:

– It was only on their tattoos that some of the boys could be identified, their tattoos! –

I thought he was going to weep but although his shoulders shook his eyes remained dry.

Used to be their stockings.

– A pint or two –

In the Long Bar on North Beach he told me the story of his relative, a girl who lived in the posher part of Portrona. Anna and Kate her friend were walking on Dempster Street in the evening which had been fine, but at midnight a sudden storm of rain and wind caused them to seek shelter in the fish mart on the quay until the weather abated. They then ran home and went to bed.

Knocking on Anna's door wakened her and Kate was on the step, having heard her brother was on the *Iolaire* on the Beasts of Holm.

They hurried down to South Beach and the first thing they saw was a horse-lorry carrying a load under a tarpaulin. A man told them the heap was the bodies of some of those drowned.

They thought they would walk on and turned along the road to Holm.

– The lorries were going past us with the dead. You hardly saw a person on the street. The wind went down and the rain stopped.

All along the shore, we saw the bodies where the sea had put them; the lorries lifting them and preparing them . . . this awful New Year, I shall never forget –

Donald drains his pint glass and pushes it away.

– *Chan eil blas air*, It has no taste –

We leave him to join a funeral cortège of carts to Eye, me to take up my patrol of the shadowed streets of the town. There is a neat pyramid of what I have come to call widows' bonnets in the window of Mhor the milliner's shop. I enter.

Mhor is sitting behind the broad counter, teasing and twisting black flowers out of crêpe and velvet. Her assistant, a girl of twenty, stands beside her. She is not wearing any sign of mourning, so I venture to talk to her about the tragedy. With serious and open face, she tells me her story; the indelible memory all ashore have of their first hearing of the disaster that will set their lives, their town and their island on an irrevocable new bearing throughout the twentieth century.

– I walked home from Portrona after the shops shut at nine o'clock, along with Norman, who is going to marry my sister Effie. Norman was bringing in the New Year with ourselves.

The *Sheila* had not arrived when we left the town and we had no idea that another boat was crossing the Minch.

A number of girls were in the shop that evening, having come in to Portrona to meet their brothers and sweethearts.

Peggy Crichton from Eye was in, over to meet her young brother, Donald. He had not been long away and Peggy was very glad he was coming home, because the two of them had to run a big croft and kept the house going as well.

Nobody from my village was lost, strangely, and maybe this is why we did not hear of the tragedy as soon as other places.

We were seeing a lot of gigs and carts and bicycles passing along the main road into town and we wondered where they were going, it being New Year's Day and all the shops shut.

At last, a young girl from the road end came into the house and said that a big boat had gone on the rocks in the harbour and a lot of men were drowned.

My father said at once, The Beasts of Holm!

Norman jumped on his bicycle and headed down to his home village, for he knew his brother was expected. On the way, he met some people who told him his brother was safe, having been one of the lucky ones transferred to the *Sheila*.

My mother had planned to visit Mrs Crichton in Knock that day as she had not been there since Murdo Crichton married my sister in New York. My brother took her in the cart, not knowing about the loss of young Donald on the *Iolaire*, not knowing of the disaster itself.

Young Donald's mother was pointing out to my mother across the bay to where she and Donald had been cutting seaweed the previous spring. The spot is very close to where the *Iolaire* sank –

These are Mary Ann's own words to me as we stood on either side of the polished counter in the silent milliner's shop, where the brightest hats now show a slash of black.

– My sister is coming home to take me to New York to work in a millionaire's mansion –

Who peers through the window now but Murdo, starting to build a reputation as a maker. He is looking to test out his *Iolaire* lament.

He comes into the shop to be greeted by Mhor, black thread round a white tooth. His bard's instinct (and who can deny the gift is just that, and sometimes not wanted, like the prophetic power) makes him a sad line for her:

– Black hats on bright heads, a dark day –

Warming in the atmosphere, he sings his sonorous *Iolaire* lines in Gaelic, the words taking their melody from the crooning of a kettle hanging on a chain over the fire, awaiting the coming home of the sweetheart of the girl whose poem Murdo is making.

> Last night was torn the Eagle
> Her brood drowns beneath her wings
>
> She cried sore, the maiden
> In the morning early
> When she finds her lover
> Drowned in the seaweed
> No shoes on his feet
> As he dived and swam
>
> She bends to kiss
> His cold salt lips.

We stand silent and look at the gifted lad through the mist. He says something I do not want to hear.
– They're wanting farm labourers in Canada –
A farm labourer in Canada, the height we can offer our poets, my God, what hast Thou done to us.
I pat Murdo's shoulder, raise my hand to the two girls and blunder outside:

> The day rises
> Her hope falls
> The kettle on the chain
> Pipes a sad lament.

I have formed the habit of joining the navymen from *Iolaire* base in their favourite pub on South Beach, which they use in the regular and familiar way of the English, a home from home. It saves them having to visit their neighbours in their houses? Today, I talked to a new face, eager to speak to any who would listen.
I pushed a nip of whisky across and mentioned the disaster,

only to release a flood of words, which made a strong impression on me. I did not reveal my own presence on board but told him that I had lost friends and relations:

– Lots were drawn among *Iolaire*'s crew to decide who should go on Christmas leave and who would have to wait for New Year. I came out of the hat for Christmas but I swapped with Seaman Lane, a married man, who had not been home for Christmas for two years.

When the *Iolaire* crossed to Kyle on New Year's Eve, she was partly manned by those members of the crew decided by ballot to go on New Year's leave, plus myself who had given up my Christmas to Seaman Lane –

His mates from the base do not want to hear his lucky ballot story. Who can blame them, now, their guilt felt daily on every street with eyes boring into them? But he has to speak and finds me more than willing. He tells me that as the youngest crew member on *Iolaire*, it was his duty to lay the anchor chain in the chain locker when they put to sea, and said that Portrona Harbour mud had an awful long-lasting stench.

– That's the job of the coiler on the fishing boats, except that he has clean rope. The harbour mud in Portrona is made up of one hundred years of herring guts.

Seaman Lane was found below the Sandwick cemetery, he made it ashore, but he died of the cold. Could have been me! –

I recalled then the bard telling me of the body he'd found, leaning against the cemetery fence as though asleep and I think, It was Lane, just back from his unlucky Christmas furlough.

What a weird little world we seem now and then to inhabit.

– Should it not have been me? –

– Don't talk daft, there's predestination –

– What's that? –

– Don't let it trouble your C of E conscience, just thank God –

– My mother will pray and light a candle for him for me –

– Good lad –

– When the *Iolaire* crossed to Kyle, she was manned by those members of the crew decided by the ballot to go on New Year's leave. I cannot say who they were, as there was considerable confusion on the quayside at Kyle and we became separated as we went for our train to Inverness –

– Was the *Iolaire* crewed on the way back to Portrona by men coming off Christmas leave? –

– Yes, mainly –

– Including the officers? –

– Only sixteen of us went on New Year's leave, so the chief officers took the ship both ways, from Portrona to Kyle and back again to the island.

It is intriguing that there was at least a partial crew change at Kyle, with a certain amount of undermanning. How this changeover, added to the lack of full crew, affected the behaviour of the ship on her return voyage we can only speculate. We know *Iolaire* has been stationed in Portrona for only a few months, has never entered the harbour at night, and was not only undermanned, but undermanned with a crew unfamiliar with the route, many of them tired out from a two-day train journey.

The question arises, did *Iolaire* travel to Kyle specially to convey island libertymen home to Portrona? Or was she going over anyway, to send some of her men on New Year's leave and pick up those who had been away for Christmas?

Had *Iolaire* not gone to Kyle, the island sailors would have been transported safely home on the mail boat over the next few days. Was she sent specially, a totally inadequate mode of transport, or did the accident of organising her crew's Christmas leave mean she took the chance of carrying far too many men in dangerous conditions?

Who gave the order for *Iolaire* to carry so many men, thereby breaking totally all navy safety regulations?

– With nearly three hundred men and their gear on the aft and promenade deck, with the waves breaking over her, it's no wonder they were swept off like flies –

He gulped his nip the way we do here, tears came into his eyes and he spluttered. I pushed a half pint into his hand to clear his airways.

– She was a brute of a boat to turn; she was top heavy with the guns fitted fore and aft. When we went to St Kilda, I nearly died of seasickness. Another thing, she only had lifesaving stuff for the forty odd crew –

He told me an odd thing:

– My bunk was right under the officers' mess and they only had one gramophone record, which they played all the time: Schubert's Sonata in A Minor that will always mean the *Iolaire* to me –

The day of the public inquiry dawns cold and clear with a promise but springtime will not come to this island this year; for many, never.

In my Sunday suit and white collar I sit in a corner of the pews of the Sheriff Court. This becomes my personal place, avoided by other members of the public during the hours and days of listening to question and answer, of trying to discover what will assuage the rage, the grief, the sense of doom that envelops the pitiful town of Portrona just now. For the rest of the island, each village has withdrawn behind its dead windows, its eddies of peat smoke; fortunate the man who has cattle to feed and the woman who has children to ready for school; you can put the numbness away whilst the routines of ordinary life are performed.

The routines of lawmen, sheriff, Crown and public engaged in legalities I permit to pass over me. I sit as one drugged, as though coming round from a surgical procedure; my mind is calm and waiting quietly to absorb those details, the tiny pieces of information that will scrawl a mark on my brain that waits to receive like a dusty blackboard in a lecture room.

Words in their many, many thousands in many accents pass over me and some few here and there leave their trace; create flickering scenes of short duration inside my closed eyelids, with the addition of words; a cinematographic film, with sound.

After preliminaries of names and positions of those in Portrona to keep a public inquiry: Sheriff, advocates, procurator fiscal, solicitors (glad to see a local lawman is appearing for the bereaved families, it gives those who have truly suffered a voice), we hear of the arrival in Kyle of two trains with a total of three hundred and twenty sailors for Portrona. At the same time, the commander in Kyle is informed by telegram from Inverness that five hundred and thirty men have left there for Kyle, this figure including men for the other islands.

The navy needs to look closer at its sums, not that it matters now.

The hundreds of us shoving gently up and down the platform, seeking chums from other carriages, our muscles relaxing after two days' sitting, the boys from the different villages wanting to travel over on the boat together, get the yarns of the war, plan what to do at home, build a white house, see the children, the wife and the caravy, plant seed in land and bodies.

Never was heard such a roar of Gaelic voices on Kyle of Lochalsh pier.

This man here, the commander, he lined us up then, Portrona men, marched us off to *Iolaire* and to the mail boat, lucky lucky lot, overspill from *Iolaire*, the boys at the end of the column, marched on board the *Sheila* for a safe trip home and a lifetime thinking of the fickle finger of God; the men of the Aird, the fortunate, all home safe.

We knew the *Iolaire* was faster than the *Sheila* and would get us home first, a long lean rich man's yacht against a butting stubby steamer.

The libertymen of the Aird surface late on New Year's Morning to discover they have had predestination thrust upon them.

Feel the smooth white warm-soft blanket on your bare skin, hear the rustle of autumn straw beneath you. Now your life is altered forever by fearful cries which burst into the house, into your room and reverie, your very box bed.

> We call predestination the eternal decree of God by which he has determined in Himself what He would have every individual of mankind to become, for they are not all created with a similar destiny; but eternal life is fore-ordained for some and eternal damnation for others. Every man therefore, being created for one or the other of these ends, we say is predestined either to life or death.

Versions of the Calvinist message absorbed at fireside and pulpit over the years stray through your head. You wiggle your toes for reassurance, touch a bare back if you have one beside you: God's will be done, be still and know who I am. It's all right, all preordained.

The boys are drowned on the Beasts of Holm, Long Live the Boys.

How about this (I think well, as I listen to the legal droning about me): If you are predestined, then you are special, someone of distinction. If you know you have been lifted up by divine decree, then you are raised beyond the poor meaningless life here below to a new state of dignity and importance, brought nearer my God to Thee.

You have become a vital actor in the world drama, one of its writers, even?

Two reasons creep into my exhausted brain, that may go together in some weird way, for we island folk bury deep our feelings about the dreadful happening on the Beasts of Holm. We are yet a deeply superstitious race and fear being contaminated by talk or thought of such an awful and malign event, a calamity that must have been intended as a punishment.

There is too our religious acceptance, although how deep this goes in the minds of such recent pagans as us is difficult to define. We are constantly abjured to accept the will of God, however terrible and mysterious, with Job-like patience. Understanding does not come into it, yet our main religion bases itself triumphantly upon thinking and understanding, whilst explaining nothing that happens in us at a deep-feeling level. The disaster is being presented as a test of belief, divine-decreed to enable us to prove our spiritual superiority.

My instinct says the women will handle it better. My God, they have to, for it is they who are truly suffering. Did men not bring this upon them?

The solicitor for the bereaved cross-examines, seeking the sense of the numbers reported arriving in Kyle and the telegrams notifying same. He is placing local rumour on record, but the Kyle commander is more than adequate:

It is untrue that the commander of *Iolaire* made any complaint about taking the men across. There is no truth in the story that the *Iolaire's* captain received two telegrams from the Admiral in Portrona because he refused the first instruction. He was perfectly sober. No lifebelts could be procured at Kyle.

We islandmen were slightly disorderly from the point of discipline, adds the bodach, but what did he expect?

The *Iolaire* crew were sober then, but what about us? For the first time I sat up in my pew in the Sheriff Court to hear the next witness, a Kyle man who works as a porter on the railway station:

– There was no sign of drink on the boys when they came off the train. There is a bar in the town, but it only sells beer, and it is a poor chance that any of the sailors got near it. And nobody saw anyone from the crew of the *Iolaire* in town that day either –

Weird how one of your own sounds more honest, it's maybe the accent?

They call the man who sails the Minch six nights a week and we all listen as he expounds the ins and outs of that treacherous journey.

He begins by explaining why *Iolaire* bumped the quay at Kyle on arrival and goes on to reply to questions about the course taken by the yacht, that ended with such tragic force on the Beasts of Holm.

He talks of the strong current at Kyle making one who is not familiar bump his ship against the pier.

Nothing to that crash with the quay coming into Kyle, then, but was there ever much in it?

Our old-time lawman of the town, one for law and the ladies, now a bit broken-toothed for either, niggles at the detail of the course taken by *Iolaire*. The people's champion he was, once, making up maybe for the deadly days of Black Donald MacRoe, who has gone down in our history as the direst villain of all, more evil even than Mac an t-Srònaich.

The only tale of his life I have personally is one from the end of it; MacRoe lying paralytic drunk in a close, after his fall from grace due to the Bernera rioters, the wee boys of Portrona around him, pissing on him from their tiny clibeans and chanting:

– Cuiridh mi às an fhearann thu, I'll put you off the land! –

– One of the witnesses says that the *Iolaire* passed a little more than a mile off Caback Light? Was that the proper position and course? –

The captain of the *Sheila* answers without adding anything:

– She would be more than a mile off Caback Light. We are generally three to four miles off –

So where exactly was *Iolaire* when passing Caback Light?

The suggestion is that the witness (my chum from Lochs, a seaman born and bred in sight of Caback) is making an error of judgment of two or three miles.

Iolaire was wandering to say the least.

– Is Portrona a difficult harbour to enter at night? –

The steamer captain answers with the confident complacence of the man who knows it all:

– Well it is for the man that does not know it, a man who has not actually taken a vessel in –

That's it, that's our case, a man who has not actually taken a vessel in . . .

– In many cases they stand out all night until they get a pilot to take them in . . . The *Iolaire* is longer than the *Sheila* . . . there might be difficulty if he was too close on the land before trying to turn –

Too close on the land before trying to turn and her top heavy with guns and lifeboats of her war rig, as well as being as long as New Year's Day Night.

– When you came up to Portrona Harbour did you have a lookout? –

– I always have a lookout –

This is where the navy falls down, the lookout was down below trying to get a tired crew out of their bunks to enter the harbour when she struck.

There was nobody on lookout when the *Iolaire* rode up the back of the Beast at ten minutes to two on First January Nineteen Nineteen.

The commander was in his bunk and all, just a lieutenant on the bridge. One of our boys spoke to him after, him tied to the bridge railings:

– This is a terrible job –

– You could be worse –

– I could not be worse, awaiting my doom –

Don't speak ill of the dead, the lieutenant went down with her and so did the commander.

Another commander speaks up for the navy and its way with lookouts:

– It is not at all customary not to have a lookout when entering harbour –

Never said *Iolaire* had a lookout, just that she should have had.

– The lieutenant we are told sent the lookout man below to get the hands to stations? –

– I should think that is highly impossible. The fixed lookout is usually forrard. He is never moved until the ship is brought to anchor –

The captain of the *Sheila* had his lookout with him on the bridge, because the weather was so bad. *Iolaire*'s lookout was never forrard and was actually down below calling the crew when she struck.

Had the night been decent and the lookout at the bow, for sure he'd a seen the Beasts looming but they would be on them so quick.

A theory: the ship is too far to the north, she turns to port to pick up the Arnish Light, runs down on it and totally forgets the Beasts lying between?

Why in the Name is the so-called beacon on the Beasts a dead one?

Your man the navy commander is never going to give in:

– Would sending the lookout below endanger the ship in any way? –

– Oh no, because the proper lookout man would still be on his perch –

– On this occasion it is said he sent down the only lookout man – The stone-walling answer comes pat:

– I think it is highly impossible –

Highly impossible, what would Shakespeare make of it, highly impossible; or Doctor Johnson?

As always, the cunning word of the officer overrides that of the ranker, how else could this world be run? God (and the Devil) override poor Job.

I half-listen to the sad evidence of the man in charge of the life-saving apparatus; his failure to get the horse out to pull it, the bunch of matelots from the battery who hauled the ton of stuff to within a few hundred yards of the wreck. All this taking three hours and when they approach the cliffs there is nothing to see or hear apart from the shouts of the hardy young Niseach clinging to the mast of the sunken yacht.

He was rescued by the navy trawler in the morning and will probably live to see a hundred, remembering each day the awful never-ending night. His shoulders and hands will heal but his mind never, men drown by the score beneath his feet.

MacLeod, another Niseach wrapped one end of a heaving line around his wrist and handed the other end to a man by the rail whose eyes did not yet show fear. He plunged into the maelstrom below and struggled to tread water. He was waiting for the third wave. It came and he thrashed on its peak, rising over the barrier of smooth rock, and he landed. Now he gripped a crevice, fought the undertow, tried not to swallow too much water, working for the balance of air and water in mouth and throat. He crawled farther on and he was clear. He turned to signal to the others to brave the line of survival he had created for them.

Some did, as I know, and it looks like the strongest made it, those who knew the sea and have bodies fit for it, a couple of score of us, the fortunate ones. Luck is needed for God's will to be done.

My mind comes back from the hero's story to the smell of varnish in the Sheriff Court.

Is it strange that so many of the preachers take the text Be Still and Know that I am God for their sorry sermons of comfort on the tragedy that devastates their innocent flock? It takes me to Job and his sufferings unearned, with a need to find some solace that the ministers cannot give.

Many a warm Sunday night before, drugged in the odour of varnish and camphor of the smart Meeting House built by the people of the Aird with their own hands (the women creeling the shingle from the tideline on their supple backs, the elders eagerly spending the five dollar bills from the Americas on cement, timber and paint) did I listen to sermons on the very topic.

Now this.

Why did God invent predestination (or was it Calvin; can we blame the Geneva man for everything?). Surely God, having laid down the rules for all eternity, had sentenced Himself to existing in total boredom forever and ever?

Ah, but as Job tells us, God permitted evil to enter the world, gave Satan scope to torment those that offended him (the innocent?). Job took the trouble, despite all, to get a bard to write his story for us.

To make up for having sent Evil into the world (he had to, otherwise both He and we would be bored out of our existence) God sent Jesus to teach us Love.

All I can say is, it does not seem to have worked up to now. Which suggests there is a lot of freewill that preachers and others here don't ken about. Raising questions. Unthought questions, such as Why do ye keep kicking your children in the teeth?

They would never express it so I shall do it for them, it is a fair question to arise from His most faithful flock.

They tramped miles over the moors in their thousands last century to listen to the men on the top of Mùirneag, the Maiden, the mountain we have isolated, conveniently for missionaries, right in the middle of the dark island we continue to inhabit so grimly. Which pap the men chose to stand on, I know not.

Like the early days; only wet desert for dry, rain for sun, pneumonia instead of sunstroke; the wilderness repeated two thousand years later.

They have turned, in village after village, back to the scriptures of old. But now they meet in houses, crowded to the gunnels, those unable to enter standing listening at doors and windows.

Just like the routine for a funeral; approaching a house where a meeting is going on, you could just as easily be attending a burial service.

And it is happening for many, their locked emotions are finding a voice, their stiff bodies are loosening and dancing again, their music the ineffable Gaelic psalms. I have heard grace notes this past week you would not believe.

Grace notes . . .

Read the *Portrona Gazette*:

On Thursday night at the weekly prayer meeting in the Free Church at Uig several of the worshippers fell into a trance as has already occurred at revivalist services held in other parts of the island.

Special services are being held nightly in the district of Eye. A resident states that these meetings are held in private houses in rotation. They are joint services attended by the ministers of both congregations. Frequently the attendance is so great that worshippers have to stand outside, around the doors and windows, unable to gain admittance.

The service generally begins about nine p.m. and continues until the small hours of the morning. When the ministers leave, the meeting is continued by the singing of psalms and it is during this part of the service that worshippers are physically affected. Many people are doubtful whether the strange experiences recorded have any deep spiritual value.

The singing of psalms; their only original art form left to them or allowed and from it they derive comfort and confidence to cry out. Was it not Aristotle who said emotional arousal is accomplished by making and listening to music? And hear also Ecclesiastes:

> It is better to go to the house of mourning
> than to go to the house of feasting –
>
> Sorrow is better than laughter
> for by the sadness of the countenance
> the heart is made better.
> The Joy of Grief . . .

The jurymen are all from the town of Portrona itself, nobody to represent the interests of the vast wet island hinterland, we maws sometimes being seen as of lesser account, despite much evidence to the contrary. Not worth a quibble, at least not from me; I am becoming exhausted by it all; once or twice waking thinking maybe I'd be better off floating out the Minch with the majority of the lads.

Sheriff Mackintosh informs the jury now they shall be wary of assuming the position of censors and distributing blame, as a great many casualties at sea must forever remain enigmas.

And the Lord said to Satan, have you considered my servant Job, that there is none like him on the earth, a blameless and upright man, who fears God and turns away from evil? He still holds fast to his integrity, although you moved me against him, to destroy him without cause.

Did Satan himself, Black Donald, sink the *Iolaire*?

He destroys both the blameless and the wicked.

Now Job is a wonderful man; perhaps the only one of his kind, an optimist of that colour we scoff at today and yesterday too, likely.

God allows Satan to torture him, yet Job expects God to help him in his affliction!

What a man is Job; he realises that God is at odds with Himself in some way, having permitted his wicked minion to test Job.

They had a wager on the outcome, He and Satan.

God lost.

What a man is Job.

Scraping his sores with bits of clay, his entire life destroyed. How would such man meet the tragedy of the *Iolaire*, say he lost his two sons that remained, after the Somme, and Loos; and Ypres had taken the other three?

I know that my vindicator liveth.

The jury of townies is back:

'We find unanimously that the *Iolaire* went ashore and was wrecked on the Beasts of Holm about one fifty-five on the morning of 1st January, resulting in the death of two hundred and five men; that the officers in charge did not exercise sufficient prudence in approaching the harbour; that the boat did not slow down and that a lookout was not on duty at the time of the accident,' saith the jury.

They recommend consideration be given to the question of putting up a light on the Holm side of the harbour. That's the one that would have saved us all from this, the simple solution, having a light on both sides of the harbour instead of two lights on one side.

The jury desire to add they are satisfied no-one on board was under the influence of intoxicating liquor.

My brain is as though I had been to three all-night weddings in a row, drunk with lack of sleep, or after a double watch at sea in a gale, being called again after an hour's kip. It has presented me with a solution, to my Job's equation, which applies to the *Iolaire* disaster and every other case of tragedy unfair and unexplained: It is impossible for the mind of a good God to produce evil deeds.

But what if He acts without thinking? The way we do. If divine unconsciousness and lack of reflection exist, then we can form a conception of God which puts His actions beyond moral judgment and allows for no conflict between Good and Evil.

That will have to do; Cha tuig sinne e, as the elders assert, not for our understanding but my equation comforts me.

Returning at near-dawn from an all-night meeting, numbed pleasantly in my head from the glorious psalms, walking through the cold dark for hours till I arrive at Inaclete on the outskirts of the town and then know where I am going; just like on Ist January, the shop of all small goods and basic food, with her waiting behind the counter.

There is a middle-aged woman before me, black-clothed, an oilcloth bag clutched in one hand, getting the breakfast for the children; an ounce of loose tea in a poke, expertly spun by her behind the counter, a bigger poke of sugar, two of yesterday's loaves, back ones, no butter; she slips a wedge of cheese into the widow's bag unseen, except by me. That was the instant that made up my mind.

The widow leaves and she goes into the backshop, reappears holding a clothes hanger, on which my crisp naval uniform hangs. I had abandoned the brown paper parcel with my wet uniform at the door of the shop for the scavengers, but now here it is, washed and pressed.

My elated state makes the rest easy. Opening the slide in the counter (which she expects me to do), I accompany her into the backshop.

– Let's burn it –

She nods and fetches a bottle of paraffin from the barrel which supplies the lamps for the houses in these parts that still lack gas or electricity.

She leads me outside, into the back garden, shows the place where the rubbish is burnt and together we immolate the uniform suit. As it burns, we embrace and watch the sullen flames rise.

Characters Real And Not

THE MOST FAMOUS MAN Stornoway ever produced and we never heard a word about him for two hundred years until one of his descendants did the digging and told us. Both their names will be found at the beginning of this book.

Yes, James Morrison, the man who knew more than most about the greatest ever mutiny, was a Stornoway cove. What's more, he wrote a splendid book about the whole exciting and romantic episode. And although deeply involved in much of the illegal action, he was clever enough to avoid having his neck stretched from a yardarm in Spithead.

The reason we know so much about Jim Morrison is not only because of his close involvement in the mutiny but the fact that some SY [Stornoway] schoolmaster (Anderson?) gave him an education along with an urge to write everything down.

Whether they like it or not (and many of them do not, rest assured), all your writers and experts on the *Bounty* since 1789 depend, almost desperately, upon the detailed and highly perceptive words of the seaman from Stornoway.

More than nine hundred books have been written about the mutiny on the *Bounty*, nine hundred, and although I have not checked them all out, I'll take curer's gamble that James Morrison's name and work appears in all of them.

That's number one reason for producing yet another book

on the subject; but this one is about the fellow who was over there and saw it all.

There you have it; our main man was *real* and he has plenty to tell us.

Not all of the characters are real, of course; this being a novel of sorts, there are others whom we invent so they may move our story on for us.

The main thing about them is their basis in reality; Anna MacLeod or Flett, our romantic lead, is firmly based upon many thousands of girls like her, who appeared on the scene during the herring boom, did the work that put the town on the map of the world, and then quietly disappeared into history (as indeed we all do).

The same applies to Donald MacDonald, skipper of his own vessel, beginning to learn the ways of getting on; work for yourself, take a chance, borrow to purchase a second-hand boat to start, work the Stornoway season, make your first foray to the East Coast, through the Pentland, down to Wick and further, it may be. There is nothing very fictional about Donald MacDonald in the context of a nineteenth-century Lewis fisherman pushing his way to the front, looking for his fair share of nature's gift.

The really fictional characters are the exotic women. Whence comes Madame Wolkova, art expert of Petersburg and entrepreneur of the European herring trade?

It seems there was a cailleach Ruiseanach (Russian lady) used to come to Stornoway every year to cure herring. She could hold her own with any man and smoked cheroots so foul-smelling there was generally a small space around her. How much she knew (or knows) about art, European or other, we have no idea, but it is a nice thought. Also, it gives her an entrée to the castle, where Lady Emily (Emmeline, when it comes to art) is desperate for sophisticated company.

Northern Europe throve on the gleaming hordes of herring for six hundred years. The Dutch were the first and the British the last to benefit. The herring is the most basic of fish; other fish eat it as well as man, yet it tastes ambrosial. There is magic about it.

The Dutch Golden Age grew out of the herring fishing. It gave them Rembrandt and many other glories; we may secretly speculate that Madame Wolkova's art history lessons in Petersburg led her to the humble skeds on Number One Quay?

It was due to salt and the genius (simple, but then genius is) of Willie Benkelzoor, who took his salt barrels all the way to sea with him and stored the herring fresh and lively out of the briny; first taste is all. The mystery of them; are they here, there, will they come at all this year?

The Balts needed fish and the Dutch supplied them in abundance. They also went south, for salt (has anyone examined the effects on the European economy and population of six hundred years of using salt?); to Spain and the Canaries and even the Caribbean to get salt for Europe's herring.

Unpredictable as they are, they shifted grounds, benefiting last the latecomer to the industry, the British, especially the Scots, who learned well from the hard-headed Hollanders and at last triumphed by the simple passing of a law: thou shalt gut herring clean with a knife; the humble cuttag was born and so started one hundred and fifty years of the Scotch cure that saw the great European gamble to its close with Stornoway at its centre.

There is at least one other character we must refer to here; my own favourite. I have always had a soft spot for the Stornoway entrepreneur (and there have always been such men, taking on the incomers at their own game and with admittedly built-in advantage beating them, sometimes).

His trade depends on what is there. For MacAllan, of course, it was the herring; what else, in the middle of the great nineteenth-century boom. And to cap it all, does he not fling his bonnet over from Number One to the castle (a long way, admittedly, with a try at finding out what makes a lady from the South so keen on staying here).

This is what gives him his advantage: he is the only person in Portrona who ever thought to wonder why a 'blue stocking' from farthest England, with a good education, wants to spend all her time in a place like Lewis?

Maybe it is the beginning of that fascination with the 'exotic' that has landed us with so many of her kind over the years?

Be that as it may, it follows that MacAllan is quite right: this is a fascinating lady with a mind of her own and who knows to what excitements the development of a relationship might lead? Especially during the bleak winter months, with nothing to pass the time but trying to keep part of a mausoleum warm enough to enjoy the simple fruits of artificial hothouses, fine fish and game and a well-stocked cellar.

MacAllan's etiquette grows apace and with it his little world of socialising; his power grows with his influence over Lady E; on his recommendations are Portrona folk invited to the occasional soirées.

Alistair MacAllan is some cove, I tell you, I leave a lot more to your imagination. He is also, of course, a pure fiction. As is Emily or Emmeline, take your pick.

Post-modern culture has become novelistic, mass-producing narratives for our insatiable appetite for television, book, radio, film.

Facts are events to which we have given meaning. Different historical perspectives derive different facts from the same events.

As said previously, more than nine hundred books have been written about the mutiny on the *Bounty*, which featured centrally a Stornoway man who disappeared from history for two hundred years. We have rehabilitated to a certain extent our Jim Morrison.

But a ship that sears the memory of Stornoway and Lewis and will forever do so, has had no book written about it, although it was responsible for the death of not a few men but the enormous number of two hundred and five, mostly young men from the island of Lewis.

We have attempted to right this wrong here for the first time and we have done so with a clear desire not to falsify but yet to try to paint, through the new self-consciousness, something about the distinction between the brute events of the past and the historical facts we make out of them.